ASHES TO ACCOLADES

THE AUTHOR

Bill Sandiford would describe himself as a late developer! He left school aged 15 with no qualifications, but subsequently gained a Maths degree and had a successful career as an Operations Analyst. In retirement he has written a novel which draws on his love of music, especially the classical guitar, and shows a sympathetic understanding of the challenges facing child refugees from a war-torn country. He is a keen fly fisherman, and enjoys painting watercolour landscapes as well as being a Maths tutor.

ASHES

TO

ACCOLADES

Bill Sandiford

Matador
9 Priory Business Park,
Wistow Road, Kibworth Beauchamp,
Leicestershire. LE8 0RX
Tel: 0116 279 2299
Email: books@troubador.co.uk
Web: www.troubador.co.uk/matador
Twitter: @matadorbooks

ISBN 978 1800462 748

British Library Cataloguing in Publication Data.
A catalogue record for this book is available from the British Library.

Printed and bound in Great Britain by 4edge Limited
Typeset in 11pt Adobe Garamond Pro by Troubador Publishing Ltd, Leicester, UK

Matador is an imprint of Troubador Publishing Ltd

To Ruth
For her endless dotting of i's and deliverance of teas.
Thank you!

Where words fail, music speaks.

Hans Christian Andersen

Chapter 1

IN THE BASQUE
PROVINCE OF VIZCAYA

May 1937

The City of Bilbao

The sun blazed out of a brilliant sky, eddies of shimmering heat rising up from the cobblestoned square of the open market.

Mikel placed a bucket of clean water on the ground in front of Raphael, his little brown pony. He watched as the animal sucked noisily.

It was Saturday. A day without school! On Saturdays Mikel would delight in the steady toil before daybreak, helping Papa to load the pony cart with fresh fruit, vegetables and milk. This morning, he'd been entrusted to hitch Raphael to the cart. And then he'd climbed aboard with Papa for that brisk thirty-kilometre trot from Guernica, down into the ancient city of Bilbao.

The bridle jingled as Raphael shook his mane in a vain attempt to rid himself of a hideous swarm of face-flies. They'd been pestering the pony since sunrise, but now it was worse. A two-hour journey along the main highway, and with a heavy cart to pull, had left the animal steaming. Flies were settling around his watery eyes, basking in his sweat.

Mikel tried to swat them away, but it was useless. They were back in an instant, utterly remorseless.

"Good boy," Mikel whispered gently into the pony's ear. "Good boy, Raphael."

Papa dragged the last of the vegetable crates off the back of the cart.

"Nearly finished, Mikel! And then we'll see about a cup of coffee!"

Papa hoisted the crate onto his shoulder and headed off towards the busy market stalls. There he would deliver the load and collect his money from the traders.

The cart had been full to the brim this morning with a good crop of vegetables and two incredibly heavy milk churns. Mama had added a few bunches of irises and carnations. At the last moment she'd managed to find space for some potted plants; deep purple bougainvillea and scented jasmine. It would all help to support the family budget.

Squinting in the bright sunlight, Mikel scanned the sprawling marketplace. It was always fun to visit Bilbao. He loved the crowding, chattering masses of busy people, the teams of working mules, the children playing games in narrow streets, and the River Nervión with its waterfront shops and cafés.

He caught sight of Papa making his way back towards the cart. It was good to see Papa wearing his old familiar smile again. Talk of war over the past few weeks had made him act differently. His sudden outbursts of anger, followed by long frozen silences, hollow and sterile, had clouded all their lives. Mama had looked anxious too, and even Gorka, Mikel's little seven year old brother, had been easily upset.

But now Papa looked content and at ease again; his old flat cap pushed back on his forehead, a faded red cravat loosely tied around his neck, his shabby jacket secured by a single button, and that wonderful moustache falling to well below the corners of his mouth.

"Look what I've got, Mikel!"

"What is it?"

"Guess!" Papa came closer.

"I don't know!"

"It's a spider crab!" Papa laughed, brandishing the pink, spiky creature. "A gift from the fish lady in exchange for your mother's flowers. Fair trade, eh!"

"Ugh!" Mikel exclaimed. "It looks like a devil!"

"Good to eat, though!" Papa wrapped the spider crab in an old sack and tossed it onto the cart. "We'll not be going home empty-handed, Mikel!"

He pulled down an oat bag and handed it to Mikel.

"You know what to do with this," Papa said. "I'll go and fetch more water."

Mikel took another swipe at the flies. Then, very gently, he hitched the strap over Raphael's ears and eased the oat bag down to below the pony's muzzle. Raphael lowered his head, pressed the oat bag onto the ground and began to munch.

"Come on, son!" Papa placed a fresh bucket of water down beside the cart. "Let's fasten up, and see if we can get some lunch."

"But Papa… Raphael!"

"He'll be fine, Mikel. The fish lady has promised to keep an eye on him."

Mikel wound the reins securely around a metal post and gave his old friend a reassuring pat.

"We'll be back soon, Raphael," he whispered.

A Waterfront Café

It was a world of dreams; enticing and mysterious. Narrow, crowded streets filled with colour, sound and movement. A wonderland of cafés, bars and antique shops. Pavements lined with stalls piled high with books, torn and stained with age. Trays filled with collectors' coins, postage stamps and trading cards.

Mikel paused, gazing with curiosity at some caged birds; canaries, budgerigars and doves. How exotic they looked. He moved forward and sidled up to an elegant macaw parrot, uncaged but lightly chained to a perch. And what a beauty he was; bright yellow breast, wings as blue as the sky, and a crown of vibrant green. Unable to resist, Mikel reached out and gently touched the big black beak. It felt rough, just like the slate blackboard at school.

"Careful, Mikel," Papa said. "One little peck and you'll say goodbye to that finger."

They moved on. Soon they were passing the western edge of the old medieval town. Two minutes later they were strolling along the waterfront beside the wide, swirling Nervión River. Ahead lay Papa's favourite café, its green canvas awning overhanging at the front and offering shade to people seated outside.

And there sat the old shoeshine man with a nose shaped like the macaw's beak, his long jet-black hair swept back and reaching down to his collar. Mikel had often seen the shoeshine man in this part of the town. Today, he'd set up his collection of boot brushes, tins and polishing cloths under the café's awning. Poised over a pair of brogue lace-ups, he applied the sticky black polish with a few quick swipes of his bare hands. There was a kind of detached aloofness about the way he worked; purposeful, focused, and apparently oblivious to the world of hustle and bustle going on around him. The shoeshine man suddenly reached up and ran his polish-stained fingers lightly across the top of his head. *How strange,* Mikel thought. No wonder the old shoeshine man's hair always looked so black and shiny!

At that moment, as if caught by an invisible hand, Mikel came to a dead stop. He could not speak, and nor could he move. He just stood, listening intently. And in his heart, he knew that he would always remember this day, this very instant; the moment he'd heard the rich, strident sound of a guitar played like he'd never heard before.

"It's flamenco, Mikel!

Mikel felt the warmth of his father's hand leading him towards the café, the sound of the flamenco guitar becoming louder with every step.

"This isn't like the guitar music you play, Papa!" he said excitedly.

"No, Mikel. However hard I try, I will never be able to play the guitar like this."

On entering the café Mikel was struck breathless, his head giddy with the rush of hot air, thick with the scent of coffee and that potent treacle-like sherry Papa would sometimes buy for special occasions.

But he was faced with a human barrier: a crowd of onlookers, all pressing forward and trying to be closer to the source of that wild and compelling rhythm.

Mikel was almost choked with suspense, seized with the terrible notion that he might miss the opportunity to see for himself the maker of this exquisite sound.

"Papa, I can't see!"

Lifted onto Papa's shoulders, he now had a good view of the guitarist, a short, stout man in a glossy black suit and sombrero hat. But Mikel's attention was drawn to the guitar itself. He stared fixedly, captivated by its graceful curves, the ring around its sound aperture laced with pearly inlays of fruit and flowers, all beautifully engraved. Mikel gazed spellbound, marvelling at the way the man's fingers raced up and down an ebony fingerboard, the metalled frets sparkling, bathed in a shaft of sunlight from a side window. How the thumb and fingers of his right hand ripped into those strings, but with great skill, driven by the assured boldness of a master musician.

"He's a gypsy, Mikel. A gypsy from Andalusia."

The guitarist let out a long and melancholy moan, as if to engage more closely with the music, attuning with its life-force. Stamping with the heel of his shoe, his voice suddenly swelled, the walls of the café echoing as if to the shrill of a thousand tormented spirits.

"Now that's what I call singing!" Papa exclaimed. "Real Moorish music, aye Mikel?"

"Olé," someone replied softly, and with feeling. "Olé…"

The Town of Guernica

Mikel tilted back on his chair and gazed through the classroom window into a cloudless sky. High in the hills, beyond the edge of the town, he saw hundreds of trees decked in delicate shades of pink and white; the almonds were in flower. Down in the town itself, gardens were adorned with deep pink cherry blossom.

With all his heart, he longed to be out there, walking in the mountains, or down at the seaside watching huge waves rolling in from the Bay of Biscay and slamming into the rugged Basque coastline.

It seemed so unfair! Schools were supposed to be closed, the teachers having been called away to fight in the war. Only Father Imaz had been left behind. But Father Imaz was not a teacher. He was a priest.

Children younger than Mikel had been excused from school. Gorka was only seven, so he was allowed to stay at home with Mama. He would likely be playing out in the garden, or walking Raphael around the grazing field.

Mikel was nine. And sadly, that meant school!

Reluctantly, he turned his attention back to the front of the class. Father Imaz was still at his lectern, reading from the school Bible. He was dressed as usual in his long black cassock, the buttons at the front reaching right up to a high black collar around his neck. Unhurriedly, he turned another page.

For the past few weeks, Mikel thought he'd noticed a change in the priest's appearance. His face seemed thinner and more drawn. Someone had said that General Franco hated Basque priests almost as much as he hated Basque soldiers.

Could that explain why the brightness had gone from Father Imaz's eyes?

Mikel's attention wandered to Ainhoa. She was seated with her back to him, just a few desks further forward, her hair neatly gathered under a white band, secured with a big floppy bow. How very perfect she looked, sitting so straight with arms folded on the desk in front of her, and obviously intent on capturing the priest's every word. Mikel's pulse was apt to race a little at the thought of Ainhoa.

Father Imaz closed the Bible at last and clasped his hands tightly together across his chest.

"I want you to remember, children, that God will never forsake us. Because Guernica is an important town; a meeting place for Basque tribal chiefs since the dawn of time. God will always protect the people of—"

He broke off as the monotonous drone of an advancing aeroplane began to fill the classroom. Mikel turned again and peered out of the window. He saw nothing but blue sky. But the noise of the aeroplane grew steadily louder, and there was menace in its tone. In the deep recesses of Mikel's consciousness, veiled yet potentially terrifying, came the realisation that something wasn't right. It was flying too low. Was it going to crash?

Now the whole class was up on its feet, the children running to the windows and peering out.

BANG!

The explosion was followed by another, even louder than the first. At that moment, Mikel saw an aeroplane roar across the school playground at treetop height. It had two engines. He even managed to catch sight of the pilot's face looking down at him! Another tremendous blast followed, and this time Mikel felt the shock. A dense wave of impacted air slammed into his body. He dropped to the floor.

"God!" he gasped, burying his head in his hands. "Help! Help! Help!"

But the sound of his voice was drowned by another rapid succession of eruptions, shattering all the classroom windows and blowing away the door.

"Stay down!" Father Imaz screamed.

Another almighty **BANG!** and at that moment, Mikel could hear nothing. Gradually, a high-pitched humming noise, pulsating in sympathy with the beat of his thrashing heart, began to worm its way back into the forefront of his mind.

He stayed down for several more seconds before rising to his knees. Some other children had begun to stir. Covered in dust and grime, they appeared like writhing ghosts coming up from their graves.

As Mikel's sense of hearing began to recover, he became aware of the harsh crackling of things burning outside.

He drew a deep breath, and a stench of high explosive filled his lungs. He coughed and spat, his mouth and nostrils filling with acid and vomit.

Father Imaz staggered around the classroom, face blackened and cassock hanging in tatters. He stooped low, picking his way through a mound of wrecked desks and chairs.

"Ainhoa! Are you there? Are you alright, my child?"

Ainhoa was Father Imaz's favourite girl; his star pupil.

Mikel reached up and clung to a brick ledge. Scrambling to his feet, he peered out through a gaping hole that had once been a classroom window. It looked like hell out there; fire, black smoke and scorched earth. He saw an elderly couple running, screaming, from the ruins of their home, their bodies aflame.

This was too much.

He shrank back, collapsing down amidst shards of glass and lumps of building debris, his mind a confusion of fear and anguish.

He had almost begun to gather himself when he heard the unthinkable. The distant drone of more low-flying aeroplanes. More bombs… lots more. But they sounded further away.

Mikel was struck by a terrible thought. The eastern side! Mama… Papa… Gorka… Raphael… He must get home!

At lightning speed, he was up on his feet and heading for the doorway: a dark, jagged chasm in the classroom wall.

"Mikel!" the priest cried in a husky voice. "Mikel… stay! Don't go outside!"

But Mikel was as good as gone.

He tore past several shapeless piles of wood and brick rubble, dodged around an oily black bomb crater, the earth inside still burning fiercely, and began sprinting up the narrow country lane towards home.

Oblivious to the bombs exploding a kilometre or so off to one side, he sped past a motor car lying upside down in a ditch. What was left of its tyres was belching filthy, stinking, cloying plumes of smoke right up into the sky.

Just when it seemed nothing in the world could stop him, he slackened the pace and came to a halt. He turned, went back a few steps, and peered again at the car. His worst fears were realised. Ejected from the shattered windscreen, there lay the remains of a human body. A woman's hair, tangled amidst a sticky red horror, had flowed out onto the road, and for the first time in his life, Mikel caught the hideous stench of burning flesh. Dazed and nauseated, he stepped back and began to shake uncontrollably.

Market day! Papa was supposed to be down at the town centre, looking after his vegetable stall. Raphael, the little brown pony, would be there too. Or might they already have made their way home?

What was the last thing Papa had said before leaving the house this morning? Hadn't he promised to pick Mikel up from school on his way home from the market?

Against a background of throbbing indecision, he turned away from the direction of his home. With the sound of repeated explosions behind him, he sprinted off towards the town centre.

Along the roadsides he saw traumatised men, women and children. Most were seated on pavements, crying, dazed and unsure of what to do next. Uprooted and splintered trees lay scattered all around them.

Within minutes, he found himself approaching the market square.

The sound of exploding bombs had begun to ease. But then came another devilish noise: the high-pitched scream of more aeroplanes. They were flying towards him, very low down, and in a side-by-side formation. Fighter aircraft!

They began opening up with machine guns.

"Get down!" someone yelled: "Get down, or they'll cut you to pieces!"

Mikel ran headlong through the open door of a barber's shop, and flung himself down on the floor under the counter.

He heard the thud of bullets impacting outside. A shell ricocheted off the pavement, **PEEOWW**! It tore through the shop counter above his head. A young soldier, no older than a teenager, threw himself into the shop and landed on his stomach beside Mikel. His rifle skidded away across the floor.

"Keep still! For God's sake, don't go out; more bombers are coming in!"

He'd hardy finished speaking when there was another **BANG!** Mikel felt the air punched down into his lungs and then, just as quickly, sucked out again.

"Bloody swines!" the young soldier threw out violently.

Mikel lay still for several more minutes as wave after wave of aircraft attacked the town centre.

Suddenly they were gone; another lull in the bombing and strafing. What to do now? Where to go? Papa and Raphael... they would be waiting for him in the square! Just a few hundred metres more! Mikel leapt up and dashed outside.

"Boy!" somebody yelled. "Give me a hand, will you?"

Mikel froze. Glancing to his side, he saw another soldier. He was pulling with all his might, trying to drag two bodies off the road, blood streaming out behind.

"I... I can't!" Mikel stammered. "I've got to..."

Then, as if suddenly liberated from a deep paralysis, he turned and raced on. Struck by an instant stab of shame, he felt robbed of all compassion. Tears of disgrace welled up, cascading down his cheeks and nose.

Approaching the market entrance, he slowed to a walking pace. The scene that confronted him was impossible to imagine. The market square was unrecognisable. The big stone buildings that had once surrounded the area were reduced to skeletons. Flames leapt up from every side, the square itself a smoking chaos of twisted metal girders. Blocks of shattered concrete and shards of broken glass were strewn everywhere. Fragments of heavy wooden beams were tossed up at crazy angles. Not one single building was left with its walls or roof intact.

Mikel saw a crowd of people wandering in an aimless daze. An old man was seated on a concrete block, hunched forward, supporting himself on a walking stick. A trickle of blood ran down his wrinkled forehead.

Fixing Mikel with a wild stare, the old man pointed his stick up to the sky.

"Guernica is finished," he wailed. "The Germans, they have bombed us!"

Mikel lunged onwards. He must find that corner of the square that had been reserved for Papa's vegetable stall. Above the groans of grief and pain, he heard the sound of yet more bomb blasts. They were distant and muffled at first, but then the explosions came closer, increasing in severity. At that moment, the sudden high-pitched whine of an aero engine blasted his ears. He looked up to see another of those wretched fighter aircraft passing right over his head. Higher still, and moving in the same direction, were several waves of more two-engine bombers.

He fell to the ground as a bomb exploded off to his side, sending a sheet of flame streaking out across the square. What remained of a partially ruined building suddenly collapsed in a filthy, yellowish cloud of smoke and debris.

Mikel raised his head. In the midst of it all, he saw a priest down on his knees in prayer. His cassock was torn, stained grey by dust and detritus. A small group had gathered around him, all kneeling. They were very close to where Papa would have set up his stall.

Mikel scrambled forward on all fours. He passed a number of partially clothed bodies, charred and blackened, smoke still rising from them, the stench indescribable. A pain of suffocation beat in his chest; his breath stifled in his throat. Only God could save him now.

Exhausted, he pushed on towards the kneeling priest, blundering over the last few metres in a kind of stupor. Breaking into a paroxysm of sobs, he reached out and touched the shredded hem of the cassock.

In a sudden flash of recognition, he cried out, "Father!"

Father Imaz turned, his skin deathly pale beneath the streaks of black soot that lined his sombre face.

"It's alright, Mikel. Your father went home early. He will come back to collect you soon. When all this is over."

Farewell to Guernica

The old cart moved slowly along the rutted track. A signpost pointed the way ahead, towards Bilbao. Mikel sat with his knees clasped close to his chest, his backside aching as the rough timber planking trembled beneath him.

He gazed down at his dirty legs, the skin on his knees scuffed and lacerated, the blood half congealed. He scraped at one of the smaller scabs with his fingernail. It loosened and came away surprisingly easily, leaving the skin smooth and pinkish beneath. He studied the crusty specimen closely, rolling it over between his thumb and forefinger, and then flicked it over the side.

Heaving a sigh, he gazed upwards at a flock of seagulls soaring in tight circles, growing smaller as they rose into the warmth of the morning sun. *The ocean must be close.*

He glanced towards his mother. She sat with her legs outstretched, leaning her back against the old orange box that Papa had used as a driving seat for as long as Mikel could remember. She was cuddling Mikel's young brother, Gorka, on her lap. Gorka was still fast asleep.

Mikel reflected on this image of his mother and felt sure it would stay with him. She'd never looked so beautiful; the embroidered sleeves of her white blouse extended a little beyond the cuffs of her finest dress; her dark hair parted down the middle, curling upwards at the sides to reveal a tiny earring. She was staring past him, trancelike, in the direction of the home they'd left behind. Glancing over his shoulder, Mikel followed her gaze.

Guernica was out of sight now, hidden behind the hills. But a yellow smog lingered over the ruins of the town like a poisonous cloud; a dirty smudge against the clear blue sky.

It had been several days since the air raid and Mikel had lost all sense of time. He remembered being at school on the day of the attack. Father Imaz had made a solemn promise that God would protect Guernica and its people.

How could a priest be so badly wrong? Mikel felt an icy coldness take hold of him as he remembered the terrifying noise of those bombs raining down for more than three hours. He sighed again, spasmodically, his whole body shaking violently. He must try not to think about the past.

He turned back to look at Mama. And now she met his gaze, her eyes still red and misted with the pain of it all.

"You'll have a sore bottom, Mikel," she said. "Why not go and sit with Papa?"

"No, I'm fine."

Mikel longed to talk to her about what had happened. But could he bear to see her cry?

He looked away to his side. A sudden breeze swept across the lush meadowland. Flexing with the wind, a tract of long grass darkened and appeared to race like a crazy spirit over the surface of a vast unbroken sea of green pasture. It moved swiftly, twisting and turning into the distance until it disappeared, blending with the distant hills. And there he saw tiny specks of white moving on the grassy slopes. Sheep… They would be migrating up into the mountain grazing lands, just as Father Imaz had taught at school.

Mikel fixed his attention on Raphael, the little brown pony, now so thin and slow. When did poor Raphael last have an oat bag fastened to his bridle?

And when had Mikel himself last enjoyed a bowl of chickpea soup, a plate of rice, or a piece of oatcake? Where were they going to find their next meal? When would they be allowed to return home? And Papa's guitar; why hadn't they brought Papa's guitar with them? So many questions. But Papa had become strangely silent. He'd hardly spoken a word since the bombing. Where could Mikel turn for answers?

"The guitar, Papa!" he exclaimed. "We didn't bring your guitar!"

Hunched forwards, with one hand resting on his thigh, the other loosely holding the reins, Papa urged the pony on with a click of his tongue.

"Papa?"

Papa turned his head, just a little.

"We had to get away, Mikel. There wasn't time."

Suddenly restless, Mikel rose unsteadily to his feet. The cart lurched. He tottered forward, grasping Papa's shoulder for support.

"Hold tight, Mikel!" Papa reached out to steady him. "Watch your step!"

Here was another sight; Papa's eyes, now grave and distrustful. Papa turned away and faced the road ahead.

"We could go back and get the guitar," Mikel persisted.

Papa heaved a deep sigh.

"You must make a new one, Mikel. I'll hear you play it one day."

A whitewashed cottage appeared off to the side, its red and green shutters closed, not a soul in sight. This was unusual for mid-morning. Maybe they'd been frightened by the noise of the bombs, the aerial attack led by what Papa had called Hitler's Condor Legion, which had shattered all the homes of Guernica. Maybe these country folks were hiding themselves away, trying to pretend that it had never happened.

Bilbao harbour would be near. But why should they have to go there? If only someone would speak to him, explain what was going to happen.

"How long will it take us to reach Bilbao?" Mikel tried to sound cheerful.

Papa shook his head sorrowfully.

"You've forgotten already, Mikel?"

Mikel felt his father's arm around his waist, drawing him closer.

"How often have we travelled to the city together, just you and me?"

"Lots of times, Papa, but not down this road; this is slow!"

"No, Mikel. It will be *quicker* this way. The main highway is blocked."

Papa's embrace tightened.

"So… our last journey together. For a little while anyway. Aye Mikel?"

Last journey? How could that be? How could everything change so quickly?

The vast ocean opened to Mikel's right. He'd seen it before many times, twinkling and shimmering in the sunlight. But today it looked cold and grey.

"I don't want to go, Papa!" The words burst woefully from Mikel's lips, unrestrained and without thought. "I don't want to go away!"

Papa glanced round at him, and Mikel felt himself drawn to those tired, distraught eyes.

"You *must* go, Mikel! You must go with Gorka across the sea, to be safe!" Papa tugged at Mikel's arm and pulled him down onto the driving seat beside him. "Mikel, listen to me! Hundreds of people are being executed, almost as fast as they can be put on trial; ordinary people, just like Mama and Gorka! The Generalissimo is taking everything away from us, even our language!"

A tear rolled down Papa's cheek, blending with the rough of his moustache. Mikel wanted to back off; anything to keep Papa from crying.

"And our industries!" he went on grimly. "The Generalissimo is even sending our coal and steel to Germany. And all because his friend, Chancellor Hitler, wants to prepare for war… his *big bloody war*!"

What did Papa mean by Hitler's 'big war'? And why did Generalissimo Franco hate the Basque people so much?

"Mikel, you're almost a man now," Papa said in a gentler voice. "There's nothing left for you here. It's too dangerous. And we need you to look after Gorka. He's just a child, Mikel. Your mother's worried about Gorka. She needs you to take care of him."

"But… but why, Papa? Why can't we all stay *together*? Aren't families supposed to—" Mikel broke off, stifled by the look on Papa's face.

"No! You *must* understand, Mikel! It wasn't just Guernica! Durango was bombed too, and soon it will be Bilbao. The Generalissimo and Chancellor Hitler are out to destroy us! There isn't a single town in the Basque Country that is safe!"

Mikel stole another glance at that endless stretch of open water, the Bay of Biscay.

"But where will *you* go?" His voice trembled as he fought against the tears. "And Mama? How will I know where to find you?"

"We'll be waiting for you, Mikel. At the harbour. We'll always be waiting for you."

When Mama spoke, her voice sounded very faint.

"Father Imaz has arranged everything," she murmured. "We must put our trust in Father Imaz."

Santurtzi, Bilbao Harbour

Resting his cheek against Raphael's muzzle, Mikel stroked the pony's breast and inhaled his musty scent. The poor creature would be thirsty. But Mikel daren't leave the cart to go in search of water; Gorka was much too young to be left on his own.

Squinting up into the glare of the mid-day sun, he saw Gorka standing on the cart and gazing out across the harbour.

"Which ship are we going on?" Gorka beamed with excitement.

"How should I know?" Mikel snapped.

It wasn't right! How could Gorka appear so happy, so eager to leave?

Mikel scanned the line of merchant ships, the closest just a stone's throw away. They looked horrible; rusty and ugly, not like the big ships he'd seen before at Bilbao harbour, nicely painted and manned by cheerful sailors. He glanced up again at Gorka.

"Mama and Papa have gone to find out which ship is ours! You must stay on the cart, Gorka! I'll get the blame if you get lost!"

Suddenly, without warning, the quayside echoed to the powerful blast of a ship's horn. Caught off guard, Mikel froze, shocked rigid, as a cold sweat broke out over his whole body. Raphael reared up, tossing his head wildly and pounding the cobbled stone surface with his front hooves. The cart heaved and swayed perilously.

Gorka tottered uncontrollably and dropped down onto his knees.

"Mikel!" he yelled. "Mikel… Stop him!"

Seizing the bridle, Mikel eased down on the reins and breathed gently into the pony's ear.

Raphael's fit of fright began to fade. Head lowered, he began to murmur that characteristic low resonating sound from deep inside his throat.

"Stay with me, Mikel," he seemed to say. *"Don't leave me alone with such an awful noise, and with all these strange people."*

Was this to be the last time Mikel would feel Raphael's closeness, the warmth and love of his childhood friend?

"Gorka!" Mikel cried. "Can you see them yet?"

Gorka sprang up and looked around.

"No! Too many people…"

Mikel scanned the crowd. This was nothing like the Bilbao he remembered from other times. People were pouring onto the quayside from buses, lorries, pickup vans, high-sided wagons drawn by horses, and smaller pony and mule carts. There were shiny motor cars too; drivers sounding their horns, reaching out of windows and waving pedestrians aside. They were getting nowhere.

There were children too; hundreds, thousands of them. They were carrying bundles, bags, satchels and suitcases. Some were crying; others were silent, their faces pale and vacuous.

"Someone's looking at us!" Gorka yelled.

Following Gorka's gaze, Mikel spotted a young girl standing alone in the midst of the chaos and confusion. She stared back at him, her face transfixed. It looked like Ainhoa. Could it possibly be? Was she lost? Should he go to her? But he'd left it too late. Grasped by the hand, she was hurried away by a couple of panic-stricken adults.

So where were Papa and Mama? They'd been gone for ages.

What if they couldn't find places on the ships? For a moment Mikel's hopes began to rise. He might have to stay at home after all, bombs or no bombs.

Then a voice. "Mikel!"

It wasn't Papa's voice, but familiar just the same. He heard it again.

"Mikel! Gorka!"

At that moment he saw Father Imaz; the man everyone had wanted to cling to throughout that interminable bombing attack. He was pushing his way through the crowd, the hem of his long black cassock ballooning in the breeze. He looked weary, his face glistening with perspiration as he drew closer.

"Mikel!" he panted, taking hold of the cart's draw-arm for support. "Your father, Mikel! Where is your father? Tell me! Quickly!"

"He's gone with Mama. Over there…" Mikel pointed towards the furthest ship.

Smoke rose up like a cloud of black soot from its funnel. Swept along by the wind, the smutty plume rolled across the sparkling water of the inner harbour and out towards the open sea. Father Imaz shook his head frantically.

"We have to leave… *now*, Mikel!"

"No!" A chaotic tide of resentment welled up inside Mikel. Why should he obey the orders of a priest whose words had already proved false? "I won't go! I'm not going anywhere! Not without saying goodbye to Mama and Papa!"

"Mikel…" The priest's expression hardened. "Our people are aboard already! The ship is set to depart, Mikel! You must come with me! Now! Both of you!"

Gorka began jumping up and down on the cart.

"They're here!" he cried. "Look, Mikel! Mama and Papa; they're coming!"

But Mikel could hardly steel himself to look. Leaning his head against Raphael's warm, clammy neck, all hopes of returning to Guernica began to slip away. He heard Papa calling.

"Father Imaz! We've been trying to find you, Father!"

"Señor Aguirre!" Father Imaz cried. "I must take the boys immediately!" The priest reached up and hauled Gorka from the cart, setting him down near Papa and Mama. "Time is short, Señor!" he gasped.

"Which one is ours, Papa?" Gorka grinned.

"You're sailing on the biggest ship, Gorka!" Papa replied. "And you're going to England! Isn't that right, Father Imaz?"

Papa sounded in good spirits now. He must be putting on a brave act for the priest. And for Mama too, of course; Mama looked distraught.

"How many children, Father?" she murmured.

"Oh, many hundreds," the priest replied. "The ships are sailing for England, France and Belgium."

Father Imaz turned towards the nearest vessel. It was smaller than the others, and very rusty.

"But not that old tub," he muttered, fidgeting with a crucifix suspended from his neck by a long cord. "That one's going to Denmark." He studied the ship for a few moments longer. "Ours is bigger!" he suddenly exclaimed. "Much bigger! We shall have *plenty* of room on our ship! Now, where are the boys' belongings?"

Mama appeared to come alive with a jolt.

"The box!" she cried.

Papa jumped up onto the cart. Lifting the lid from the orange box, he withdrew a big canvas bag and handed it down to Mama, then leapt to the ground.

"Spare clothes," Mama smiled through her tears. "For both of you. Some goat's cheese, and your favourite white asparagus, freshly picked. Eat it soon! Smoked sausages, a little ham... a little..." Her voice faltered, fading away as Mikel took the heavy bag from her.

"Time to say goodbye," said Father Imaz, placing a hand on Mama's shoulder. "The boys will be well looked after, Señora." He turned to Papa. "And they'll be well educated, Señor Aguirre! Some teachers from Guernica are travelling with us!"

Mama knelt down and gathered Gorka into her arms.

Mikel hesitated. Hadn't he already said goodbye, in his heart? He leaned forward quickly and kissed Mama firmly on her temple. He tasted salt, and pulled back again.

He was being childish and stupid. He must act like a grown-up! Try to appear strong and dutiful! He turned to Papa.

"Goodbye Papa," he said simply.

Papa reached out and took his hand. Oh, just nine years old, it was Mikel's first handshake! Feeling a little embarrassed, he glanced down at the cobblestones; anything to avoid the sadness in Papa's eyes. Then, suddenly, he felt himself swept up into Papa's arms, enfolded in a warm, tight embrace.

"Take care of Gorka," Papa whispered.

"Who would have thought it?" Mama said softly. "My two young men going all the way to England."

"Come along, then!" Father Imaz cried.

Mikel felt the priest's hand on his shoulder, urging him

away towards the crowd. A tumultuous profusion of disturbed humanity awaited him. After a few steps, Mikel paused and turned back.

"Your guitar, Papa!" he cried. "We didn't bring your guitar!"

"It didn't survive, Mikel! You must make another one, just like we said!"

Papa's lips were trembling, his face swept by a strange mix of outrage and despair; in Mama's expression, a profound sense of misery and absolute loss. The ship's horn sounded again. Little Raphael stood firm, his head bobbing slowly up and down… a fond farewell.

"Hurry, boys!" the priest exclaimed.

Mikel took Gorka by the hand. They turned together and followed Father Imaz into the crowd. After a few steps, Mikel heard Papa's voice again.

"Make another guitar, Mikel! Bring it with you when you come home!"

With a tightening in his heart, Mikel glanced up, and through a film of tears he saw a blurred image of the mighty ship that would take him across the Bay of Biscay to a place called England.

On Board Ship

The vessel now seemed a far cry from the one Mikel had boarded just a couple of hours ago. Whilst passing through the tranquil waters of Bilbao harbour he'd felt safe, thrilled by the experience of being at sea for the very first time. But now, with the deck pitching and rolling beneath him, he was suffering badly.

Having already spewed the minuscule contents of his stomach overboard, there was little more he could do except cling tightly to the side rail and endure this awful feeling of seasickness.

Further along the deck, some older boys were also up at the rail.

"Over there!" cried one of the lads, pointing aft. The sound of his voice was barely audible above the moaning wind as it beat around the superstructure.

Mikel turned and followed his gaze. Beyond the ship's wake, hurled up on the crest of a wave, he saw the smaller vessel that Father Imaz had called a bath tub. It had been the first of the flotilla to set sail, but Mikel's own ship had overtaken it. Now, the rusty old tub had fallen behind.

Further to the horizon, Mikel could see nothing of Bilbao's harbour or the warehouses on the quayside. The Basque mainland had almost disappeared, except for now and then a glimpse of some faraway mountains, their white tops glistening in the late afternoon sun.

Mikel peered down towards the heaving black swell at the side of the ship. Where were Mama and Papa now, he wondered. And where would they sleep tonight? Would they stay in Bilbao and sleep out in the open, as many others had done since the bombing? Or would they return to what was left of Guernica? Papa had reckoned that a town already levelled was unlikely to suffer another pounding.

They might be close to home at this very moment. Mama would be seated on the pony cart and looking out across the water towards him. Mikel thought of her canvas bag lying in a storeroom somewhere below deck. She'd labelled it carefully: *Mikel and Gorka Aguirre*. He would treasure that canvas bag always. But he didn't like to think about the contents. Sausages and ham… ugh!

Struck by another sickening contortion from somewhere deep inside his abdomen, Mikel held his breath and waited for the acid tide of vomit to fill his mouth and nose. But this time, nothing came.

Several more boys had arrived, all clutching the side rail. Gorka was not among them.

Gorka had gone inside with the rest of the kids; hundreds of them. He would be running around the corridors, making a nuisance of himself with the crew, showing off to all the girls what a good sailor he was on a rough sea.

But Mikel didn't care. He was content to be out in the open where he could grieve in private, and without making a fool of himself. Besides, there were long queues at the lavatories. They were blocked and in a terrible state.

"It's gone!" one of the boys suddenly yelled. "It's not there!"

Mikel turned his attention back towards the aft section. He could see nothing but huge waves; great billowing masses of rising and collapsing rollers. The rusty old bucket had disappeared!

A loud crackling sound emerged from the public address system, close to where he stood. It was a man's voice, broken and incomprehensible. After a few moments he heard another sound: a loudhailer from somewhere high above his head.

"All hands! All hands! We're going about!" Then, after a pause, "Medics! Report to the bridge! Medics to the bridge, immediately!"

Mikel felt the deck shudder beneath him as the bow of his ship came slowly round. And now the waves were coming from behind, throwing up the stern to such a height that it seemed the deck might break in two.

"Hey! You lot!" someone yelled. "Get inside!"

Mikel glanced along the gyrating, sea-drenched deck and saw a sailor moving towards him. He wore a large yellow hat, and a long yellow cape reaching down to his boots. Clinging to the side rail and advancing hand over hand to keep his balance, the sailor called out again.

"Come on! It's *dangerous* out here! Get inside, before you all get washed overboard!" Wrapping an arm around the rail, he pointed towards an open door. "Get in there! All of you!"

One by one, the boys let go of the side rail and lurched towards the safety of the cabin.

Mikel lingered. What about those other children, the ones in that rusty old bath tub? He wanted to be close to them. Hadn't he watched their parents standing on the quayside, trying to look cheerful as they'd waved their kids goodbye?

"Come along, young feller!"

Mikel felt his arm seized in a powerful grip.

"No!" he sobbed. "I can't! Please! I want to help!"

Seeing the look of alarm on the sailor's face, Mikel began to sense the danger. It was time to give way.

Releasing his hold on the rail, he felt himself being hauled, slipping and sliding, towards a dark hole in the wall. He stepped awkwardly over a bulkhead and into a large cabin that stank of vomit. A heavy metal door slammed shut behind him. He turned, holding tightly to the handle, and in the dim light he saw a hundred or so children sprawled across the floor, many slumped against the walls. There was no childish chatter, only crying and retching.

Some grimy circular portholes filtered the sunlight. Two electric light bulbs on the ceiling flickered, their wire mesh cages dangling and swinging ominously from side to side.

As his eyes grew more accustomed to the gloom, Mikel saw a space between some kids seated on the floor at the farthest side. He would make his move... now! Thrusting himself forward, he sidestepped as best he could around the wretched bodies and puddles of stinking vomit, struggling to remain upright as the floor heaved and rolled beneath him. Exhausted, dizzy and almost overcome with nausea, he slumped down quickly, squeezing himself into a narrow gap between two girls.

Mikel closed his eyes. Pressing himself against the cold steel wall behind, he felt the power of the sea. The floor rose up as if propelling him to an unimaginable height. It hung there for several moments before falling back, so that his whole body became almost weightless in the downward plunge.

He tried to imagine the scene outside; those poor children tossed into a mountainous sea, clawing desperately at the barnacled and rust-encrusted bottom of a massive, upturned hull, their screams for help blown away by the vicious wind.

"Save them," he murmured under his breath. "Please... please just save them."

A small voice interrupted his thoughts.

"Mikel?"

He turned to meet the eyes of the girl to the left of him.

"Ainhoa?"

Her smile went straight to his heart. But a crushing weight pressed down on his soul, and he could think of nothing to say.

Once again, the public address system began to hiss and

crackle. Then, just as before, it fell silent. There followed another broadcast from the loudhailer, muffled but still audible.

"All hands! All hands get below!" There was a pause before the voice continued, "Recovery vessels alerted!" And then, in a more sombre tone, "No survivors! Repeat, there are no survivors."

Chapter 2

THE WEST MIDLANDS
OF ENGLAND

8 Years Later – November 1945

Refugee Camp

Father Imaz was a good man. He'd converted a ramshackle Nissan hut into a workshop, kitting it out with carpentry tools so the refugee boys could develop their woodworking skills. Access to G-clamps, chisels and a smoothing plane had opened up fresh horizons for Mikel; a new world of craft opportunities.

And now his very first guitar was almost finished. But he wasn't happy with it. Having worked on the tuning mechanism for several days, the instrument still sounded dull and wouldn't hold pitch.

"Damn!" he muttered.

If only it wasn't so cold! But at least the workshop was dry. The rest of the camp was a wreck. The refugee kids had vented their frustration on the place. There were broken windows everywhere. The ablutions facilities were a nightmare; cracked washbasins, and never any hot water.

Mikel cupped his hands and blew hard on his numb fingers.

Thankfully, all the other carpentry enthusiasts had gone to lunch. He could work alone now, without interruption. He stood back from the bench and scanned the workshop.

A couple of small wooden lamp stands, nicely turned but not yet varnished. Some partially assembled chairs and bookcases. An unfinished writing cabinet, probably abandoned, stood in a corner gathering dust.

Flexing his fingers, Mikel turned his attention back to the guitar and gave the tuning pegs a quarter turn each. They held firm; no slippage. He took a tuning fork from his apron pocket, struck it lightly on the bench, and listened carefully to the pitch… Bass E. He lifted the guitar and plucked the bass string. It twanged horribly.

There was only one thing for it: a new soundboard with thinner wood. He'd read in a book that thinner woods might produce better sounds.

He gave a start as the outside door burst open behind him. He spun round, chilled to the marrow as a rush of freezing November air swept into the workshop.

His heart sank. It was Imanol: the bright young man Ainhoa had chosen to be her boyfriend.

"Ah, so there you are," Imanol said casually. "I might have guessed."

Imanol looked snug in his thick overcoat and a fur-lined hat with floppy sides covering his ears. He slammed the door shut and strode briskly up to the workbench.

"Christ alive," he muttered. "It's bloody freezing in here."

"It's not that bad." Mikel laid his guitar down on the bench. "Not when you're working."

It hurt like hell to be standing this close to Ainhoa's boyfriend. Imanol was from a wealthy industrial family. If he could get himself repatriated back to Bilbao, he'd be set to become a successful manufacturing baron.

"You know it's Ainhoa's birthday," Imanol said.

"Yes, of course I know. She's eighteen."

It was difficult for Mikel to believe that Ainhoa was the same girl he'd shared that miserable sea voyage with eight years ago. She was now a fine young woman.

"Yep… eighteen," Imanol replied, reproachfully. "And she's expecting you to be at her birthday dance."

"Dance?" Mikel's heart gave a sudden heavy bound.

"In the main hall… tonight!" Imanol threw out the words like a viper spits out venom. "Surely you must have heard about it!"

Mikel shuddered at the thought. He'd already known about Imanol and Ainhoa sloping off together in the middle of the night. It had plagued him for months. Watching them dance together? It was enough to turn his stomach.

"I'm not sure," he muttered. "I'll see how it goes."

"Oh, come on, Mikel! You can't spend all your life tweaking bloody guitars."

"I told you… I'll think about it."

"Well, you better had! She told me to remind you. If you don't turn up, I'll get a sodding earful."

Mikel untied his apron and tossed it down beside the guitar. The creative energy had gone out of him.

"Ah well!" Imanol gave a shrug. "Message passed. Duty done. By the way, I heard your brother's going to the party."

"Gorka? Yes, I'm sure he is."

"So be there! He needs looking after. We don't want him stealing all the bloody girls!"

Imanol moved away and yanked open the door. Another chill of frigid air surged around Mikel's body. It was like being sprayed with crushed ice. Imanol paused and glanced back.

"And another thing," he said, "have you heard the latest?"

"What latest?"

"The Home Guard… it's being disbanded."

"Why not? The war's over, isn't it?"

"The local platoon's doing something this afternoon. Some kind of celebration. They've got a regular army guy coming in to give a talk. Father Imaz says we can join them. What about you?"

"Maybe. What's the talk about?"

"Don't know for sure. Weaponry, I think."

Imanol gazed up into the arched roof of the Nissan hut.

"God knows what'll happen to this place when they've gone. Bloody dump! I expect they'll pull it all down once they've finished with it."

Mikel drew himself up, his lips and face stiff with cold.

"Where's the talk?" he said.

"Main hall, two-thirty. It's the only place to go if you want to stay warm. They'll have a couple of coke fires burning. Ainhoa's party starts later… same place at four. See you there!"

Imanol was suddenly gone, the door slamming shut behind him.

Mikel sauntered over to a side window. He gazed out upon a scene of melancholy. Winter had come early to England. A bitter frost had gripped the country even before the leaves had fallen. The sight of those ex-army Nissan huts, now mostly derelict and with graffiti scrawled across their bleak corrugated metal walls, served only to remind him of his yearning to be home.

He watched as a couple of refugee lads, hands buried deep inside their overcoat pockets, shuffled out of the canteen and headed off towards one of the accommodation huts. A sharp wind had blown up since dawn, and the meagre sunlight that now bathed those two desolate figures was pale and cold.

Mikel felt an uncomfortable hollowness in the pit of his stomach. He drew a deep, sighing breath, and with a twinge of self-deprecation remembered that he'd missed his lunch.

An army lecture about weaponry? Stripping and reassembling rifles? Sounded a bit dreary, but at least none of the girls would be there. It would be good to get Ainhoa off his mind. Oh God… Ainhoa! That wonderful store of mysterious secrets. The very thought of her was enough to drive Mikel mad with jealousy. But guns and ammunition… that was a man's thing. Definitely not something to interest Ainhoa. And besides, the main hall would be warm. So why not?

Weapon Training

Turning up the collar of his charity-handout overcoat, Mikel approached the large black Nissan building known throughout the camp as the main hall. Ice that had formed overnight was beginning to thaw and the road had turned to mud. It would freeze again before sunset.

Despite having arrived at the camp eight years ago, Mikel had never once set foot inside the main hall. Refugee kids had broken into the building on numerous occasions, but they'd never returned with anything interesting. According to reports, it was just a large expanse of wooden floor, along with a few tables and chairs, a couple of blackboards mounted on easels, and an old chest full of maps and other useless stuff.

The hall had served as a base for the local Home Guard throughout the war years. The platoon commander had often complained to Father Imaz about things going missing, including maps and aircraft recognition posters. The Basque refugee quarters were always being searched. Gorka's bedroom would usually be first on the list, but nothing had ever been found. Gorka was fast becoming known as a sneaky operator. He was always bragging about having enough money to buy things, but never revealed the source of his income.

As Mikel drew closer to the hall, he saw smoke rising from its two chimneys, one at each end. At least it would be warm inside. Tea and biscuits, maybe… Isn't that what the Home Guard feasted on when they weren't out on exercise? Having missed his lunch, a few biscuits would be welcome.

The double doors at the front of the hall were shut. A dozen or so refugee lads had gathered outside at the base of the steps. They stood silently, like penguins, huddled together against the biting wind. At that moment, Mikel heard a familiar and very raucous sound coming from inside the hall.

"LEFT, two, three, four! LEFT, two, three, four! Left, right, left…" And then, after a pause, "Idle hair! Idle boots! Idle bloody everything! Pick up the step! Pick it up!"

It would be the Home Guard's weekly drill practice, the

local platoon being put through its paces, and probably for the last time.

One of the refugee lads sidled up to Mikel.

"Afternoon," he mumbled, offering a cigarette. "You can thank your brother for these."

Mikel shook his head.

"Why can't they do their bloody marching outside?" somebody groaned.

"Because it's warmer inside," replied another. "Won't be long now; they'll be finished in ten minutes or so."

A shiny military car swept into view and drew up at the hall entrance. A young uniformed army officer manoeuvred himself awkwardly out from the passenger's side carrying a walking stick.

"Afternoon, lads," he chirped. "Waiting for the weapons briefing? Come on, then!"

All spruced up, with peaked cap and a brown leather shoulder strap placed diagonally across his chest, he limped up the steps and pushed open the double doors.

The refugee boys filed into the hall behind the officer, and the harsh sound of heavy boots stomping on the wooden floor came to a swift 'halt!'

"Thank Christ for that," one of the lads muttered.

"Room! Atten…tion!" bellowed the drill sergeant.

"At ease, gentlemen," said the officer. "Good news! Your instructor today is Corporal Pringle, a man with war experience. Corporal Pringle survived Dunkirk, and then went on to serve in my battalion during the D-Day landings. What Pringle doesn't know about gunnery and ballistics isn't worth knowing. Enjoy the afternoon, gentlemen!"

The drill sergeant saluted. The officer returned and strode from the hall with a very uneven gait.

"Right, you lot!" The sergeant pointed to a makeshift classroom at the side of the hall, where several desks had been placed. "Get yourselves seated! Now!"

Soldiers from the Home Guard platoon moved swiftly and took their seats on the back rows.

It was a slightly worrying scenario. A blackboard and easel had been positioned at the front of the class. Pencils and paper had been neatly placed on the desks. A burden of oppression fell upon Mikel, stifling his hopes for a quiet hour of easy listening.

"Come along if you're coming, lads!" the sergeant bellowed. "Don't just stand there picking your bloody noses! Get yourselves sat down!"

Escape was now impossible.

Mikel pushed his way past some boys scrambling for the remaining seats at the back of the class. He headed for the front row, sat down quickly, and instantly regretted the decision. He was exposed and vulnerable.

The double doors opened again, then slammed shut with a mighty echoing bang. Mikel turned to see the instructor, a wizened army corporal with ribbons of war emblazoned across the breast of his tunic. The instructor stood for a long moment, surveying the class from a distance. He marched smartly forward, his expression serious. He seemed preoccupied, as if persecuted by some unending wartime torment, a nightmare of unyielding despair.

He came to a stop in front of the class, his eyes narrowing. Mikel held his breath.

With a contorted smile, the instructor reached behind his back and snatched a bayonet from a sheath attached to his webbing belt. Holding the silvery blade aloft for all to see, he ran his bony finger slowly down its full length.

"What's this, then?" he croaked.

"It's the blood-run, Corporal!" someone called out.

"The blood-run…" the instructor echoed in a low, yet strangely menacing, tone.

Oh, that awful grin, the lips widening to reveal traces of tobacco trapped in the clefts of his blackened teeth!

"What's it for, then… the blood-run?"

A pulsating rush of blood surged through Mikel's stupefied brain as the instructor's rat-like eyes settled on him.

"Come on, lad! What's it for?"

"I… I…" Locked in the grip of terror, Mikel felt like an idiot, his insides turning to water.

Mercifully, someone else called out.

"It reduces cavitation, Corporal! It facilitates withdrawal of the blade!"

Then a sharp metallic *click* as the instructor pressed the bayonet down over the end of a rifle barrel, locking it firmly into place with a twist of his sinewy hand.

Once again, those demonic eyes fell upon Mikel. Another question was about to be shot at him. A wave of debilitating fear surged up through his spine, clawing at his pounding heart. Would he know the answer? Would someone else call out on his behalf? Imanol was to blame for this! Imanol and Father Imaz: they had made this happen!

Ainhoa's Dance

A trumpet blast from two large gramophone speakers crashed into Mikel's brain. How he longed to be away from this place.

Setting his teeth against the discordant din, he fixed his eyes on a thin vortex of cigarette smoke. He watched as it curled slowly upwards, passed an electric light bulb dangling from a long flex, and eventually disappeared into the gloomy shadows of the arched corrugated roof of the main hall.

He detested all this razzmatazz; the flurry of skirts as the girls spun and twisted to the accompaniment of America's latest big-band sound, the boys showing off and prancing around like crazed chickens. They had no idea what *real* music was like. Classical music was so much kindlier. And then there was flamenco. There was nothing to compare with the glorious resonance of the Spanish guitar, especially in the hands of a natural genius like Azpiazu, the Basque maestro.

A hand slammed hard on the table where Mikel sat. It was like a slap in the face; the shock, instantaneous, made Mikel catch his breath.

He looked up and saw his brother, Gorka, towering over him and grinning from ear to ear.

"Gorka!" Mikel exclaimed. "Don't creep up! You could kill somebody doing that!"

Gorka dragged a seat from another table and sat down facing Mikel.

"Brother!" Gorka gave Mikel a withering look. "You look like a paralytic deadbeat!"

"That's not fair. You know I can't dance."

"Won't dance, more likely. Anyone can dance!"

Gorka flipped open the top button of his double-breasted jacket and subtly revealed a hip flask.

"Maybe this'll help," he grinned. "Want some?"

"Where did you get that?"

"That's for me to know," Gorka smiled slyly.

He glanced furtively over his shoulder, then took a quick swig and slid the flask back into his inner pocket.

"Better not let Father Imaz catch you," Mikel grumbled.

"Ha!" Gorka slipped a cigarette between his lips and searched his pockets for a light. "It's a poor thing when you can't manage a dance on Ainhoa's birthday."

"I told you, Gorka. It's not my style."

Two cackling trollops suddenly appeared and hauled Gorka up from his chair. The unlit cigarette popped out of his mouth and rolled across the table. Gorka staggered for a moment, recovered his balance, and then threw a silver cigarette lighter down in front of Mikel.

"Go on, brother!" he laughed. "Help yourself!"

A moment later, he was back on the dance floor.

Mikel watched as Gorka twisted and turned, his tie sent flying as he bounced and spun rhythmically to one of those new American jitterbug routines. Gorka reached out and drew both girls into a writhing embrace. They screamed ecstatically.

Mikel studied the girls carefully. Slim and serpentine, they moved like snakes. He'd seen one of them before, her face daubed with cheap rouge, flaunting herself around the camp. She'd be one of those refugees from Durango, a small market town to the south of Guernica; just another of Gorka's many one-night stands.

But Gorka was right. Ainhoa deserved better than to have a miserable deadbeat at her eighteenth birthday party.

Where was she, anyway? Mikel leaned forward and scanned the floor. Ah… there, gyrating like a top, her pink skirt swirling to reveal her shapely legs. How lovely she looked. He caught a fleeting glimpse of her white panties, his pulse quickening, a flame rising up from his belly to his chest. *Easy now! Steady! Can't you see who she's dancing with? She's not yours, Mikel.* Ainhoa belonged to the bright young lad whose parents could afford to send him monthly parcels filled with new clothes, home-baked cake, and boiled sweets. *Yes, Ainhoa would do well to stick with Imanol.*

Another refugee couple were sitting close by, kissing and cuddling. In fact, they were practically making love to each other! Beyond them, Mikel saw Father Imaz standing alone. He appeared thin and haggard, the war years having taken a toll on his health, but now he was smiling broadly, apparently amused by all the commotion on the dance floor.

Mikel glanced at the clock above the double doors. Nearly five. The workshop would be quiet; an opportunity to think about reconstructing the guitar. He would creep away now, while the gramophone was still playing.

But his departure was badly timed. As he rose to leave, the ear-shattering din ended abruptly. He looked up and saw Ainhoa moving towards him. She was pulling Imanol by the hand.

Mikel sank back in his chair and felt a deep throbbing in his breast. If only she knew how much he longed for her company at this moment.

"Mikel!" she smiled.

Ainhoa gave a sprightly toss of her head, swishing aside a lock of dark hair from her eyes. And now Mikel could see her glowing cheeks, her two tiny earrings.

"We're thinking of going window shopping," she chuckled. "Fancy coming, Mikel?"

Window shopping? And play second fiddle to Imanol? Not likely! And anyway, could he bear those drab city streets, the gloomy bomb sites with rows of boarded-up windows, the long queues of people waiting for too few buses? Would he ever forget the humiliation he'd suffered last Christmas when everyone had been talking of victory, the war in Europe almost at an end? Sensing the excitement, Mikel had roused himself to go down to the city all by himself. But a bus conductor had turned him away, calling him a filthy little gypsy, and allowed others to jump the queue ahead of him. Would he ever forget the tears and anger that had kept him awake that Christmas Eve?

"No, Ainhoa." Mikel forced a smile. "I'm in for an early night. You go."

"Back to the smoothing plane, aye Mikel?" Imanol said in a dead voice.

Ainhoa's happy smile faded. Then, with Imanol tugging at her hand, she turned and began moving away.

Mikel leapt up.

"Ainhoa!" he called after her.

She glanced back, her face brightening.

Mikel paused, uncertain of what to say next. Would he ever have the courage? Would he ever command the strength to really know her?

"Happy birthday, Ainhoa," he said weakly.

Then she was being pulled again, led away by the young Imanol to mingle with the rest of the company, all spruced up in their smart American-style suits and frilly skirts.

There came a loud *clank* as the double doors sprang open. A sudden draught of fresh air moved swiftly through the hall, dissolving away the dense haze of cigarette smoke.

The place was emptying fast. Mikel felt as if he was being brushed aside, abandoned by his own brother and rejected by his kinsfolk. Perhaps, secretly, he really *had* wanted to join in with the dancing, to let go a little, just as they had done. But it was too late now, and suddenly he felt horribly lonely.

He waited for everyone to leave, then ambled slowly over to the double doors to gaze out into the twilight glow of evening.

Gorka was moving away, his arms locked around the two newfound girlfriends. What would Mama have thought of it? But Gorka was nearly seventeen now. He must learn to act responsibly.

And then Mikel spotted Ainhoa and Imanol, hand in hand as they sprinted through the mud and slush towards the hut where Ainhoa slept. A cold shiver of anguish passed over Mikel's body.

"Ah… Mikel…"

Mikel spun round. It was Father Imaz.

"Just the man I wanted to see," the priest said kindly. "Not going out with the others?"

"No, Father."

"But you'll miss out on the metal-hunting! Spent shells… Bits of aeroplane… Souvenirs like that might be worth a fortune in years to come."

"I'm not interested, Father. Actually, I've seen enough wartime junk."

"Yes… yes, of course, my boy. And no more contrails in the sky, thank the Lord."

"You wanted to see me, Father?"

"Yes. I have some news for you. And I want to find out how that little wooden marvel is coming along."

"Not good, Father; I'm thinking of making a new soundboard. The wood needs to be thinner. Then I'll need to glue some bracing struts inside the body. It has to stand the high tension of the strings."

Father Imaz turned to Mikel and smiled.

"Very good," he said thoughtfully. "I've always been impressed by your capacity for hard work. And your brother?"

"He's good," Mikel replied.

"Hmmm…"

They stood silently together for several moments in the fading light.

Mikel spotted Gorka and his two girlfriends approaching a Nissan hut on the far side of the compound. He felt a slight quiver of panic as one of the girls uttered a loud screech of sensual delight.

"Yes… well…" the priest mumbled. "A word, Mikel. My office; say, in ten minutes?"

Taking Leave

It was with a strange mix of curiosity and nervousness that Mikel approached Father Imaz's office. Over the past eight years, living as a Basque evacuee, separated from his parents and marooned in a children's colony somewhere in the West

Midlands of England, Mikel had never set foot inside this private retreat.

In a flash of inspiration, he'd decided to bring along his guitar. Father Imaz would want to see what progress had been made. If it hadn't been for Father Imaz, the guitar project would never have got underway. He'd even managed to track down a tuning fork. With luck, the priest might forget about that other unsettling little problem: Gorka's unseemly behaviour earlier in the evening, and at other times.

The door of Father Imaz's tiny office was partially open. Mikel knocked gently, peered in, and saw the priest seated behind a small desk.

"Come along in, Mikel!"

Mikel's eyes scanned the room. It was cramped but snug and homely, with a coke stove mounted on a concrete hearth off to the side. There were several shelves stuffed with old books, and walls decorated with various pieces of Christian iconography.

"My spiritual home," Father Imaz smiled, gesturing towards a chair. "Take a pew, Mikel."

Mikel sat and cradled the guitar on his lap.

"We need to talk." The priest clasped his hands together on the table.

"About Gorka?" Mikel returned. A pang of guilt went through his body.

Father Imaz leaned back, his dark, curved eyebrows arching slightly.

"He's been avoiding me for some time, Mikel; ever since I caught him switching on the air raid siren for a joke. Gorka could go one of two ways, you know that?"

"Yes, Father."

"It's not your fault, Mikel. But do try to keep an eye on him."

"I will, Father."

"He's been stealing."

"What?"

"Little things; cigarettes and loose change. Perhaps alcohol."

"I didn't know."

"Don't let him end up as something he doesn't want to be, Mikel."

"I won't, Father."

"I know you'll try," the priest sighed, the tone of his voice suffused with doubt. After a short moment, his face brightened. "Your guitar…!" he exclaimed. "May I?"

Mikel passed the guitar across the desk.

Father Imaz played a chord. He tuned the guitar quickly and strummed again, lightly.

"Doesn't sound at all bad!" he said in a slightly surprised manner. "You know this one?"

A soft blend of chords filled the room; slow, gentle and echoing pleasantly.

Drawn under its spell, Mikel felt himself lost in waves of perfect harmony. It stole through his inner consciousness, stealthily and powerfully taking hold of him. It sounded so wonderfully refined, and should never be allowed to end. A big lump seemed to grow and tighten in his throat. He was struggling within himself, fighting to suppress a tide of raw emotion building deep inside. He mustn't let the priest see him crying. He must not cry! He would fight against it!

It was almost a relief when Father Imaz brought the piece to a close.

"Bach…" the priest said reverently. "The Chaconne in D minor." Then, in an almost whispering voice, "Heart-rending, isn't it?"

"I… I didn't know you could play," Mikel said, fumbling for the words. "It's… it's beautiful." Reaching up, he quickly wiped away the wetness from under his eyes.

Father Imaz handed back the guitar.

"You've heard of the Esteso factory?" he said.

"Esteso? No, Father."

"It's a famous guitar workshop in Madrid. They've been making guitars in Madrid for hundreds of years. You *must* go there, my boy. You'd learn a lot. You must visit the Esteso guitar factory in Madrid, when the time is right."

Mikel clenched his fists. For how much longer must he wait before the time was right? He'd been away from home for eight long years! Mama would be wondering where her two boys had got to!

"I have some news for you, Mikel; some of it good, some not so good." Father Imaz leaned a little closer. "What if I was to say there's a way to gain your independence? A job, so you can support yourself."

Independence? A job? A passage home! Mikel had dreamt of it since the outbreak of war, since that very first night in the air raid shelter, breathing the damp air, thick with the smell of unwashed bodies! And money to buy clothes, instead of waiting for the six-monthly charity handout!

"Where, Father?" Mikel seized the priest's sleeve. "What work? When?"

"Whoa… steady!" Father Imaz shrank back.

He pulled open a side drawer and produced a large brown

envelope. Mikel watched, his heart pounding, as the priest ripped it open and shook the contents out onto the table.

It was like treasure! Cash notes and coins, two small tickets made from thin cardboard, and a piece of folded paper; everything necessary for Mikel's voyage to a fresh life, a new journey of discovery.

"You're a lucky young man," the priest smiled. "I've found work for you in the Garden of England!"

"The garden of…" Unable to believe what he'd just heard, Mikel sat for a long moment, his brain locked in heavy, fretful thought.

"I could offer it to somebody else," Father Imaz said reproachfully.

"Oh… no, Father; it's just that…"

"I've told you before, Mikel, you must forget about returning to the Basque Country. Hitler's defeat has worsened the situation at home. Spain is becoming isolated. France is closing its frontiers, and all the other countries are withdrawing their ambassadors from Madrid. The Generalissimo is a repressive leader, Mikel. People are being killed all the time."

"Yes… yes, I know, Father, I read about it in the newspapers. And I'm grateful. I really am."

"You should be. We're trying to find places for everyone. And it isn't easy. Two million British families living in bomb-damaged houses, many more searching for new jobs, new homes, and—"

"What about my brother?" Mikel interrupted.

"Absolutely imperative!" The priest flung out the words with an acid, almost injured air. "How could I possibly forget about Gorka? The little rascal hiding in the shadows of the blackout, throwing metal washers into the road and making me grapple on my hands and knees in the pitch darkness for the fortune I thought had fallen from my pockets. And now he's getting involved in the black market, feasting off other people's greed and gullibility. I've tried to find jobs where you can be together, Mikel. That's why farm work in Kent seemed ideally suited to you both."

Mikel reached across the table and singled out one of the tickets. He turned it over.

"What does the word *warrant* mean, Father? It says *warrant* on the back."

"What you are holding in your hand is a rail pass. It will be exchanged for a proper ticket on the day you travel. The work in Kent doesn't start until the summer. So, there's still plenty of time for you to do something with that guitar of yours; to bring it up to concert pitch, perhaps?"

Summer… it seemed an age away. But at least things were beginning to move. In just a few months from now, Father Imaz would be gone from Mikel's life. A guiding light within the Basque refugee colony over the past eight years was destined to become a distant memory.

Mikel looked up and saw the priest's eyes upon him, mysterious, darker than dark and beyond understanding.

Father Imaz lifted the piece of folded paper from the table.

"There's something else you should know," he said in a low voice. "Here, Mikel; you must read for yourself."

Mikel felt its texture. It was very creased, as if it had passed through many hands.

He opened the letter slowly, a burden of anxiety raging inside him, and began to read:

From: The National Joint Council for Spanish Relief.

To: Father Xavier Imaz, Basque Children's Refugee Colony, Rowley Regis.

Pursuing the whereabouts of: Señor Andoni Aguirre and his wife Señora Miren Aguirre, parents of Mikel and Gorka Aguirre.

Last known permanent residence: Amurrio Farmstead, Guernica.

Summary of conclusions: The above persons took temporary residence in Bilbao following the bombing of their home town, Guernica, on 26 April 1937. Extensive enquiries have failed to confirm their safe evacuation either prior to, during, or following the collapse of Bilbao on 18 June 1937. You will doubtless be aware of the high death toll that accompanied the Nationalist advance into Bilbao. The Committee extends its sincerest commiserations to their surviving sons, Mikel and Gorka.

"I'm sorry, Mikel," Father Imaz said gently. "Sometimes the news is good. But I'm afraid my enquiries often produce letters like this."

For a long moment, Mikel could say nothing.

"Bilbao fire-bombed…" he whispered faintly. "I… I read about it. More than fifty thousand people killed… blown to pieces."

For the past eight years he'd dreaded this moment, hoping against hope that it would never come. He suddenly felt cold and began to tremble, the tears running free, unashamed.

"Mikel," Father Imaz said softly, "I know it won't make any

sense to you right now… but believe me, worse things have happened under Heaven."

Mikel took a deep halting breath.

"I… I don't want to think about it anymore, Father."

Chapter 3

THE GARDEN OF ENGLAND

September 1946

New Horizons

Mikel's eyes were closed, but he sensed the light of daybreak. He could hardly face the thought of leaving his bed, of venturing outside into the cold damp air and trudging over to that miserable ablutions block with its broken windows, rusty pipe work, and cracked washbasins.

Last spring he'd come across a swallow, bleeding and fluttering helplessly, snagged by its spindly leg in the cleft of a shattered pane. He'd released the bird gently, cradling it in the palms of his hands before letting it fly away. How wonderful, he'd thought. How absolutely wonderful to see it skim away, leaving behind just the minutest smear of blood on the tip of his finger.

The dormitory was still quiet. It must be early. He would stay beneath the covers and doze. He would explore this strange world of half-sleep where dreams and reality combined; where his imagination was free to roam, and take him anywhere he pleased.

He might enter the world of that migrating swallow whose life he'd saved, streak back across the heaving Bay of Biscay to Guernica and swoop low over the ancient church of Santa Maria la Antigua. He would settle on the shrivelled oak tree where Basque leaders had met for more than a thousand years. Or follow the Nervión River all the way to the city of Bilbao, and alight on that green canvas awning overhanging the front of Papa's favourite café.

What a store of memories! The old shoeshine man, with his long hair swept back and as black as jet; that rich and heady aroma of coffee and treacly sherry. And best of all, the intense, almost brutal, power of that flamenco guitarist; the remorseless hammering of his heel and the guttural shrill of his singing voice.

It seemed amazing to Mikel that he could still conjure up such detailed images from the past.

But his mind was drifting again. He was losing his concentration. The pulse of the guitarist's heel was giving way to a different sound… the rapid pounding of knuckles against a wooden door.

"Michael? You awake, Michael?" It was a female voice. "Mam says you'd better be up, or Charlie Oldham will be having words with you!"

Now his eyes were open wide and staring up at the ceiling, but not the familiar pitch of the dormitory roof with its iron gable supports. This was a low ceiling, painted white and crossed by a heavy black wooden beam. Mikel went rigid, seized in the grip of confusion. Glancing to his side, he saw a tiny window with leaded frames and patterned curtains.

"What time is it?" he yelled, still wrestling with the mystery.

"It's gone five! And Mam says she'll give your eggs back to the chickens if you're not quick!"

"Tell her I'm coming!"

The events of yesterday began to flash through his mind. The roar of a steam engine, the sound of its mighty power echoing through a railway station; the huge traction wheels losing their grip and spinning furiously before eventually locking themselves firmly to the rails. He'd never been so close to a steam engine. Basking in the immense heat radiating from its massive body, he'd stood entranced, delighting in that glorious scent of burning coal and sulphur. It was like a man-made monster, hissing, spitting, and enveloping him in clouds of vapour.

He recalled a platform sign, *London Victoria*, moving slowly past the carriage window; Gorka falling into conversation with some women sharing the same compartment; some young kids up at the windows, delivering a running commentary on what Hitler's bombs had done to London's East End.

And that repulsive stench of cigarettes! Unable to stand it any longer, Mikel had released a long leather strap on the carriage door, allowing the window to drop down with a loud bang. Leaning out, he'd felt the sting of hot ash from the engine on his face, and watched as the steamy grey smoke from the engine's funnel had swept through vast orchards… acres upon acres of trees laden with fruit.

Fruit trees! Charlie Oldham!

"Remember, boys… you must report to Mr Oldham,

the fruit bailiff!" It was the last thing Father Imaz had said as he'd waved them goodbye from Birmingham railway station yesterday morning!

Mikel threw back the bedcovers and swung his legs over the side. He reached for Mama's canvas bag. He must get cleaned up. A small washbasin stood in the corner of the room.

Razor in hand, he stood for a long moment gazing through the little window. The sun was rising, a low mist forming in the distant hollows where lines of poles stood draped in greenery. Pushing open the window, he drew back, startled, as a pair of doves fluttered noisily from the eaves above his head. They soared upwards, their feathers soft pink in the early morning light, and settled on the conical roof of a dovecote at the bottom of the garden.

Glancing down, he saw a young woman crossing the lawn. She paused and lifted her face to him. Mikel drew a sharp intake of breath. He was stark naked. But then he realised that from where she stood, she could not possibly know.

She smiled fleetingly and then turned to scatter feed. Some chickens quickly gathered, strutting and pecking in the grass.

Peering at himself in the shaving mirror, Mikel felt the smoothness of his skin.

He'd seen that young woman before, last night. He cursed himself, annoyed by his failure to recall her name. *Marie? Mercy?* But the events of yesterday were still a blur, the long train journey having sapped his strength.

He remembered a station master's cry: "Faversham! This is Faversham!" It had woken him on the train, and just as well. Father Imaz had said they must leave the train one stop after Faversham; someone would be there to meet them.

As he'd stepped down from the train, he'd mingled with a multitude of women and kids carrying pots, pans and great bundles of bedding. Swept up in the crowd, pushed and jostled along the platform, he'd feared for the safety of his guitar, holding it close to his body for protection. He'd stood with Gorka outside the ticket office, watching the crowd move away on foot. The sound of children's laughter faded into silence as the last of the stragglers disappeared around a bend in the lane.

An attractive young woman had emerged from the waiting room. Pulling down smartly on the cuffs of her navy blue jumper, she'd strode purposefully forward. The evening sunlight transformed her short auburn curls into a halo. Everything about her had seemed so beautifully ordered.

"I reckon you'll be the Basque boys," she'd said.

"Yes, we be!" Gorka had laughed.

She'd introduced herself as…

Mikel paused, razor still in hand… It was coming to him. Maisie? Yes! Maisie!

Gorka had dominated the conversation, chatting with Maisie every step of that long trudge from the rail station to the village. It had felt like miles.

Where is Gorka now? Mikel wondered. And what clothes should he put on? Something smart to create a good impression? It would be best to play safe. He would wear the refugee-issue suit Father Imaz had given him. How Mikel loathed second-hand clothes!

He took a final look at himself in the mirror. Yes, very presentable. Then, bending slightly to avoid a low beam over the landing, he descended the steep narrow stairs into a spacious living room.

A large circular table, beautifully polished, dominated the centre of the room. *Rosewood,* he thought, *brilliant for guitar-making.* On the table stood an oil lamp mounted by a flute of soot-stained glass, and beside it a bowl piled high with red apples. He glanced around at the uneven white-plastered walls; the framework of heavy timbers, black and cracked with age; more leaded windows, edged by floral-patterned curtains, neatly tied back; some polished brasses on leather straps hanging from the mantelpiece; a large open fireplace set with logs, its hearth fronted by a shiny brass rail. Surely those logs must be decorative; frosty mornings had yet to come. Mama would have approved of the tall pendulum clock ticking away in the corner. And yes… that unmistakable scent of home-made bread! He'd escaped Hell, and arrived in Heaven.

He saw a photograph on the mantelpiece and moved closer to investigate. Neatly framed, it showed an airman leaning casually against the propeller blade of a fighter aeroplane.

The floor creaked behind him. He spun round.

"So, our young man eventually decides to surface!" A short and very rotund woman stood in the doorway. "Come along, my lad. Your breakfast's getting cold!" She turned away and shuffled from the room.

"I… I'm sorry, Miss!" Mikel followed her into a large kitchen. "I was tired. It was all the trains and—"

"You sit here!" She pulled a chair out from under the table. "And you call me Missus, right? I'm Missus Chapman, not Miss!" There was a husky, rasping quality to her voice, probably on account of her excessive weight.

There were jars on the table, amply filled. Some were red,

others black, each with a paper top tied with string. Curious, he reached out and lifted one.

"They're Maisie's," Mrs Chapman said. "I make the bread, Maisie makes the jam." She set a plate down in front of him. "That plate's hot, mind! And those tomatoes are home-grown."

Mikel breathed the aroma of fried bacon, eggs, tomatoes… and mushrooms! Yes, he really was in Heaven!

"It's all fresh!" she went on. "We're doing all right, Maisie and me, despite all the rationing. We work hard for it, mind. We keep our own chickens, and a veggie patch."

Mikel broke an egg with the side of his fork and began scooping up one delicious mouthful after another with the blade of his knife. He paused, aware that Mrs Chapman was eyeing him closely, and felt some warm egg yolk dribbling down his chin. He wanted to run from the room, to disappear. This was no refugee canteen, but a proper home!

"Well, you're a hungry one!" A smile flickered between her rounded cheeks. "Can't imagine what they feed you on at those refugee places. Just look at the state of you; all skin and bone!"

"Are you Maisie's mother, Missus?"

"Short memory, too!" Mrs Chapman turned to busy herself at the stove. "Yes, Maisie's my girl. She just about had to carry you up the stairs last night. Don't suppose you remember much about that."

"I don't remember anything, Missus. I was—"

"Out for the count, I'd say!" She glanced back. "We'll have to build you up, my lad! Work in the fields is hard!"

"My brother, Missus… Is Gorka here?"

"Gorka?" Mrs Chapman chuckled. "A good name, that!"

Breathing heavily, she came closer and ladled a big dollop of scrambled egg from a large black saucepan onto his plate. "According to that allocation list from the Spanish refugee council, your brother should have been staying here with me. Looks like my Maisie had different ideas about where he'd be staying. He's over at old Mrs Rudd's place now. Shouldn't think it matters who goes where; not so long as everybody's happy."

Mrs Rudd: the name seemed vaguely familiar to Mikel. Last night, on the way from the railway station, Maisie had paused outside a tumble-down cottage with ancient brickwork and worn-out thatch.

"You can stay here with Mrs Rudd," she'd told Gorka. "Mrs Rudd is very elderly. She'll be glad of your help in getting rid of the rats."

Up until that moment, Gorka had been buoyant and very chatty, but his smile had quickly vanished at the mention of rats. Half faint with hunger and exhaustion, Mikel hadn't thought to question it. Maybe now was the time to raise a complaint on Gorka's behalf. Mama would have gone crazy if she'd known Gorka was sleeping with rats.

"I'll change places with Gorka, Missus," Mikel said suddenly.

"Too late for that, young man," Mrs Chapman grinned. "Truth be known, you *were* down to stay with old Mrs Rudd. But seeing as Maisie didn't hold with your brother's constant jabbering, she arranged it so you'd be with us instead."

There was a loud *clack*, followed by a sudden draught of cold air. Mikel turned and saw Maisie supporting herself against the open door and kicking off a pair of knee-length boots. She moved nimbly across the stone-tiled floor towards him.

"Only eight eggs this morning, Mam." She put a lumpy cloth bag on the table. "Morning, Michael. You made it out of bed, then?"

Mikel felt his heart beat a little faster as Maisie's eyes shone warmly down upon him, her voice laughing and teasing him in a kindly sort of way. He should make a fuss about Gorka's lodgings, appeal to Mrs Chapman for leniency. But he felt captivated by Maisie's smile, the freshness of her face. For a long awkward moment, the words stuck in his throat, and before he could open his mouth Maisie had turned to her mother.

"We'll need to do something about that new Rhode Island Red, Mam," she said. "He's upsetting all the hens. White Peg got herself trapped in the privy with him last night. She might have got drowned, likely as not!"

"Why, the little devil!" Mrs Chapman slammed the heavy saucepan down on the oven top. "I won't have him carrying on like that, not with *my* hens. I'll get Charlie Oldham to sort him out; he'll wring the little blighter's neck, most likely!"

Mikel, lured by the steaming fragrance of scrambled egg, gazed down at his plate. He lifted a fluffy portion on the end of his fork and then gave way to temptation, wolfing it down, one mouthful after another. He scoffed remorselessly, hardly pausing for breath. By the time he'd done, Maisie had sat down beside him.

"There's no need to rush, Michael," she said. "You'll get indigestion if you carry on like that."

Loosening the cloth bag, she rolled out some eggs, and then gathered them into a tight group on the table in front of her. She glanced at him, the warmth and softness in her eyes going straight to his heart. He wanted to know Maisie better... much better; to run in the shadow of that store of mysterious feminine secrets that had always darkened his mind. It was hopeless, of course. Why should Maisie find him, a skinny stripling without a proper home, in the least bit agreeable?

"I saw Charlie Oldham this morning, Mam," Maisie said suddenly. She was still looking at him, her knowing, glistening eyes seeing right into him. "I'm to take Michael to Four Oaks field."

"What will I be doing?" he said.

"Well!" Mrs Chapman exclaimed. "You won't be strumming that guitar of yours, I can tell you that much!"

"Go easy, Mam!" Maisie said reproachfully. "Michael will do alright. Tom Gristle needs a bit of help, that's all."

"Working with Tom Gristle!" Mrs Chapman wheezed. She moved closer. "Now look, young man, Lord only knows what Tom will think if you turn up in a suit and tie. You'll need to change into working clothes!"

"But... but what will I have to do, Missus?"

"Four Oaks is where they grow apple trees," Maisie smiled. "They'll be staking apple tree saplings, likely as not."

"There's a spare shirt in your bedroom!" Mrs Chapman gathered up the plate. "Top drawer! And watch what you do with the wages. They'll pay you a fixed rate for the week so long as you keep to the hours. You give me half, and the rest is yours. Right, my lad?"

"Right, Missus..."

To Work

Filled with excitement and anticipation, Mikel walked quickly, eager to get started on his first day of paid work. The sun was well up now. It was like witnessing the very first dawn, the air heavy with the pungent smell of hops and damp soil. Every tree was different to the next. Yes, even the trees were worth looking at! He was actually noticing things: spiders' webs saturated with morning dew and sparkling with the brilliance of diamonds; birdsong from the thorny hedgerows. He wanted to call out to Mama and Papa, make them understand that he was happy now.

He glanced round at Maisie. There was a kind of magnificence in the way she strode along in her knee-length boots, the picture of English pride and respectability. Maisie was so wonderfully perfect; small and tense, so utterly alive. She glanced up at him, breathing rapidly, her face flushed and beautiful.

"Michael," she gasped. "Do you think you could walk a bit slower?"

Reluctantly, he slackened the pace. Ahead lay the prospect of a job, and a weekly wage.

"How much further?" he asked.

"Not far," she panted. "We're almost there now. Four Oaks is just over the hill."

Soon, she was falling behind again.

"Phew!" she exclaimed. "Slow down, Michael!"

"How much will they pay me?"

"Pay you?" She quickened her pace, closing the gap between them. "Oh, about half a crown a week, I should think.

That's for staking fruit trees. You can get more in the hop fields, especially if you're a tally-man."

"A tally-man? I'll be a tally-man, then!"

"You'd have to serve time as a bin-man first."

"That's alright. I can do anything, Maisie. Bin-man, tally-man; they're all the same to me!" Mikel widened his stride, revelling in the chance to prove his worth.

"Michael!"

Coming to a stop in the middle of the lane, Mikel waited for her to catch up again.

"I don't think you've any idea," she said. "Being a bin-man is harder than you think. The hop pickers need to be watched carefully, all the time. They play tricks, Michael. They fluff up the hops so the measuring bins get filled too quickly. They gossip a lot too, especially the ones from London."

"Yes, I know!" He moved on, but much slower now. "I saw them on the train yesterday. And how those London ladies enjoy their cigarettes! I spent the whole journey leaning out of the window. I was ready to do anything just to get away from all that hop-picker talk and cigarette smoke."

"Well, there you are then," she smiled. "And there'll be more of them arriving today. Hop picking earns them a lot of money. Enough to buy school uniforms, anyway."

Mikel felt transformed, full of energy, perhaps more than ever before. Only one other person had ever made him feel like this. Of course, he'd been saddened at having to say goodbye to Ainhoa. But now he was making friends with another girl. Maisie… she was so lovable, so radiant… so beautiful, like a flower in the sun.

"Those kids on the train," he said, "do they have to work in the fields too?"

"Not if they can't reach the hop branches," she chuckled. "The little ones sometimes help to fill the measuring bins. If they can't manage that, they'll fill biscuit tins instead. Not the babies, of course." She looked up at him, still smiling. "Babies are exempt from work."

Exempt… another word to add to his English vocabulary. He was getting good at speaking English.

"Those kids looked so happy," he said. "I thought maybe they were going on holiday."

"They don't sound so happy when they get hop pollen under the skin!" she laughed. "It really stings. The pollen gets everywhere, even in the sandwiches."

They were moving quite slowly now. It was like the duties that lay ahead didn't matter quite so much. It was a relief to be this close to Maisie, a great, great relief. She was so very good-looking… her hair, her little turned-up nose… everything about her, in fact.

Maisie blushed and glanced away.

"Yes, you have to be good with people to be a bin-man," she went on. "And you especially need to know how to deal with children. They get bored and start playing around."

Mikel felt his heart tightening with a yearning for Maisie's closeness. It was unthinkable, of course. Uneducated and inadequate… A refugee from a poor country…

"I… I like your mother," he said awkwardly. "I mean, she's a good woman… very kind."

Maisie came to a stop. She gazed up into the sky, a far-away look in her eyes. A quivering shadow from the topmost branch of a giant oak played on her face, the joy of the day fading from her. He'd been too familiar, over-reaching himself by saying too much, too soon. And now he felt ashamed. The long silence between them was strange and frightening to Mikel. Then, at last, she turned to him.

"It's good for Mam to have a man around," she said in a dull tone. "But... but if only you could have met my daddy. My daddy was one of 'the first of the few'. He never came back, you see."

"One of the..." Mikel broke off. He swallowed hard, his nerves ripped like silk. That young pilot in the picture on the mantelpiece! He groped for the words before going on, a little unsteadily. "I... I'm so sorry, Maisie."

"That's alright; you weren't to know. Daddy had only just qualified as a fighter pilot. Mam said the inexperienced ones were often the first to be shot down."

The memories of Guernica came flooding back to Mikel with a startling reality. That acrid smell of high explosive and burning. And now another image: the wreckage of a wartime aeroplane, its gloomy cockpit riddled with jagged cannon shell holes. The stench of boiling engine oil, fuel and vomit. A medic clawing at the blackened cables, struggling to extricate a dying airman.

"Anyway, Michael," she murmured, "I've got to show you up to Four Oaks field. Charlie Oldham will be there. We don't want to be late, not when Charlie Oldham's around."

They walked on in silence. He wondered if Maisie would know anything about his own background. She would probably know quite a lot. Father Imaz was always sending letters of introduction on behalf of the refugee kids in his care.

"I like your guitar," Maisie said suddenly. "What music do you play?"

"Oh, not very much; I'll never be a professional guitarist. My father tried to teach me, but I was too young." Mikel glanced up and felt the warmth of the sun. It reminded him of another place. "I once saw a guitar being played in a café," he went on. "And then I knew what I wanted to do with my life. I've never wanted anything else; just to build beautiful guitars, and to hear them being played by the world's greatest performers."

"So, what's your *favourite* music? Flamenco, I suppose."

"No, not especially; I like classical music better. I once heard José de Azpiazu playing the classical guitar. I've always wanted to play like Azpiazu."

"Hum… Azpiazu," she frowned. "No, I can't say I've heard of Azpiazu. He sounds very Spanish."

"Basque!" Mikel laughed. "Azpiazu was born in San Sebastian. Started out as a painter and won lots of art prizes. He didn't become a professional guitarist until he was twenty-four."

"Twenty-four!" Maisie came to a halt. "So, there's hope for you yet, Michael Aguirre!"

She moved to the side of the lane and pushed open a large wooden gate.

"Here we are," she said. "This is Four Oaks!"

Maisie led the way into a vast field.

There was a kind of military precision about it; rows upon rows of fruit trees, and each row never-ending. Off to the side, some restless crows were cawing loudly, fluttering above a small copse. A pair of wood pigeons streaked overhead and sped away towards some gently rolling hills on the distant horizon. So, this was what people meant when they spoke of the *Garden of England*?

"Do you see?" Maisie pushed gently against the slender trunk of a young sapling. "The baby trees have to be staked to keep them upright."

"But… there are so many!" he cried. "How can I possibly be expected to look after all this?"

"You won't be on your own. You'll be working with Tom, remember? You'll like Tom. They say he's never been out of the village, not even for a holiday. Tom's as old as the hills. But you watch him swing a sledge hammer! Come on, Michael; they'll be waiting for us." Maisie strode on ahead.

Mikel's shirt clung uncomfortably to his back as he stumbled after her, his big moment fast approaching. His first day of work.

But there was an unwelcoming look on the faces of the two men waiting to meet him. They stood silently, eyeing Mikel up and down as he approached them.

"This is Mr Oldham, Michael," Maisie said, gesturing towards the taller of the two. "Mr Oldham is the fruit bailiff."

Charlie Oldham was powerfully built, obviously an overseer with considerable authority. Mikel's mouth felt dry, his throat parched, as the bailiff gazed back at him with a look of astonishment on his big red face.

"And this is Mr Gristle," Maisie smiled, sidling up to a much older man. Short, stooping and rather bow-legged, the aging farmworker stood dressed in his shirtsleeves, a silvery pocket watch secured to the lapel of his very respectable waistcoat. "Tom is my very best friend!" Maisie gave the old man a gentle hug.

Tom Gristle stared at Mikel through a pair of wire-framed spectacles, a crooked smoking pipe sprouting from his rough grey moustache.

The two men turned to each other for a long moment, and then back to face Mikel. There came a long, rasping, guttural sound as old Tom Gristle withdrew his pipe, tossed back his head, and gave vent to unrestrained laughter.

"'T'ain't nothing to laugh at!" the bailiff boomed angrily. "A body like that… 't'ain't nothing to laugh at!"

"Well!" Maisie said rather stiffly: "If you can't at least be *civil* to a Spanish refugee!…" She turned and began striding away, back towards the gate.

"'Ere…!" Charlie Oldham yelled after her. "Where are you off to now, lass?"

"To old Mrs Rudd's!" Maisie cried, without glancing back. "Michael has a brother, you know. Someone's got to look after the new boys!"

"Maisie!" Mikel cried out. "What's happening? About Gorka?"

"Oh, no need to worry about Gorka! He'll be working as a bin-man, I shouldn't wonder!"

Chapter 4

FOUR OAKS FIELD

7 Months Later, April 1947

Hard Times

Easing aside a slender bough, still moist and slippery from the early morning rain, Mikel felt the blossom buds hard beneath his fingers. Moving carefully, he tucked the bough behind him. Charlie Oldham, the fruit bailiff, was always on the lookout for broken twigs and bruised spurs. Wages could be docked for careless work, and a labourer found guilty of causing serious damage would face dismissal.

"There you go, boy!" Tom stabbed the ground with the pointed tip of a long wooden stake post. "Hold it firm, now!"

Grasping the post in both hands, Mikel drew a sharp breath at the searing pain in his fingers. This was nothing new; his hands and fingers were always burning. The tarred binding twine was forever slicing into them, leaving the wounds open and raw. With more than five hundred trees to stake and bind every week, there was no end to the torment. His fingers burned with everything he touched; even a wet slippery stake post could feel like a burning brand.

Tom moved off a few paces to retrieve the sledge hammer from where it lay in the wet grass. He'd developed a pronounced limp since last autumn.

Mikel glanced in the direction of the copse; the oak trees black and skeletal, their tops swaying in the gusting wind. There was no sign yet of any springtime greenery. His gaze wandered over the huge orchard, those endless rows of apple tree saplings. They stood naked and exposed; survivors of a winter cold enough to break stone.

Mrs Chapman said it had been the snowiest winter for over a century. Blizzards and drifting snow had blocked roads and railways. Coal supplies had run low so power stations had closed, leading to electricity cuts. Everyone blamed the government. The Minister for Fuel and Power was receiving death threats! Vegetables froze in the ground; food shortages and rationing were widespread. Thank goodness for Mrs Chapman's log fires and stored fruit. Her cottage had become a place of refuge. But now the snow had gone and it was back to work again; an unremittingly hard, and very boring, grind of a job.

The grass beneath Mikel's feet was sodden, his socks drenched, the wind on his face numbingly cold. A shudder struck at the core of his body, rippling down his legs and intensifying that repulsive sensation of wet woollen trousers against tender skin. Their cloying roughness made his flesh creep.

"Upright, boy!" bawled Tom, his drooping pipe trembling in the thicket of his rough grey moustache. "'T'ain't no good if the post ain't upright!"

Mikel felt his cheeks reddening. He'd been caught daydreaming, and not for the first time this morning. Steadying the post as best he could, he squeezed his eyes closed and braced himself.

Tom's hammer came down with a loud thud, the vibrations shooting upwards through Mikel's arms and reaching deep into his chest, the pain in his fingers severe. Tom struck again, unerringly. And then once more. Three hammer blows followed by a pause; an unspoken signal that the post was now clear of overhanging branches. Tom would bash away on his own now, and get the post down to the correct height, ready for binding.

Tucking his hands under his armpits for warmth, Mikel ambled over to a heap of freshly hewn stake posts. He'd tried wearing gloves, but the bailiff didn't approve of them, saying blossom buds were easily damaged by careless use of gloves. Besides, gloves were no good when it came to knotting the binding twine.

At the base of the pile he found the ball of coarse twine, larger than a football. He drew off a long length and slashed at it with Tom's bone-handled penknife, once, twice. But the twine wouldn't part. He formed a loop, gripping it tightly. Setting the blade against the twine he pulled hard, but the twine was wet and began to slip through his clenched fingers. A reddish stain appeared, melding with the brown of the tar. It was blood! He closed his eyes, pulled harder, and saw a flash of white light. And then stars! Hundreds, thousands of tiny pinpoints of light, never still but moving unceasingly against the darkness of his inner eye.

He must steel himself to get through this day, endure it for just a few more hours; then home to Maisie. His heart leapt at the thought. Life without Maisie would be horrible, like trying to stay afloat in a dark, meaningless flood of nothingness.

Bear with it, then; pull again with the knife… pull harder! He saw another flash of white light. Then another tug and the twine gave way at last. Reaching up with the back of his hand, he wiped the sweat from his brow.

He glanced over at Tom. The old man stood with his hands clasped over the top of the stake post. He was gazing down at the ground, his breathing slow and laboured.

One day last December, when the ground had been rock-hard and progress slow, Tom had thrown the sledge hammer down by his side.

"Perishing cold!" he'd exclaimed, taking the pipe from his mouth. "Don't suppose it'll be like this where you come from, aye boy?"

Seizing the opportunity to talk about his *real* home, Mikel had tried to describe winters in the Basque Country, when brave young men would go trekking on Gorbea Mountain, some never to return after becoming lost in the snow.

"It rains a lot, just as in England," Mikel had told him. "But in summertime, the valleys are like oceans of green. My mother would take us for long walks. We'd pick red poppies and white asparagus. Sometimes we'd hear thunder rumbling in the mountains. Never in winter, though; not like in England. We only heard thunder in the summertime."

Tom had seemed to reflect on this for a while:

"Nay, lad," he'd said after a few moments. "That was no thunder. That was *voices*!" Then, slipping the pipe back into his mouth, he'd reached down for the hammer. "I'd get myself back to that sunshine if I were you, boy. It's your sweet life, mind!"

It was ghastly to think a man like Tom should have to spend his whole life staking fruit trees. According to Maisie, Tom had never been away from the village, apart from to visit Canterbury once or twice in his youth. He would probably die with a sledge hammer in his hands. The villagers would have to come and prise the hammer from his grasp. Then they would cremate him and spread his ashes here, at the base of an apple tree sapling in Four Oaks field; a fitting end to a life of devoted service on the land.

Mikel glanced down at his throbbing hands. Thank God tomorrow was Sunday; the one and only day of the week which might provide the freedom he needed to enjoy Maisie's company. If only every day could be a Sunday.

"When you're quite ready, boy!" bawled Tom.

A Sleepless Night

Maisie sat gazing at her reflection in the dressing table mirror. Her cheeks were flushed, her eyes sparkling. But she was troubled in spirit.

It had been a night of broken sleep; a vague awakening to the realisation that she was now eighteen. What would life have to offer?

As a child, even the darkest days of winter had been filled with interest and discovery. On bleak frosty mornings, often before sunrise and still in her nightgown, she would flit across the crisp frozen lawn and down to the chicken hut. Lifting the hens from their perches, she would laugh to feel them wriggling between her hands, always in anticipation of finding some eggs for breakfast. Usually there would be at least three; one for Mam, one or two for Daddy, and one for herself.

Winter walks with Daddy were amongst her fondest memories. Hand in hand, and all togged up in their welly boots, they would press ahead through roaring winds and driving rain, crossing fields of wet grass and stepping joyfully along narrow winding lanes spread with mud. Sometimes they would pause, gazing in wonder at the shiny red berries twinkling in the hedgerows, or cautiously gather twigs from blackthorn bushes decked in clouds of white blossom.

In springtime, they would roam through forests glimmering with creamy primroses and banks of blue speedwell. Wood anemones were her favourite flowers, with their delicate white petals and yellow centres. How wonderfully rich and splendid was this thing called nature, especially when just a few days of springtime sun could transform a bare woodland floor into a dense carpet of bluebells. And to think she had experienced all of this without a care in the world.

But her precious daddy was gone now. The foreign boys had arrived. And their presence had awakened in Maisie new kinds of feelings, sometimes secretive and unwilling to be laid bare.

Those two brothers had come to mean a lot to her. There was a kind of earthy scholarship in them; a familiarity with the world that was worth more than anything she'd ever owned. Even the prizes she'd won at school, the trophies of a privileged upbringing, were as nothing compared to her feelings for Michael and Gorka. So, where was it all leading?

She hated to admit it, but living with Mam could be oppressive at times. Also, she was becoming bored with her job at the Faversham library. Not that there was anything wrong with being an assistant librarian. She'd made some good friends there. Besides, it paid well, and there was a good chance of promotion.

Maisie breathed a deep sigh. For the first time in her life, she'd come to know what it meant to be in a state of uncertainty. She felt trapped, like a fish in a goldfish bowl, and her heart flashed with the certainty that there had to be more.

She loved the sound of Gorka's voice, the way he would exaggerate his Basque accent, clipping his sentences just enough to get a laugh. Gorka was so exciting to be with; her resistance melted away under his physical advances. Not that anything had ever happened, not really. Anyway, Gorka was heaps more fun than the other boys in the village.

With Michael, it was different. Sometimes, late in the evening, she would slip into the shed and watch him at work on his guitar, chiselling, gluing, sandpapering and burnishing with such an extraordinary intensity that he would often fail to notice her. She would stand quietly at the side, breathing the sweet scent of freshly planed timber, watching the light from the oil lamp reflecting in his sloe-dark eyes. How she admired Michael's skill as a craftsman, delighting in the sound of his guitar playing.

"Come on, Maisie!" Mam called from the bottom of the stairs. "Church service starts at ten!"

"Coming, Mam!"

Leaning closer to the mirror, she pouted her lips and carefully applied a tiny measure of lipstick. With a quiver of disquiet, she contemplated the future. *Follow in Mam's footsteps? Marriage? Children?*

Casting a final glance at her image, Maisie rose from the dressing table and moved swiftly out onto the landing. She almost floated down the stairs.

"Ah! Here she comes!" Her mother was up at the stove. "Porridge?"

"Not this morning, Mam."

"No porridge!" Her mother frowned disapprovingly. "Never mind. It'll keep for tomorrow."

Maisie flushed with irritation. Like Goldilocks, her porridge had to be just right; not too thick, and definitely not too thin. She made her way to the bread bin.

"I'll make some toast. Want some?"

"Not me, child."

Maisie carved a couple of slices and pushed them under the toaster.

"It's a new vicar that's running the service this morning," her mother said, gently sliding a boiled egg onto Maisie's plate. "He's come up from Stowting. You remember Stowting?"

"Stowting?" Maisie took her seat. "Don't think so, Mam."

"Course you do! It's where that air crash happened back in January. Surely you remember that?"

"Oh, yes. I do remember that."

Maisie poured herself a cup of tea.

Everyone in Kent knew about the Stowting accident. Several passengers had been killed after an aircraft ran short of fuel. Loads of villagers had turned out to help.

"Well," her mother went on, "word's getting out that this new vicar's a bit of a hero. He was the first at the scene, according to old Mrs Rudd."

Maisie dropped her egg into an eggcup, and cleanly sliced

off the top with a knife. With a sideways glance she saw that Michael's breakfast place had been set, but nothing touched. He'd be enjoying a lie-in, likely as not. Sunday wasn't just a sacred day. It was the only day the Basque boys could take break from work.

"Michael up yet, Mam?"

"Up and gone, my girl. No breakfast. No tea. Just wanted to get on with that blessed guitar of his!"

"But Mam, it's freezing in the shed! He'll catch his death!"

"I told him to put the electric fire on."

Her mother set the toast down beside Maisie.

"Michael can have that," Maisie said. "I'll take him some toast and jam."

Her mother gave a shrug. "You'll spoil that lad!" She placed a tray on the table. "Better take some tea as well, I suppose," she went on. "Lord knows if he'll bother to drink it."

Maisie finished her egg quickly and downed the tea. She poured a fresh cup for Michael, smeared some raspberry jam on the toast, and loaded the tray.

"And don't be spending too long, girl!" her mother said in a severe tone. "Church beckons; we'll need to be gone soon!"

But Maisie was already on her way. Lifting the latch on the kitchen door, she stepped out under a leaden sky. It was bitterly cold and drizzling with rain. She crossed the lawn at a measured pace, taking care not to spill the tea.

It had been good of Mam to grant Michael the run of the shed. Unrestricted access to carpentry tools had galvanised Michael into making the shed his own personal den. Mam had even moved Daddy's gramophone player, along with his entire collection of classical records, into Michael's bedroom. How Daddy would have approved! The very thought of her father's happiness brought a blazing light into Maisie's soul, her heart quickening as she pushed open the shed door.

Michael stood leaning over the workbench. He glanced up, his expression awash with alarm.

"Maisie!" he cried in a kind of apoplectic frenzy. "Help! Quick!"

She put the tray down on the floor and moved swiftly to his side.

The body of the guitar was in the grip of several large metal clamps.

"The soundboard! It's not going to fit! Push down on the edge, Maisie!" He pressed his fingers on the outer rim of the guitar. "Here!"

Maisie gasped and drew back, appalled at the sight of Michael's fingers, horribly cracked, swollen and bleeding.

"Michael!" A surge of pity welled up inside her. "Your fingers! Your poor fingers!"

"It's alright, Maisie! Please… just press… here!"

She reached over and pushed down on the rim as Mikel worked his way around the edge, tightening the G-clamps one by one to secure the new soundboard.

At last, he was finished.

"That's it! A new guitar… with bracing struts!"

"Perhaps now you'll let me see those fingers," she said. "Come back to the house. I'll put some cream on."

He glanced down at the guitar.

"The glue will harden in an hour. And then I'll need to smooth away the excess."

He turned to her, his beautiful dark eyes wide and shining.

"Thank you, Maisie," he said.

The White Lion

Maisie sat alone in a darkened corner of the pub and fidgeted nervously with the handbag on her lap. The snuggery was crowded with menfolk. She recognised most of them; fieldworkers mainly, some as young as fifteen. They kept darting curious glances across at her. Then they would roar with vacuous laughter. The air reeked of fags and sour beer; the noise was deafening.

She should never have agreed to meet with Gorka. It was so unfair! Having asked to see her in the pub, he might at least have made the effort to be here on time. This was no way to treat a girl!

If he didn't arrive within the next five minutes she would leave, and never speak to him again. If it wasn't for the warmth of the big log fire, she'd have gone home ages ago.

The pub door opened.

"'Ere, watch out!" some mindless hooligan yelled. "The Spanish Armada's arrived!"

Gorka appeared and rolled his eyes around the bar area, searching. A group of young lads bunched around him, slapping him on the back and embracing him in a very cordial manner.

"Oi, Gorka!" somebody cried out. "She's over here, mate!"

Gorka pushed his way through the crowd towards her, smiling broadly as if being late was some kind of clever joke.

"Good of you to turn up!" Maisie flung the words out. "Another minute and I'd have been on my way home!"

"Sorry, Maisie." He settled on the bench beside her. "A few things to sort out. I've ordered you a drink; lemon shandy."

"Aren't you going to ask how long I've been waiting?"

He was about to answer, but a ruddy-cheeked orchard

manager suddenly appeared with a pint of beer in one hand and a half pint of something weaker in the other.

"There you go, Master Gorka!" he beamed. "These are on me. Have a good time, both of you!" He gave Maisie a strange wink and then jostled his way back into the mob.

"Do I know that person?" Maisie said.

"I doubt it," Gorka replied in a low tone. "Cheers anyway, Maisie." He drew a mouthful. "So, what's the latest?"

"What on earth do you mean?"

"Everything," he replied. "I want to know everything, especially about you."

Maisie's heart skipped a beat, the noise of the pub fading into the background.

"You're incorrigible," she murmured.

Gorka's soft, full mouth hung open a little as he fixed her with his beautiful doe-like eyes.

"Incorrigible?" he echoed. "Is that good? No! Do not answer that. Tell me about my brother. Is he incorrigible also?"

"Michael?" Maisie took a sip of shandy. "Hmmm," she murmured, "this is quite nice."

"And my brother," Gorka persisted, "is he nice also?"

"He works very hard, as well you know, Gorka."

"Yes, I do know. Mikel is a very good person, especially when there is work to be done."

"Not just daytime work," Maisie said defensively. "In fact, he's working right now, in Mam's shed."

"Guitar?" Gorka smiled.

"It's coming along very nicely, Gorka. I wouldn't be surprised if he makes another one. He might even go into business."

"Hmmm," Gorka said thoughtfully. "But I'll bet he doesn't do this."

He reached out and gently stroked her arm.

Maisie's heart beat a little faster.

"Gorka…"

He lifted her hand and kissed her fingers lightly, sending a shiver of excitement right through her.

"Gorka!"

"Or this…"

His hand was on her knee.

She edged away. He might certainly kiss her hand, but he may not touch her!

"Stop behaving like a maniac!"

Gorka laughed out loud, withdrew his hand smartly and took another mouthful of beer.

Maisie's eyes flashed to the open fire, her cheeks burning.

Gorka leaned back and gazed up at the ceiling, a faraway look in his eyes.

"I have to tell you something, Maisie. And I want you to be the first to know."

"Don't tell me you're dying, Gorka. You're not old enough for that."

"I'm moving to London."

"No! But why?"

"Jobs, Maisie! A man should go where the jobs are."

"But… but… you're almost part of the furniture!"

"I want you to know, because I need you to come with me."

"What? I can't!"

"Why not? You told me you were bored. You wanted a change from library work. Isn't that what you said?"

"Well, yes… I mean, no. I'm not sure. These decisions take time, Gorka!"

"But I have a good plan for you in London. It will be the best job in the world!" Leaning closer, he whispered in her ear, "Shorthand and typing."

"Shorthand and…" Maisie drew back. "Gorka!"

"It takes time, Maisie; yes, that's true! But you could learn to be a secretary in less than a year. I even know where you can take lessons. There's a school in Canterbury. You can go there at weekends and learn to be a shorthand typist, and then you can come to work with me in London. Honestly, what could be better than that?"

"Gorka…" Maisie paused, mystified, stumped for words.

"Anyway," Gorka went on, "London is a good place to live. I mean… living with old Mrs Rudd! She's a good sort, Maisie. But honestly…"

"We'd miss you," Maisie said.

"Come with me, then. There's something for everybody in London. Even for you, Maisie."

Once again Gorka reached under the table. He laid his hand gently on her inner thigh.

"Oh, Gorka," she murmured.

"No, don't say it," he whispered. "I'm incorrigible, right?"

A Divisive Influence

There came a sudden blast of cold air. It scurried all around Mikel, beating him from every side. Looking up, he saw Tom a long way off, shuffling away towards a tiny shelter that stood at the bottom of the orchard. Tucking his hands into his pockets, Mikel set off to follow. He walked slowly at first, and then, feeling the sting of cold rain on his face, he quickened his step. Soon he was running, imagining himself to be a steam engine, puffing and panting as he moved swiftly along a long narrow corridor between two rows of apple trees, the long wet grass lashing at his socks and trouser legs.

The shelter was open at the front with a corrugated tin roof sloping down towards the rear. Breathing heavily, Mikel bent low to enter and squeezed himself onto a narrow bench beside Tom. They sat in silence together, gazing out at the rain. It fell in sheets, driven by an icy wind from the direction of the copse, and rattled on the roof like a never-ending cascade of metal nails. The rain poured through the gaping entrance of the shed, drenching Mikel's trousers below the knees. The saturated wool clung mercilessly to his legs, its rough texture scratching and pricking his skin.

"Sandwich, boy?" Tom loosened some binding twine from around a brown paper lunch pack.

"No... thanks, Tom."

He'd tried one of Tom's sandwiches before. They were made of hard white bread, laced with yellowing fat and stained with the blackened residue from a roasting tray. Leaning to one side, Mikel struggled in the confined space to pull one of last year's apples from his trouser pocket.

"This'll keep me going until teatime," he said. "Mrs Chapman always fixes a proper meal when I get home."

"Nasty old fingers," said Tom grimly, glancing down at Mikel's hands.

Mikel studied his upturned palm and fingers, gashed,

swollen, smeared with half-congealed blood and oily brown tar.

"Oh, it's nothing." Mikel quickly flipped his hand over, resting the palm on his lap. "They don't hurt much; the skin's hardening now." He shuddered at the prospect of Charlie Oldham knowing about the state of his fingers. The bailiff had a terrible reputation for sacking workers who went off sick. "I'll soon have hands like yours, Tom. Real workman's hands!"

He took a bite from the crinkled apple. It had a mushy texture and a musty taste, but was surprisingly sweet for an old apple.

"Nasty fingers, all the same," Tom said. "You need some of that *binder's relief,* lad."

"Binder's *what?*"

"*Relief,* boy! *Binder's relief!* That's what folks call it around here."

Binder's relief? It must be some kind of skin cream used by people working out of doors in the freezing cold. He must try to get some. What a thought; Maisie massaging a cool dollop of binder's relief into his hands!

"Where can I get some? Is it expensive?"

"Expensive be blowed! It's what they use to keep oxygen out of the storehouses!"

"Oxygen out of the…?"

"It's grease, boy! They smear it on the inside walls. You can't let oxygen in, not when storing fruit. You'd lose the whole crop!" Tom munched steadily as he gazed out across the orchard. "Everybody takes a turn at greasing. Mark my words; come the summer, you'll be up that ladder with a bucket of grease, just like all the rest of them. Job's got to be done quick, see, before the fruit comes in." Then, pushing the last piece of sandwich into his mouth, "Grease is good for the skin, lad. Gets the hands in good shape for the coming winter!"

Mikel tried to imagine reaching into a bucket of grease and daubing it across the inside walls of a giant storehouse. The grease would get everywhere; in his hair, on his face, all over his clothes. Mrs Chapman would go mad with all the washing. And Charlie Oldham would be watching to see that not a single patch of storehouse wall was missed.

"Rain's easing!" Tom began rewrapping his lunch pack. "That young brother of yours… *Corker*…"

"Gorka!" Mikel smiled. "I don't see much of Gorka these days. He's working with the hop gangs."

"Well!" Tom gave a loud sniff. "Hop gang or no hop gang, he's been seeing plenty of our Maisie, and that's for sure!"

"Seeing Maisie?" Mikel's heart gave a sudden quiver. "Oh no, I don't think so."

"Oh yes. I saw him the other night, bowling out of the White Lion with our young Maisie on his arm! And that wasn't the first time, neither!" Tom sniffed again before adding, thoughtfully, "Nice girl, our Maisie; might have ravished her myself when I was younger. She's my little treasure, see! Wouldn't want any harm coming to our Maisie!"

Mikel froze, his heart pounding like a mad thing. Tom was right. Maisie *had* been going out in the evenings… like last night. Mikel had gone to bed feeling exhausted, desperate for sleep. He hadn't heard the familiar *clack* of the kitchen door latch on Maisie's return. And all those other nights! The thought of Maisie and Gorka being alone together pierced anew the most secret scar in his shrinking soul; Gorka playing around with Maisie!

Leaning forward on his elbows, his mind emptying of all happiness, Mikel clenched his hands tightly, the soreness in his fingers as nothing to the pain that burned like a fiery torch inside him. He glanced up at the sun, pale and watery as it made a brief appearance through a misty veil of cloud. Tom mustn't see him in this state; no-one should.

"Well, must be getting on!" Tom rose unsteadily to his feet, pausing for a moment to recover his balance before stepping out from the shelter. Then he limped off towards the copse, leaving in his wake a winding slither of darkened grass.

Mikel felt crushed, thrust into a state of insensibility. He was filled with a sudden impulse to rush home, to spill out his heart to Maisie, to declare his love and yearning for her. He should have done so before but had backed away, unable to face rejection. Gorka was different. Gorka would have made her feel special. He would have pursued Maisie relentlessly, coaxing her with all his charm until she'd lowered her guard. Oh God... Maisie! There came another blast of ice-cold wind. It struck Mikel like a spiteful whiplash.

Locked in a dreadful vertigo, he felt weak and defenceless, like an abandoned child. Oh, the anguish of uncertainty; those powerful wounding visions of Maisie lying in Gorka's arms!

At that moment, above the howling of the wind, there came another sound; a distant harmony, almost painful in its simplicity. He'd heard it before; the beautiful and deeply moving Adagio from Schubert's string quintet. How Schubert himself must have suffered to produce such sounds. How else...?

With a tremendous effort, Mikel reached up and pressed the raw flesh of his wounded fingers into the salty tears streaming down his face.

Sunday

To Maisie, the mood at breakfast had seemed desperately bad; first Michael not saying a single word, and now her mother. It was unnerving to see Mam in such a foul temper, gasping for breath as she strode ahead up the lane. Everyone at church was going to see what a terrible paddy she was in. The service would be a nightmare; so embarrassing!

"Mam!" Maisie called after her. "We're going to arrive too early!"

But her mother barged on without even a backward glance.

Maisie shot a passing glance through the open door of the White Lion and captured a glimpse of the yellowing hop fronds festooned across the top of the bar. It looked so dull inside the pub now; dark and sombre. Since that first visit with Gorka a couple of weeks ago, she'd grown to like the pub. At night-time the place would come alive with carefree talk and laughter. With a tingle of excitement Maisie recalled the warmth of the blazing log fire; the courting couples snuggling in shadowy corners; the rowdy young men, their eyes wide and sparkling. How freely they doted on her, lavishing their affections on her, and how she loved it.

But enough of that! She must do what she could to get Mam out of this awful brooding temper.

"It's Michael, isn't it, Mam?" she cried. "I don't know what got into him this morning!"

Still no response…

Maisie felt a wave of dread, struck with the realisation that she'd have to sit through the service with her mother in a wheezing strop. As they turned the corner into Church Lane, Maisie eased her pace, the gap between them widening.

"Why get all upset, Mam? It's not fair! Mam!"

At last her mother came to a stop. She spun round and opened her mouth to speak, but a sudden clanging of the church bells drowned her words. Maisie moved closer.

"It's not our fault, Mam! We're not to blame if Michael chooses to—"

"It's not Michael I'm thinking of! It's *you*, my girl! You, and that… that brother of his! A right little charmer *he* turned out to be! I'm bothered about what folks are saying about my Maisie carrying on with that young Master Gorka!"

"Mam!" Maisie felt herself blushing, her mother's words searing through her brain like hot irons.

"Don't you *Mam* me!" Her mother's eyes narrowed. "It's not right, see? Rules are rules, and the rules say that refugee kids need support and guidance! I've got responsibilities!" Her lips trembled as a terrible wheezing sound came from deep inside her chest. "And another thing; we need the rent!"

Maisie felt trapped, unable to advance or retreat. She might have known that tongues would wag, and for all the wrong reasons. Yes, of course she'd been drawn to Gorka. She'd been attracted by the hot glint that flashed in his lovely dark eyes, his beautiful white teeth and open smile when he looked at her. Of course she'd warmed to Gorka, laughing inwardly at his silly jokes. But that was all.

"It's not like that, Mam! I couldn't... we didn't..." The words came halting, confused. "I haven't done anything *bad*!"

"How can you tell me such a lie?" Her mother's voice choked with contempt. "Do you think I'm stupid? I know what time you came in last night! You might as well have arrived home with the milkman!"

"I meant no harm, Mam! Honest!"

"That's not what other folks are saying!"

"Folks can say what they like!" Maisie filled her lungs with a hot, convulsive breath, her eyes filling with tears of anger and frustration. "What can *they* know about... about..."

She broke off, silenced by the livid look on her mother's face. A wave of indignation swept through Maisie's head like ether. Wouldn't any girl have felt that same flutter of excitement with Gorka sitting so close in the pub, laying his hand gently on her knee, begging her to leave the village and move to London with him? Hadn't she suffered enough, torn between the home she'd always known and the prospect of a new life in the big city?

"He just wanted to talk, Mam! That's all!"

"Just wanted to talk!" her mother echoed derisively. "Stupid girl! You mean to tell me you don't know he's going out with married women?"

"Married women?" Maisie gave an involuntary shiver. Her mouth went dry, as if suddenly filled with dust and ashes. She tottered for an instant.

The clanging of the church bells suddenly ceased, all except one... a solitary bell tolling on with a slow, regular beat. Maisie looked round, nervously. But they were still alone, no-one else in sight.

"Mam," she said in a strangled voice, "I really don't feel like going to church this morning."

"Best you get home, then! Do something useful in the garden! The spinach plants need putting out."

Maisie's tear-drenched vision seemed to magnify the apparition of her mother turning away and moving on towards the church. There came a silence, hollow and sterile, as the last remaining bell ceased to chime.

Her mother suddenly came to a stop and turned back.

"And you'd better have a talk with Michael, my girl! You weren't in the house last night. You didn't hear what I heard."

A wild, chaotic thought struck Maisie like a dagger thrust. Had the village tittle-tattle got to Michael as well? Is that what had made him so withdrawn at breakfast?

"What did he say, Mam? What did Michael say?"

"Nothing! He stayed in his room all night!" For a moment the hardness in her mother's expression appeared to soften a little, her eyes strangely melancholy in her sallow face. "It was the sound he made with that guitar of his. I've never heard anything like it, not in my entire life." She turned again and moved slowly away.

Maisie felt like a creature without a soul, shackled in the darkness of torment for something she'd never done.

And what must Michael be thinking now, after hearing the false gossip about herself and Gorka? Michael had always been so protective about his younger brother.

Yes, she must speak with Michael. She must go to him now, try to explain. Suddenly, Maisie yearned uncontrollably to be with Michael.

Church Cottage

Mikel sat on the edge of his bed and gazed down at the black, uneven floorboards. His eyes drifted to the guitar beside him. He looked at the instrument for a long time, staring at the tiny inscription he'd carved so carefully into the side of its mahogany arm…MA… his very own initials. But he derived little comfort from seeing them. Having fought with himself all night to stay normal, he felt drained, the blood in his veins as black as hell. Through the open window came a peel of bells, muffled and drowsy. Maisie and her mother would be arriving at church.

He could scarcely bear to think of Maisie now. But then, how could he not think of her? Maisie's absence was more than pain; it was like being dead. But he wasn't dead. Only in death would he be able to shut her out.

She would be taking her place in church, kneeling in prayer and asking God for reassurance about her love for Gorka. God would know everything. God would have seen everything. But God was merciful. He would look kindly on her, and return to her the unsullied perfection she'd once possessed. Mikel swallowed dryly. How was it that God could so abandon an innocent man, and yet be so graciously forgiving to a woman?

Mikel had only set foot in the church once. He'd gone there with Maisie and Gorka to see the newly installed stained glass window. Maisie had stood very close to Gorka in the aisle, gazing up at the new window, her face bathed in medieval hues of purple and scarlet. If only Mikel had known then what had been going on between the two of them.

"Look carefully at the window," she'd said. "Do you recognise the scene; orchards on the left, hop groves to the right?"

The new window was small; the colours fresh and assertive, dominated by shades of green and barley-yellow. The central image was that of a young country gentleman dressed in tweeds, leaning on a walking stick, a black gun dog at his side.

"Nice dog!" Gorka had exclaimed.

"Yes, Gorka, I *thought* you'd like the dog," she'd laughed. "We call the window the *estate window*, because the man you can see actually owned the estate. He was killed in the First World War, so the window is dedicated to his memory. His son runs the business now. The son's a bit of a recluse, actually. You'll hardy ever see him around the village, except occasionally when he comes to church."

Church... Never again would Mikel visit that church! He felt emotionally drained and beaten down by the utter loneliness of his position in the world. Lifting his eyes slowly, he peered through the tiny bedroom window. The sky was dazzling, almost blinding in its intensity. The rhythm of the church bells seemed to falter. And then they ceased to chime. All but one; it tolled on, mournfully.

Hooking his toes around the rung of a chair, he coaxed it nearer to the bed. Then, resting his left foot on the rung, he brought the guitar up onto his raised knee.

There came an eerie, piercing cry, like a distant scream, echoing and then fading into nothing. It was the sound of peacocks; they would be fluttering down from their overnight roosts in the treetops. Cherished and protected by the village folk, the birds were tame and left free to wander.

There was silence now. No more bells, no more peacocks; just silence. He rested the thumb of his right hand on the bass string.

A grotesque thought suddenly struck him: it was inconceivable that he would be allowed to stay in this house. How could he possibly continue to live here? Mrs Chapman wouldn't want him; not after his standoffish behaviour at breakfast this morning. In any case, he would not, he *could* not, live under the same roof as Maisie. He must go back to the refugee camp and throw himself on the mercy of Father Imaz and the Spanish Refugee Council. He would arrange it tomorrow and catch the first available train back to Birmingham. He'd rather do that than wait to be thrown out.

He pressed down lightly on the bass string and produced a single note, very soft but of good quality. He counted the beats slowly, and then played another note, higher in pitch. Then he repeated the first note on the next downbeat. And so, the Adagio of Schubert's C major quintet began to unfold. It was so amazingly simple; so profoundly beautiful. Schubert's music had sustained him on that lonely trudge to work, often in total darkness. Lifting his collar to the wind and rain, he would hear this music in his mind. It had always made him think of Maisie, still tucked up in bed and sleeping soundly.

It would never be the same again. Gorka had asserted himself on Maisie, wrapping himself around her body and sending her mad with desire. Gorka had possessed her.

Mikel played on in an agony of helplessness, determined to give everything to the music.

He heard a faint sound, the light tapping of a bird settling in the eaves. It came again, and quite distinct this time. Maintaining the tempo, he glanced up a little and saw the bedroom door opening, very slowly. And still he played; the melody must endure, or the very essence of what Schubert had created for him would be shattered forever.

Oh God, how exquisitely beautiful she was, standing there in the doorway, her face radiant in the bright morning sunshine.

With her hands tucked behind her, she pressed herself gently back against the door. It closed with a faint click. The blood seemed to boil in his veins as a fire went through him like lightning. He would bring the music to a close, but carefully, and with a satisfying finish to make it sound complete. Only then did he place the guitar down on the bed beside him, all the while gazing up at Maisie.

She moved closer, her lovely eyes shining down on him, blowing away the darkness from his mind.

"Here, Michael," she murmured. "Let me…"

She lifted the guitar from the bed, her very closeness heightening his senses. There came a low, discordant *clung* as she laid the guitar on the floor. He caught the smell of her perfume, the wonderfulness of it intensifying the flames that flickered and danced right through him, stabbing and tearing at his nerves.

As she gazed down at him, he felt her eyes teasing him, almost daring him to reveal himself, challenging him to expose the shamefulness of himself; his whole self. More sinews of fire, savage in their intensity, blazed through his body.

"But your poor fingers…" She took his hands gently, moving her thumbs very lightly across his palms. "Your poor hands; poor clever fingers."

She leaned forward, touching with her lips the tip of each finger, but very lightly. Sensing the hotness of her breath, his body trembled. She leaned closer, kissed him lightly on the cheek, and then drew back.

Was this some kind of game? An adventure for her? Mikel felt a rush of frustration. It tortured him, stretching every fibre and muscle of his body, to think how much this girl had hurt him.

Something inside him gave way, like an invisible shackle of restraint bursting apart. Reaching out, he gathered up her hair, twisting the locks around his fingers. He drew a sharp intake of breath as the hallowed strands snagged in the deep recesses of his wounded fingers. But he felt gladdened by the agony it aroused in him, thrilled by the look of surprise in her ever-widening, blazing eyes.

Would she kiss him again? It seemed the most natural thing in the world… to draw her down, to feel her mouth, moist and warm, receiving him. He fed on her mouth, the succulent sounds filling him with delight.

"Gently, Michael," she whispered.

Then she drew back a little, her hand reaching through the open front of his shirt, pushing him, coaxing him to lie back. He sought her mouth again; no more words, just kisses, lots of kisses. His whole body filled with an anguish of gratefulness. The lust for her drove him wild; a flood of madness swept over him, the tide of emotion so strong that he had no choice but to give way.

There came a joyous throbbing deep in his lower abdomen, its movement circular, propelling, and filling him with a yearning to give himself to her; everything… his heart, his blood, his whole life. Beyond the locks of her beautiful hair, he saw the heavy black beam across the ceiling shimmering through his tears. He felt the whole weight of her, the wondrous gentle motion of her body as she breathed. It was good. So unbelievably good.

He lay still, feeling warm and secure with his arms still locked around Maisie's body, the fullness of her breasts pressing down on him. Mikel had found himself. He was like a man who'd come into his own existence. He felt the thrill of a new life, a passion for living that was not childish, but which carried all the responsibilities of manhood. And he actually felt proud of himself. Yes, proud… and very, very new.

Chapter 5

AT HOME IN KENT

1 Year Later, March 1948

Fatherhood

The bliss, the irrepressible, deep-rooted bliss; to be lying on the couch with his tiny son sprawled across him… to feel that little heart beating, the tiny puckered fingers clutching at his shirt.

Work in the orchards had always demanded so much time, so much energy. But for these two precious hours on a Sunday morning, with Maisie and her mother away at church, Mikel would stretch himself out on the sofa with baby Javier lying asleep on his breast. He needed this time to feel the nearness of Javier, his own flesh and blood.

Reaching down, he felt the exquisite little head resting close to his chin and lightly stroked the wispy strands of downy black hair with his fingertips.

"Papa's little boy," he whispered.

Naming the child had been a tense affair; the only black moment of his married life. Why not *Andoni*, after Papa? But Maisie had wanted the baby christened *James*, after her own father. Mikel had suggested a compromise: *Andoni James Aguirre*. It would have sounded good. But then Maisie's mother had intervened, saying people wouldn't care much for a name like *Andoni Aguirre* in an English village. How would other kids treat him when he'd grown old enough for school? It was the kind of blind intolerance that made Mikel seethe with rage. So eventually they'd settled on *Javier*. Perhaps their next child would be a girl, in which case he would insist on naming her Miren, after Mama.

What a thought; *another* child! But no, not yet; that would have to wait. First, he must get himself a decent wage, and then a place of his own.

He felt shackled living under his mother-in-law's roof. Mrs Chapman was a tough, obdurate person. When Maisie had become pregnant out of wedlock, her mother's attitude towards him had changed. Sometimes he would catch his mother-in-law looking at him furtively, her eyes narrowing disapprovingly. And then she would turn away from him disdainfully. She must rate him very low-class; shallow and worthless.

Such animosity was bound to grow with time. Eventually his presence here would come to irritate her beyond endurance. And since there was nothing in the world he could do about his mother-in-law's deep dislike of him, he must break free. He would move to London with Maisie and Javier; establish himself as a guitar manufacturer. Of course, it would take time and money, the two things that had always seemed so far from reach. But if he kept on working hard, putting a little money by each week, then he might succeed. After all, Gorka had managed to set himself up in business.

Since moving to London, Gorka's military contacts had begun to pay off, or so he'd claimed. Surplus weaponry, uniforms, second-hand married-quarter furniture, they were all making good money in the civilian sector. Gorka had even managed to acquire some original oil paintings from a decommissioned officer's mess! But was it legal? If only Gorka would bend his skills towards doing something more reputable, like promoting professionally crafted classical guitars. Just imagine the advertising placard: *The Aguirre Spanish Guitar Workshop: instruments shipped abroad and prized by players all over the world.*

Wouldn't Mama and Papa have been proud to know their sons had formed a successful family business?

Overcome by a great drowsiness, Mikel began to drift away. Then he heard Maisie's voice.

"Don't let it get cold," she whispered, laying a bottle of warm milk down by his side. "Mam and I are off now. And be careful not to let my little boy roll off onto the floor."

"Oh, no need to worry about us," Mikel smiled. "We're big boys, aren't we, Javier? Big boys can take care of themselves."

His eyelids were drooping again. He heard the rustle of clothing and reached out, driven by a sudden impulse to touch Maisie, to keep her with him. But there was nothing to touch, nothing but empty space where she'd stood just moments ago. There came a familiar *clack* as the outside door opened and then slammed shut. Mikel felt his body relaxing, his mind slipping away, succumbing to the power of sleep.

An Unexpected Visitor

Mikel opened his eyes and glanced up from the couch. What kind of strange universe was this? It was Gorka! Gorka was standing right next to him! A smart suit and tie with a matching handkerchief, neatly pushed into his breast pocket, and that thin moustache nicely trimmed... Oh yes, Gorka was definitely in the money!

"Hey Gorka..." Mikel spoke softly so as not to disturb baby Javier. "It's good to see you. But... but what are you doing *here*?"

Gorka fixed him with a cold, menacing gaze. "Still taking life easy, brother?" he taunted. Gorka turned away, his eyes darting curiously around the room. Moving over to the mantelpiece, he swept up a photograph and examined it closely. "What's this?"

"That's Maisie's father," Mikel said cheerfully. "Flying Officer Chapman. He was killed flying a Hurricane during the war. He's my father-in-law."

"Your father-in-law? You mean Maisie's your *wife*?"

Mikel sensed the onset of a clash.

"We were married last summer."

"My God!" Gorka shook his head scornfully. "Poor Maisie. Doesn't seem right, a lovely girl like that wasting away her life in a dump like this. Nothing ever happens in this place; it's always so bloody quiet."

"We won't be here for much longer!"

It was a weak response, and Gorka was bound to latch on to it. Without money, Mikel would have no hope of moving away.

In the depths of his aching heart, Mikel began to think the unthinkable: that Gorka, his own brother, was nothing more than a heartless, self-conceited scoundrel, and that he would probably remain so for the rest of his life. Mikel felt cold, as if the blood in his veins had ceased to flow. But he wasn't about to cave in.

"We've got plans," he went on. "Up in London."

"Plans? You've got plans? You just don't get it, do you, Mikel? You'll need more than plans. It takes guts! Look at the state of you. You've missed the boat, brother. You've been caught in a trap, spliced into a marriage you can't afford, and pinned down by family ties. You'll never make enough money to break away from this. Why not let Maisie stay with me for a while? I'll take care of her; she'll be comfortable at my place. It'll give you a break, Mikel, time on your own to get yourself properly established."

"No!" Mikel cried. "No!" A hellfire of hatred and jealous rage flared up in his breast. The very thought of it… Maisie going off to live with Gorka! It burned like a white flame in the core of his brain. "It's obscene!" he cried out again in a burst of fury. "You couldn't do something like that!" It was too outrageous, almost inconceivable. "Is that why you've come here, to try to tempt her away? You wouldn't, Gorka. You… you…"

Mikel broke off. He'd heard the garden gate slam shut, and then a crunch of footsteps on the garden path.

Gorka stood gazing out of the window, his face transfixed. For a moment his expression appeared pale and deathly, his mouth drawn down sharply at the corners. He looked terrified.

"Mikel!" Gorka exclaimed in a kind of apoplectic frenzy.

"What? What's the matter, Gorka?"

The footsteps grew louder.

"For God's sake!" Gorka plucked at his immaculate collar. "You've got to help me, Mikel! I'm your brother, dammit!"

"But… what have you done?" Mikel struggled to lever himself upright. "Tell me… Gorka!"

Clutching baby Javier tightly to his breast, Mikel flung his legs over the side of the couch and stood up quickly, his body hot and damp with sweat.

"Gorka!" he rasped. But Gorka was nowhere to be seen.

It must have been a dream… a nightmare…

Mikel's blood ran cold as Javier let out a piercing cry, his tiny face wrinkled with alarm. There came a brief silence as the baby's skin turned crimson, and then he let out another cry, even more wretched than the first.

"Ssshhh! Ssshhh…" Mikel rocked the baby frantically.

Oh, the relief as Javier's bawling began to subside. But then came a loud pounding on the outside door. Was Gorka still here? And then again: *boom, boom, boom!*

The shock of it seemed to liberate Mikel's paralysed muscles. He moved quickly into the kitchen. Lifting the latch, he pulled hard and the door sprang open to reveal a man dressed in a light-coloured raincoat.

"Mr Aguirre?"

"Yes," Mikel answered hoarsely.

"*Mikel* Aguirre?"

There was only one explanation for this: Gorka was in deep trouble. The debt collectors were after him; there would be surety papers to sign, bail to be arranged!

"Forgive my intruding on your Sunday," the stranger went on. "My name is Whitaker… John Whitaker. I'm from London." Then, after a pause, "May I come in?"

Whitaker stepped into the kitchen and swung the door to close it, but it bounced open again. Whitaker pushed harder, causing baby Javier to start as the door slammed shut.

"You seem to need a carpenter!" Whitaker grinned.

Mikel ran the palm of his hand in slow gentle circles over Javier's upper back and shoulders. The infant gave a shudder.

"It's my brother, isn't it?" Mikel said. "That's why you're here."

"Your brother?" Whitaker smiled amiably. "Why, no, not at all. Actually, I've come to see you, Mr Aguirre. I'm here to offer you a job. It's a jolly important job too, and rather well paid. It would be conditional, of course; I need to be sure you're the right man."

"A job?" Mikel said dubiously. "Where? In London?"

"London?" Whitaker laughed out loud. "Oh no, I don't think so. You wouldn't like it much up there. It's like hell working in London; a busy, over-populated city full of slippery eels and sharp-toothed tigers. No, I doubt if London would be the place for you. I'd have thought a spell in the Basque Country would have been more to *your* liking, Mr Aguirre."

"The Basque Country! But how did you know…"

"Oh, but I know a lot about you, Mikel. You don't mind if I call you *Mikel*?"

"What? What do you know about me?"

"Well, I know that you are multi-lingual; fluent in English, Spanish… and Basque, of course. That you were born in August 1927 and attended school in Guernica. That you left Bilbao in May 1937, aged nine, expatriated to England. I also know that you have a strong inclination to return to your native country. Isn't that true, Mikel?"

"How do you know all this?"

"I'm sorry but I can't say too much, not right now. We work closely with the National Joint Council for Spanish Relief, that much I *can* tell you. They speak very highly of you, Mikel. Oh, and we've also interviewed your brother."

"Gorka? You're offering Gorka a job? But he already has a—"

"No, no… Your brother's a very personable young man; highly intelligent, too. But no, we won't be offering Gorka a position. You see, Mikel, brains aren't everything. We demand other qualities: loyalty to one's country, consideration for other colleagues in the service…"

"Service… what service?"

"You want to know more? Then why not come and see me later? I know you'll be interested." Whitaker reached for the door latch. "Let's say at eight o'clock this evening. I'll be at the White Lion. Make it sharp. I intend on catching the last train back to London." He gave a pull, but the door failed to budge. He pulled again and the door opened with a bang. "Do come alone, there's a good chap." Whitaker stepped outside. "And just one other thing, Mikel. I'd be grateful if you would tell no-one about my coming here this morning."

He began to move off.

"Mr Whitaker! How should I explain to my wife? About tonight?"

Whitaker stopped and glanced back.

"You need an *excuse* to drop by at your own pub? Well now, let me see. Your village first eleven has a meeting at the White Lion tonight. I expect they'll be discussing fixtures for the coming season. Why not tell your wife you've developed a fondness for English cricket? That should do the trick. Oh, and by the way, you should hire a carpenter… to fix that door!"

Golden Opportunities

Mikel lingered in the shadows, facing the entrance to the White Lion pub. The sun had set and it was now too dark to read the time. The pub door suddenly opened, a burst of raucous laughter emerging from within. Now bathed in light, Mikel glanced again at his watch… 7.55pm. A figure appeared in the doorway, bow-legged and very crooked. It was old Tom Gristle. Mikel moved forward.

"Hello Tom!"

Tom lurched past, brushed Mikel aside and, with an unintelligible grunt, staggered off into the darkness.

It was horrible to see a good friend so debased by drunkenness. Mikel felt scorned.

Peeking through the open door, he saw a great crush and heard another burst of wild laughter. Could he face it; the bawdy humour? Yes, of course, he *must* go through with it. Whitaker would be waiting for him, perhaps with the offer of a well-paid job. Mikel took a deep breath, as if preparing himself to receive a blow, and thrust himself forward into the pub.

The acrid stench of cigarette smoke was almost overpowering as he entered the hot and stuffy atmosphere of the bar area.

Manly whistles began to break out, followed by a rapid stamping of feet. Mikel felt his body go rigid. He felt his arm held fast in a tight grip. It was Charlie Oldham, his big round face redder and shinier than Mikel had ever seen before.

"Now then!" Charlie's thick, rubbery lips parted in a silent kind of laugh. "Secret business, aye?" He tapped the side of his big nose. "You'll need to get yourself down below, lad! There's a gentleman waiting to see you!" Powerless to resist, Mikel had no option but to allow himself to be dragged towards a deep, narrow basement stairwell. "Just between the three of us, aye," Charlie hissed. "Hush, hush and all that?" Then, with a final shove, "Look lively then!"

Mikel clattered awkwardly down the stairs. He grasped a side rail for support, but it was useless. Unable to slow himself, he took the last two steps in a single stride. His left foot landed on a polished wooden floor and immediately slid away. His right knee buckled and took the full impact. He remained there, head bowed, half standing, half crouching, for several long moments. Dazed with pain, he staggered to his feet and limped stiffly along a narrow, ill-lit corridor with doors off to each side. One door had been left open.

"Mikel?" someone called. "In here!"

He entered a snug little room with a round table and two chairs. Whitaker was already on his feet. Reaching out across the table, he shook Mikel firmly by the hand.

"Good man!" Whitaker beamed. "Delighted you could make it. Close the door, there's a good chap. And take a seat."

Swallowing down the agony, Mikel sank slowly into a chair, pushing out his right leg to ease the discomfort.

"I expect Mr Oldham told you where to find me." Whitaker separated two glasses of beer, pushing one of them in Mikel's direction. "He's an interesting man, Charlie Oldham. Can we trust him, do you think?"

"Of course I trust him. He's my boss."

Charlie Oldham was an animal, but was it worth risking a job to say so?

"Then let's drink to Charlie Oldham! And to you, Mikel; may you live long, and prosper!" Whitaker drew heavily on his beer. "Ah…" He grinned. "Can't beat a good local brew. But what's your Charlie Oldham *really* like, I wonder? With his workers, I mean."

A silence followed, absolute and sterile. Mikel gazed down at his hands. They were like old man's hands, gnarled and inflexible. Reaching out, he felt the refreshing coldness of the beer glass against his rough fingers.

"Though he may slay me, yet will I trust in him," Whitaker murmured.

"What?"

"Oh, nothing… just a quote. It's from the Bible. It can't be easy having to place your trust in a man like Charlie Oldham. He's a rogue, Mikel. Anyone can see that."

"I've nothing to say about Charlie Oldham. And anyway, I won't be working in the fields for much longer. There are other things I want to do with my life."

"Oh, and I'm very pleased to hear it! One likes to see ambition in a young man."

Whitaker flipped open a packet of cigarettes and offered one.

"I don't smoke."

"No, of course not; I should have remembered." Whitaker lit one for himself, and tossed the packet onto the table. "So, you want to move on with your life. Where then? Tell me, where do you expect to be in five years from now?"

"There is only one thing I want to do with my life," Mikel rasped, smarting from the pulsating pain in his right knee. "But

I expect you know what that is. You seem to know everything else about me."

"Perhaps I do; or there again, perhaps not. Why don't you tell me anyway?"

Mikel looked down at his fingernails. They were in a dreadfully poor state.

"I want to play the guitar, Mr Whitaker. And I want to play it well. I want to have my own workshop where I can construct large, deep-bodied guitars, with soundboards made from the very thinnest of lightweight woods."

"Do you, indeed?" Whitaker took a long drag from his cigarette. He was smiling in a derisive, mocking sort of way.

"Yes Mr Whitaker, I really do. I want to produce guitars for the most famous performers. I want my instruments to be tested and signed by the very best of them; Azpiazu and Segovia, for example."

"Segovia!" Whitaker leaned back in his chair. "Oh, come now, Mikel. There's no harm in aiming high... but Segovia!"

"Why not? I have done my research. I know that Segovia likes his guitars made with spruce tops, their backs and sides with Brazilian rosewood. I know that he prefers guitars made at the Ramirez and Hauser workshops. I know that Hauser craftsmen fix metal cones around the insides of their sound apertures to enhance the bass frequencies. I know these things, Mr Whitaker. I also know that Segovia likes to replace his guitars with new instruments at the end of every playing season. And one day, he will turn to me; he will come to Mikel Aguirre's workshop for his concert guitars!"

The expression on Whitaker's face was suddenly transformed into one of genuine surprise.

"My God…" he murmured. "Yes… yes, of course I knew about your interest in music, but…" Whitaker broke off. Then, with a deep sigh, he leaned forward and stubbed out the cigarette. "Listen, Mikel. There will be much to attract you in what we're offering. The financial rewards are very considerable. But I'd hate to stand accused of diverting a man away from his own true sense of destiny. Besides, there are pitfalls… potential dangers. You should think very carefully before accepting."

"How can I even think of accepting?" Mikel replied angrily. "You pry into my life. You tell me things I already know. And yet you say nothing about this job. I am beginning to think it does not exist!"

"Hmmm…" Whitaker swallowed another mouthful of beer. "You know, Mikel, in some ways I envy you living and working out here in the country. I might even be tempted to come and join you some day. What does a man earn, I wonder, as a labourer in the orchards?"

"Half a crown."

"Half a crown?" Whitaker echoed impatiently. "What sort of answer is that? What do you mean, half a crown?"

"Half a crown! More in summer, less in winter; but half a crown a week, more or less." Mikel sipped from his glass slowly, his mouth filling with the cool effervescent flavour of yeast and hops.

Whitaker looked doubtful. Maybe he thought half a crown a week too generous for a man with barely eighteen months of work experience. Mikel decided to set the record straight.

"I don't keep all the money. I give most of it to my mother-in-law. It pays for our rent."

Whitaker cleared his throat.

"Tell me, Mikel, how does a man with a wife and a child manage to get by on two shillings and sixpence a week?"

"Your job would offer more?"

"More? A new recruit in my outfit would earn more than twice that in a single day. I told you, Mikel, the pay is good."

Mikel ran through the arithmetic. Five shillings a day, maybe thirty shillings a week. Multiply by fifty. That must be about… There came a ringing in his ears, the blood rushing to his cheeks.

"Fifteen hundred shillings a year?" he gasped. "That… that's seventy-five pounds!"

"No Mikel. Not seventy-five. The job I had in mind would provide nearer two hundred pounds a year, plus expenses."

"Two hundred pounds a year?" Mikel echoed in a tremulous voice.

"Plus expenses. It's the going rate, Mikel. It's what the British government will pay a young refugee who is willing to return to his or her own country in order to gather information. You'd be working for MI6. They want you to go to Bilbao and send back information from the Basque country."

"MI6?" Mikel struggled to grasp the meaning of it. "You mean… as a spy? But… but what about Maisie, my wife, and my son?"

"Yes, of course." Whitaker sat perfectly still, his hands clasped together on the table. "Many of our overseas agents have family ties in the United Kingdom. But they manage to keep a sense of proportion about it. And there are compensations."

"Compensations?"

"Certainly! We always try to ease the burden of separation. Whilst you were working abroad, your wife would receive an income equivalent to half your salary, plus a child's allowance.

And should anything happen to delay your return to Britain, we would continue to support them until such time as you were able to come home."

"How long? I mean, how long would I be away?"

"Postings are for six months initially; extendable by mutual agreement. It would depend on how well you performed your duties."

"I'd want my wife to come with me."

"Out of the question, I'm afraid. Postings to the Basque Country are strictly unaccompanied... which brings me to another important aspect of the contract."

"Contract? You mean I'd have to sign something?"

"You'd need to sign the Official Secrets Act, Mikel. It would oblige you to tell no-one about your work, absolutely no-one. In fact, even your wife must not know."

"What? That's impossible! I couldn't just... just pack my bags and leave! Not without telling Maisie! It's a crazy idea!"

"We're not without experience in such matters," Whitaker smiled reassuringly. "We can be wonderfully creative when it comes to matters of deception."

"Deception?" A surge of anger went through Mikel, intensified by the notion that he must be ready to cheat Maisie. He tried to imagine how she would feel, the look of utter devastation on her face when she found out. "It's... it's out of the question!" he cried. "I couldn't do it!" Surprised by the rude tone of his own voice, Mikel felt his face reddening.

"But you wouldn't have to double-cross your wife. There are thousands of refugees living in Britain, just like you. Many of them are begging to go home. The British government is already sponsoring a selected number of them to travel abroad on fact-finding trips prior to repatriation. The mechanisms are already in place. Believe me, it would be easy to get you to Bilbao. Fact-finding, Mikel… fact finding prior to repatriation; why should your wife suspect anything else?"

Mikel's hands trembled as he reached again for his beer. He was about to put the glass to his mouth, but hesitated.

"Dangers…" he whispered huskily. "You said there were dangers."

Whitaker gazed back at him sternly. After a long silence, he rose swiftly to his feet.

"I must be away! Think about it carefully. Do some homework. Learn about the political climate. Get to know what's happening in and around Bilbao." He took a card from his top pocket and scribbled something down. "Write to me at this address. And remember what I said about loyalty. In my organisation it equates to a lifetime of support for your wife and child, if that's what it comes to." He lifted his overcoat. "Do you read the newspapers?"

"Sometimes…" Mikel dallied fretfully with his beer glass.

"Good! Read the foreign affairs section of every newspaper you can get your hands on. Here's something to be going on with." Whitaker threw a rolled-up newspaper on the table. "Goodbye, Mikel. And I hope to see you again very soon."

Mikel heard the door close behind him. He sat there, dazed, a strange kind of silence throbbing inside him.

The newspaper had fallen open at an article about Spain. He scanned the headline:

BILBAO'S HEAVY INDUSTRY IS PRESERVED INTACT AFTER TWO BLOODY WARS

FRANCO MANAGES TO RETAIN THE GOODWILL OF THE BASQUE BUSINESS COMMUNITY.

Mikel lifted the paper and drew it closer.

Basque factory owners are benefiting from policies which deny rights to trade unions. Wages are being kept low whilst substantial profits are being made.

So, *this* was Franco's way of dealing with Spain's shattered economy! Mikel slammed the paper down. Exploit the Basque factories at the expense of impoverished Basque workers! He began to tremble as an acid tide of bitterness swept through his veins. The Basque people should rise up and fight! They should distribute leaflets, paint graffiti on the factory walls, commit acts of sabotage and initiate strike action! The Basque flag should be flown from every church tower!

Is that what Whitaker was asking him to get involved in? No… surely not. The British government would require their spies to lie low, discreetly gathering intelligence with the minimum amount of fuss, and relaying their findings safely back into the hands of MI6. What could be easier? And all for two hundred pounds a year!

Mikel lifted Whitaker's card from the table. It was printed:

Commander John A Whitaker
Department MI6
The War Office
Whitehall
London

He turned the card over to see what Whitaker had written on the reverse:

Mikel...
Part of a code message composed by an SOE colleague
for his girlfriend after she was captured and killed
whilst on active duty...
"The love that I have
Of the life that I have
Is yours and yours and yours..."
Loyalty is everything, Mikel.
Truly... JAW

A Long Walk Home

Mikel left the pub through the back basement door… anything to avoid Charlie Oldham and his inarticulate band of thugs and drunks. He walked slowly, the pain in his right knee intense, and headed for home.

A full moon had risen. It hung low down over the eastern horizon like a giant yellow ball, bathing the countryside in a magical, silvery phosphorescent glow.

The fruit trees appeared grey and mysterious, aligned like

ranks of soldiers in battle formation; sentinels keeping watch over a landscape, precious, hallowed, and little changed by the passage of centuries.

Pausing to rest his knee, Mikel fixed his gaze on a single row of apple tree saplings. He followed it out to the visible horizon, a distance of several hundred metres in the half-light. He'd staked every one of those trees, and thousands of others besides. How breathtakingly beautiful they looked now.

But Mikel knew in his heart that work like that would eventually kill him, just as it was killing old Tom Gristle; not to mention the many other generations of orchard men who'd come before.

He turned towards the moon. As he shielded his eyes from the glare, his gaze wandered over a wide undulating expanse of hop poles. They stood in their hundreds, erect and naked.

Close by, near to the ground, he saw new hop bines beginning to sprout from the roots. They would soon be shooting upwards, curling themselves tightly around strings, wires and anything else they could grab a hold of, before flattening out across the top of the overhead trellises. In a few months from now, the landscape would be transformed. The field would disappear, hidden behind great walls of hop bines, each wall two metres thick and several metres high.

He'd been out of the house for two hours, an unusually long period of time. Maisie would be worried, and worse still, his mother-in-law would demand to know where he'd been.

His mind grappled with the enormity of what Whitaker had proposed. Six months without Maisie and baby Javier. Could he endure that? And what if his absence became extended to a full year? His whole life would be plunged into a sombre misery of sorrow and want.

How would Maisie react to being told that her husband was about to embark on some senseless adventure in Spain? What could she possibly hope to gain from it? There would be more money, of course. Suddenly, out of the blue, Maisie would find herself very well off. But would she allow him to go? Could he persuade her of his determination to come home again, quickly, as soon as the job was done?

Maybe there *was* something he could do. He could leave something behind; something so valuable, so highly cherished, that she would know instinctively that he could hardly bear to be parted from it. Maybe then she would understand. But could he endure being separated from his beloved guitar for six months, and possibly for longer?

As the moon climbed steadily higher, the germ of an idea began to form in Mikel's consciousness; a means by which he might convince Maisie of the sense of it.

Reaching down, he rubbed the stiffness from his throbbing knee, swallowed dryly, and set off for home.

The house was silent as Mikel entered. A light had been left on in the kitchen. Making his way towards the stairs, he noticed a cup left on the kitchen table, covered by a saucer. As he lifted the saucer, a poignant wave of affection washed over him. She was so wonderfully thoughtful; selfless to a fault. Gratefully, he drank the cold chocolate down.

Setting his teeth against the pain, he climbed the stairs, avoiding the squeakiest of steps. Maisie had left the bedroom door open.

She lay fast asleep, fragile and defenceless as she breathed.

He moved to Javier's cot and peered in. How exquisitely sweet to see his little son gazing up at him, smiling as if without a care in the world. His two tiny hands were up in the air, darting around aimlessly. Mikel reached down and touched his face; absolute perfection. Javier grabbed his finger, hung on tightly, and drew it towards his mouth.

At that moment, Mikel felt Maisie's arms around his waist, gathering him close to her warm body.

"Well?" she whispered "How did it go?"

"It made me think, Maisie. It has taken me a long time. But now I know for sure."

"So, you're not about to join the cricket club?"

"The cricket club? No… no. It's not the White Lion crowd, and it's not the cricket club. It's the total situation, Maisie. This is not what I want for us. I've been thinking a lot, and there isn't an easy way to explain. But I have to…"

"Have to what, Michael?" Her eyes widened.

"I've decided to go back to Spain. I want to study at the Esteso guitar factory. I want to learn how to build guitars properly. I want to be a master craftsman."

"Michael!" she gasped, and drew back.

"I know, but I have to. It's the only way I can learn how to set up my own workshop. The pay will be very good; much more than I'm getting now."

She gazed at him for several long moments.

"When…?"

"I don't know. Esteso have an office in London. I'm going to write and tell them about my guitar."

From now on, every word would have to be dragged from the pit of his stomach.

"They'll let me know when there's a place," he went on.

"How long will this apprenticeship last?"

"Maybe six months. More if they think I'm good enough."

She shook her head slowly.

"It will break our hearts to see you go, Michael. But it's perfectly obvious you'll never be truly happy unless you do this thing."

"Maisie… I…"

"Come to bed," she smiled.

Chapter 6

THE BASQUE COUNTRY

4 Months Later, July 1948

Home, Sweet Home

Mikel set out along the narrow winding path leading gently downwards through a deep meadow valley. The vibrant grasses, knee-high and thick with wildflowers, were touched with swathes of thyme. He stretched out his hand, caressing the seeded fronds with his palm. All around him the Pyrenean cattle grazed; big docile creatures, the colour of caramel. He was consumed by the sound of their bells; a soft continuous tinkling intertwined with muted clunks and clangs. It was good to be back in his homeland, but how he longed to share it with Maisie and Javier.

Gazing up towards the higher pastures, he saw flocks of sheep grazing on the harsh alpine grasses. He thought of the cheeses Mama used to make, and which Papa would sell at Bilbao market. From a recipe said to be more than four thousand years old, cheeses made from sheep's milk were

Mama's speciality. That nutty, refreshing, herbaceous flavour; so different from cheeses in England.

His daily shift at the paper mill was over and Mikel felt relieved to be away from the ceaseless racket of the wood-pulping machinery. It was exhilarating to be outside again, inhaling the crisp mountain air, fresh with the tang of wild aromatic herbs. Almost every day for the past two months he'd trodden this path, revelling in that incessant clamour of cow bells, some near, some far; a clinking, clunking, jangling dissonance of sounds, no two exactly alike.

Soon he would leave the foothills behind and join the highway, the main bus route into Bilbao. And there, in the city, he would breathe a very different kind of atmosphere, the air tainted with poisonous effluent; filth and grime from the city's iron and steel foundries, cement plants and chemical works.

Having spent several weeks in London training to be a field intelligence officer, he'd come to regard big cities as unwholesome places. But conditions in London were as nothing compared to what Bilbao had become. As a child, he'd watched people fishing from the banks of the River Nervión. Nowadays, anything but fish might be found in those putrid waters. And it wasn't just fish that were dying. Franco's relentless pursuit of increased industrial output, together with the effects of low pay and crippling poverty, was killing people in the factory towns and cities of the Basque Country.

But at least he was back. And the training was over, thank God. At one stage, he'd felt like dropping out of the course, unable to cope with Whitaker's punishing schedule of role-play exercises. The only bit he'd really enjoyed was learning how to pass on intelligence without compromising its security, and where neither agent knew the identity of the other.

The 'dead-letter box' method had been great fun. DLB exercises had to be conducted away from the classroom, out in the busy streets of London. A DLB site could be anywhere, just so long as you were hidden from view during the few moments it took to load or empty the 'box'. Not a real box, of course; just a space between two books on a library shelf, a niche in a brick wall, a rubbish receptacle, or maybe a towel dispenser in a washroom… easy! He'd learned methods for signalling to his opposite number that he was ready to place a message in the DLB, or to retrieve something from it. Of course, there had to be a foolproof way of knowing whether the material had been collected so the first agent could go back and recover the document if the second agent had failed to make the pickup; chalk marks on telegraph poles, coded symbols on the backs of park benches, and the use of fake DLBs to check the presence of enemy surveillance teams. It was all fascinating stuff, but when would he get the chance to put Whitaker's training into practice?

Reflecting on his lack of progress, Mikel felt overcome by a brooding wave of heaviness. He'd arrived in Bilbao two months ago, and still hadn't managed to collect anything worth sending back to London. Whitaker would be expecting a preliminary report at the very least. Maybe something would turn up at tonight's Basque resistance meeting. But it all depended on Peli, and Peli was nowhere to be seen.

Mikel came to a halt and looked round, scanning the curving line of the path, backwards and upwards, until it disappeared into the high mountain forest behind him. A grey smudge rose from the trees: smoke and steam from the pulping mill. But there was no sign of Peli.

"Remember, Mikel," Peli had said, "even the trees have ears in the Basque Country."

So where was Peli? Had something happened? Orders changed? Cover blown?

The mountain summit to Mikel's left was almost totally obscured by mist. The light would soon begin to fade. The mountain was casting a long shadow and plunging the whole valley into an icy coldness. He must keep moving.

"Mikel!"

The voice had sounded close, and yet Mikel could see no-one. Then he heard it again…

"Psssst… Mikel! Over here!"

Mikel looked again and saw Peli rising to his feet from the long grass.

"You see?" Peli laughed. "I told you to stay on your guard!"

"You're late, Peli! What in God's name are you playing at? I've been worrying like hell!"

"Hey… steady!" Peli brushed himself down. He ambled closer. "I clocked-off early this afternoon, just so I could meet up with *you*! I only get paid for the hours I work, you know!"

For someone who was supposed to be high up in the Basque resistance movement, Peli looked decidedly scruffy. In fact, he might have been taken for a common tramp. His waistcoat was ridiculously small, making his legs appear too long for his body; the sleeves of his jacket ended well short of his wrists; his trousers were tatty and very baggy. He wore a working man's cap shoved back from his forehead and a neck-scarf tied with an elaborate knot. His keen eyes sparkled with a sly kind of enjoyment.

"I'm sorry, Peli," Mikel said. "It's just that I was beginning to think you'd given up on me."

"Given up?" Peli pulled down his waistcoat in a vain attempt to cover the top of his trousers. "Not bloody likely!" He moved closer and slapped Mikel on the shoulder. "I intend to rely on you, my friend!"

Peli took Mikel by the arm, and they strolled on together down the hill.

"So how are you finding life at the mill?" Peli grinned.

"It's noisy!" Mikel had decided from the start that it was an awful place to work. He was especially wary of the mill superintendent, a pale, mean-spirited little man who seemed to dislike everybody, and whose only interest in life was looking after a big production chart festooned across his office wall. "It's all those machines. Sometimes I can hardly hear myself speak."

"Ha!" Peli exclaimed. "Wait until they put you in charge of the barking drum. That's where the logs get stripped; makes a hell of a racket! They'll probably move you around a bit to gain experience. You'll find it quieter in the pulp-wash area. Be wary of the boss, though. I'll swear to God the sneaky little bastard reports directly to Franco. I wouldn't trust him if I were you."

Mikel felt a churning in his stomach. He *must* get his hands on some hard intelligence, and soon. Not just the kind of idle gossip that was always circulating around the mill, but something more substantial; something to keep Whitaker sweet. When was Peli going to say something about tonight's meeting?

"You've always lived in Bilbao?" Peli went on.

"No, I was in England during the war."

"One of the refugee bunch?"

"It was more than just a bunch, Peli. There were thousands of us. I got fed up living in England. I needed to get away; had to find out what was going on in my own country."

"So, you decided to come back?"

"Something like that. I want to tell the world what Franco's regime is doing to my people."

"Ah! So that's why you want to be a reporter!" Peli laughed. "Well, maybe you should start by writing something for the Basque Socialist Gazette."

"Oh, I can do better than that, Peli. First, I'm going back to England. I'm going to contact all the British newspapers, tell them what's happening over here. Then I'm going to collect my family and bring them back to Bilbao. And I'm going to keep on talking to those newspaper editors. You know what I mean?"

"You're bringing your family *here*? To Bilbao?"

"Why not? I'll take any kind of job, so long as I can do something for the resistance movement without putting anybody at risk."

"I chose the right man, then!" Peli grinned.

"So why not tell me what's happening?" Only too aware of the dangerous circles in which he was moving, Mikel drew a deep breath. "Like tonight, for example. Where's the meeting going to be? Who's going to be there? Will I be expected to say anything?"

"Hey! That's classified!" Peli drew back on Mikel's arm. They came to a stop. "I can't release information like that! Not until the last possible moment. We can't afford to be careless;

not with Franco's stooges crawling all over the bloody place!"

After a moment, Peli's embattled expression appeared to relax a little.

"But I reckon you're reliable enough," he muttered. "Just get it into your head, Mikel: you've got to keep your mouth shut!" His hand came down hard on Mikel's shoulder. "And I do mean *shut*, okay?" He tugged again at Mikel's elbow and they moved on. "It'll be an informal meeting tonight; just the six of us. Everyone gets a chance to talk, but I'm in charge."

Mikel felt resentful and ill at ease. He must press Peli even harder. Whitaker had a special interest in Franco's factory policies and conditions of work.

"Anyone from heavy industry?"

"Someone from steel," Peli replied. "Another from shipbuilding. Oh, and some guy from the Socialist Studies Centre; a rising member of the Basque Nationalist Party, apparently… very good for publicity."

"So, that's you and me, plus three others… And the sixth?"

"A new recruit, and very lively in debate; just like you, Mikel."

"Doesn't sound much like me," Mikel smiled. "I'm the shy type: silent and deep."

"You know something?" Peli laughed. "Being shy isn't always such a bad thing. And I'll tell you something else; she's a bloody sight prettier than you!"

The city was coming into view now, with the Bay of Biscay beyond. The path was about to divide.

"You go that way." Peli pointed to the right. "Any bus will take you to the centre. Get off at the Paseo del Prado. There's a small café opposite the Botanical Gardens; the Café Domine. I'll see you there at six."

"Will I need to say anything? Introduce myself?"

"Don't look so serious!" Peli pulled forward on his cap. "You're in good hands, Mikel. I'll take care of you. Just bring something to write on, okay?" He shook Mikel warmly by the hand, then turned and headed off along the other trail. He looked like a lanky schoolboy who'd outgrown his clothes; a perfect camouflage for one of the most influential and dynamic leaders of the Basque resistance movement.

Peli stopped suddenly.

"Those English newspapers!" he yelled. "They sell all over the world, don't they? Try to get the inside story on what happened to the poor sods who got arrested for taking strike action last year. That'll do for an opener! See you later!"

He turned again and sauntered off down the hill.

Betrayal

The bus journey had been quick, having missed the tail-end of the late afternoon rush. Mikel got off at the stop closest to the Botanical Gardens. He must slow down; best not to arrive too soon. Crossing the Paseo del Prado, he waited a few moments on the grass refuge between the two carriageways.

The sun was lower now, the sky overhead perfectly clear. But the hills to the south, from which he'd descended a couple of hours ago, were shrouded in mist. Further round to the south-east he could see the summit of Gorbea Mountain set against the backdrop of a huge and beautifully formed cumulus cloud. It was a spectacular sight. He checked the time; five minutes to go.

Then he saw the Café Domine, just a short distance away. There seemed little point in holding back.

His entry into the café was greeted by a loud, reverberating clang of the doorbell. Closing the door quietly behind him, he scanned the room systematically. It came naturally for him to do so. Although nervous, the drill had become automatic; Whitaker's training was paying off.

To his left, a young barman held a glass to the light, turning it slowly, inspecting it carefully. Three men were leaning against the bar. They glanced round at Mikel, but only momentarily. Peli was not among them. To his right, an old man sat alone at a table, a lethargic brown dog stretched out by his feet. The animal glanced up at Mikel for a brief instant, and then lowered its head back down onto its outstretched paws, its eyes closed, inert, comatose. The only others present were a young couple seated further to Mikel's right, in a corner by the door. They too had seen him enter. The young man seemed amused. He leaned closer to the girl and spoke to her quietly. She drew back a little, giggling.

Sensing no danger, Mikel moved to the bar.

"Señor?" The barman showed his teeth in a wide smile.

"A Cava," Mikel said. "Extra sweet, if you have one."

"With ice?"

"Yes… thank you."

A copy of *El Deia*, one of Bilbao's local newspapers, lay on the bar. He glanced at the headline:

FRANCE TO END SANCTIONS AGAINST SPAIN: ECONOMIC AND CULTURAL EXCHANGES RE-INVIGORATED.

The barman dropped a lump of ice into a tall glass, poured the Cava and placed it down in front of Mikel.

"For the Cava, five pesetas," he said. "For *El Deia*, nothing, Señor. Please… with our compliments." He slid the newspaper towards Mikel.

Fumbling for a coin, Mikel glanced towards the rear of the café. It was a long, narrow room, dark and rather cheerless. There were a few tables, but all unoccupied; a good venue for a private meeting. He put a ten-peseta piece on the counter.

"Thanks. Keep the change."

He checked the bar area one more time. The old man was reaching for a glass of beer. He moved slowly, his hand trembling as the glass, filled to the brim, approached his quivering lips. The beer reached its target, and without a trace of a spill.

A history of hardship seemed etched into the deep wrinkles of that man's face. He would probably have witnessed the battle for Bilbao, ten years ago. He would have taken cover in the labyrinth of trenches and tunnels built around the city by the Basque Army to keep out the advancing Nationalists. He might even have sheltered alongside Mama and Papa, the sound of artillery shells exploding all around them.

The old man turned and fixed his sad eyes on Mikel. Mikel nodded and gave a smile. Then, collecting up the Cava and the newspaper, he moved towards the rear of the café. He found a table with four chairs, and settled himself sideways-on to the bar area. From this position he'd be able to see when Peli arrived. They would need a couple more chairs for the meeting. He'd fix that later.

He made a pretence at reading the front page of *El Deia*,

but felt unable to concentrate. Eventually, he put the paper down and glanced at his watch... 6.02pm.

Then something caught his eye; a guitar leaning against the wall. It looked ancient; the front very plain, its curves beautifully rounded, the waist very narrow. It might be French. But no; most French guitars of that age would probably have edges inlaid with alternate strips of ebony and ivory. He strained his eyes to see more clearly. The guitar looked rather battered, but still had all its strings. He felt a sudden yearning to gather it up, to hold it on his lap and examine the tone. Would it have the strength to take a proper tuning, he wondered. Maybe, if gently coaxed; tuning the fifth string to the sixth, the fourth string to the fifth, and then all the way down to the first string.

His own guitar had imploded violently when tuned for the very first time. He'd spent hundreds of hours rebuilding it with a thinner soundboard and bracing struts. His guitar was with Maisie now. It would be hanging on the wall above the bedrail. "I shall look up every night," she'd smiled into his eyes as they'd lain together for the last time. "I will see your lovely guitar, and I'll feel close to you."

Mikel sighed, his heart full of the agony of being parted from her. He could hardly bear to think of Maisie being so far away, and not even being allowed to write to her.

The official line on exchange of correspondence was strict: no letters during the first six months of an assignment. He'd learned on the MI6 course that families at home would receive postcards, believing them to have been sent from their loved ones abroad. Working from specimen handwriting, a professional team of scribes would make the cards appear genuine. Their counterfeit skills were legendary.

Mikel felt a stab of torment; Maisie must have received several cards by now, thinking they'd come from him. What would Whitaker's backroom boys have managed to dredge up for her? Mikel felt as if he didn't exist anymore; his life taken over by a bunch of faceless civil servants. He sat there, motionless, gazing at the old guitar and lost in fretful misery.

Then he heard a gentle voice that filled him with the notion of Maisie's presence.

"Mikel?" she said softly. "Mikel? Is that you?"

He gave a sudden start. This was real… not imagined! It was the voice of someone he'd known for much longer; as a child, when monstrous waves had battered his ship, threatening to suck him down. Mikel turned, gripped in a long, breathless stare at the woman standing before him.

"Ainhoa?" he gasped.

"Mikel! It *is* you!"

He rose to his feet, still unbelieving but savouring the warmth of her smile.

"Ainhoa? But what… how…?"

"I'm meeting someone!"

The tangle of confusion in Mikel's brain began to clear.

"Of course! Peli!"

"Ssshhh!" Ainhoa glanced cautiously towards the front of the café. "Yes. But *you*, Mikel; I can hardly believe it!"

Reaching out, Mikel took her hand. Their fingers were still locked together as they sat down.

"Imanol… is he with you?"

He felt a flash of rage against himself. God, how he longed for Maisie at this moment!

"Imanol? Well, yes, but…" Ainhoa seemed to falter. "We

were married a year ago. Before leaving England."

"So, Imanol's here… in Bilbao?"

"We had no choice, Mikel. He was offered a partnership in his father's business; a steel mill with hundreds of workers."

"That's good, Ainhoa! I always knew you'd do well!"

"Yes," she said in a subdued tone. "Yes, I suppose it is good."

Ainhoa gently withdrew her hand, a gesture that seemed to magnify the look of sadness in her face.

A short silence followed.

"Oh, Mikel…"

"Ainhoa?"

Where was the happy face that had once lit up his world?

"It's alright," she murmured, tears starting down her cheeks. "I'm alright… really."

It tormented his soul to think that he might actually be the cause of her anguish. He pulled a handkerchief from his pocket and offered it.

"Is it me?"

"You? No Mikel, it isn't you."

"What then? You can tell me, can't you?"

Ainhoa shook her head sorrowfully. "But how could you possibly understand, Mikel?"

"Please…"

"Well, it's just that it all went so badly wrong."

"I don't understand, Ainhoa. You've got so much going for you."

"Really? You can't imagine it, Mikel. Living in an industrial wasteland with a husband who thinks he's so wonderful, so bloody important." She cast her eyes down, staring at the table, her cheeks flushed with rage. "Imanol won't listen to reason! He doesn't understand what's happening to him! He's like a toy puppet; a servant of the fascist government. First the bombing of Guernica and Durango, and then the occupation of Bilbao; my poor mother and father! All those concentration camps. More than twenty thousand people executed. What kind of a peace have they created for us, Mikel? I thought the rest of the world would support us. God knows we deserved some kind of recognition after all that. But no!"

She glanced up.

"Have you seen the newspapers, Mikel? The French are getting friendly with Franco. And the Americans! They're talking about a joint alliance against communism!" She shook her head mournfully. "What would my mother say if she could see me now, married to one of Franco's industrial elite, a son-in-law who pays his workers a pittance so they can hardly afford a proper meal?"

Mikel leaned back in his chair.

"Have you told Imanol you feel like this?"

"Imanol?" Her eyes widened with a look of apprehension: "My God, Mikel, have you any idea what they do to people who speak out against Franco?"

"So that's why you got involved with Peli?"

Mikel felt his heart pounding. He must be insane. It was against everything he'd been taught to mention his security contacts. Ainhoa darted another quick glance towards the front of the café. She turned back, her face brightening a little.

"I got to know about Peli through the Resistance Council," she whispered. "You see, Imanol likes me to accompany him at business receptions. I get treated like a VIP, Mikel! And when the industrial fat-cats get drunk, I listen carefully to their spiteful little stories, then pass it all on to Peli. The United Nations must be learning a lot about Franco and his methods; especially the way fascist police treat workers who are trying to change things for the better."

Mikel gazed into her moist, sparkling eyes. He recalled those lonely years at the refugee camp, Ainhoa listening to him pouring out his childhood anxieties, his worries about Mama and Papa. His heart had once flamed with passion for this woman.

"And you, Mikel?" she said.

"Me?" Mikel pursed his lips. He must find a suitably evasive reply, and quickly. "Arrived two months ago. Just a temporary visit. I'm aiming to come back again… maybe in a year or two when things have settled down."

"But your links with Peli…"

"Peli? Oh, Peli found me, actually; he seemed to think I could be useful in some way."

Mikel cursed himself. He was totally unprepared, gabbling like an idiot and saying too much.

"What do you know about Peli?" Ainhoa continued.

"Not a lot."

"He never told you about his parents?"

"Peli? No, I don't think so. Why should he? I've only known him a short time; barely a month, actually. He's a work mate."

"Peli had a rotten time of it," she sighed. "His father was one of hundreds taken by Franco's police during the strikes of 1941. His mother committed suicide after learning what they'd done to her husband. Peli was left to fend for himself and his five younger brothers and sisters; it must have been awful."

A telephone rang out from the bar area. It stopped abruptly. The barman called out.

"Señor Aguirre? Is there a Señor Aguirre?"

A flare of panic shot through Mikel like a fiery bullet. He glanced at his watch… 6.20! He turned to Ainhoa. She stared back at him, her eyes filling with terror and anguish.

"You must answer," she said, touching his hand lightly. "It's certain to be Peli. I expect he wants to cancel the meeting."

Mikel rose and placed his hand tenderly on Ainhoa's shoulder. He moved quickly to the bar area, acutely aware that every eye would be upon him.

"Señor Aguirre?" The barman gave a curious look as he handed over the phone.

Mikel felt anger and frustration. Peli should have known better than to contact him. Here, of all places! It was a breach of basic security! But he must relax, try to keep cool. People would be watching… listening.

"Yes?" he said softly into the phone.

"Señor Aguirre?" It was a woman's voice.

Mikel hesitated, his mind thrown into a vortex of confusion. He heard the sound of a sob. Was she weeping? Should he take a chance, confirm his identity? Or should he put the phone down… walk away? Another sob, the woman's breathing spasmodic, uncontrolled.

"Oh please…" The tone of her voice was so heartbreakingly pathetic that Mikel could scarcely bear it. "Please," she went on. "Oh please answer me."

"Yes… this is Aguirre," he said.

"Señor!" She seemed to gather herself. "I am Peli's wife, Señor. They… they have taken him!"

"What?" Mikel rasped. "What do you mean, taken him?"

"Please… Señor Aguirre!" She broke down again, crying miserably into the phone. "They will question him! You must leave that place. You must get away now, quickly, before…"

Suddenly there was an almighty crash from behind. Mikel spun round and saw an avalanche of shattered glass flying through the air. The café door had burst open, and with such force that it had rebounded from the hinge-wall, smashing the door panel to smithereens. Then a blur of movement as a troop of uniformed policemen surged into the café.

Two of the policemen bolted off towards the rear of the café. Ainhoa sat with her back to them, unmoving. Mikel watched as they hauled her roughly to her feet. He let the telephone fall and threw himself forward; he would kill rather than see Ainhoa hurt! But he was grabbed by the elbows and spun round, his chest and stomach viciously slammed against the bar. He felt handcuffs ratcheted hard around his wrists, shackling his arms tightly behind.

Glancing fleetingly over his shoulder, he saw a look of horror stamped on the old man's face; his watery eyes red and bulging, lips quivering and mouth gaping open. The brown dog was up on its hind legs, jittering and jumping as if engaged in some hideous circus dance, howling and clawing at the old man's knees, desperate to reach the safety of its master's embrace.

Mikel's heart fluttered like a wild bird caught in a trap as they dragged him to the centre of the bar area. A heavily built policeman swaggered towards him, a long baton in his hand, a heavy revolver at his side.

"A good afternoon's work, Señor!" he sneered. "I find one

little rat lurking at home with his wife. After a little coaxing, he is able to tell me where I might find other little rats. And here they are, hiding in a café!" He pressed the end of his baton hard into the side of Mikel's face. "You are indeed a wretched little rat, Señor Aguirre. And you have much to tell us, have you not? Oh yes, we shall know everything about you soon enough."

A howl of protest from Ainhoa filled Mikel with an almost superhuman strength. He let out a ferocious gasp. Twisting and turning, he managed to shake off one of the guards. Then a sharp blinding crack, as if a wooden stave had been struck hard against a heavy stone block. Mikel knew, instinctively, that his skull had been smashed. He felt his knees buckling, the ground rising up and slamming into his face with a sickening thud. Then they were dragging him, his legs cleaving a way through shards of glass strewn across the café floor.

He caught a glimpse of a dark, windowless van, its rear doors open and waiting to receive him. With a monumental effort, Mikel craned his neck just enough to see a cumulus cloud, its edges tinged with crimson. There came a roll of distant thunder. The mountains… they were calling to him. His head flopped down as he felt himself being thrust with brutal force into a gaping black void.

Chapter 7

AYRSHIRE IN SCOTLAND

5 Years Later, January 1953

Scalding Tears

"Come *on*, Javier!" The sound of his mother's voice was almost carried away by the wind and lashing rain. "We mustn't be late; not on your first day at school!" She tugged at his hand. "Oh, do try and keep up, Javier!"

"I can't!" The calves of his legs burned like fire, rubbed sore by the tops of his welly boots. "I don't want to go to school!" A sudden gust lifted the collar of his raincoat, slapping him hard across the cheek and making his eyes sting.

He peered through the rain, searching for the island that rose from the sea like a distant volcano. But the mouth of the loch was hidden behind the torrential rain and dull grey mist. The hills on the far side of the loch were closer, but even they were barely visible.

Winter weather could be frightening to Javier. On stormy nights he would lie in bed listening to the breakers pounding against the shore, just a stone's throw from his bedroom window. He would imagine the waves rearing up like black monsters, threatening to sweep across the narrow lane that separated the shore from the wooden cabin where he and his mother lived with Uncle Gorka.

The sea wasn't always rough like this. On calmer days he would stand at the water's edge and feel the smooth pebbles beneath his feet, breathing the strong scent of seaweed and listening to the wavelets brushing lightly against the shore. He would go to the sea whenever he felt miserable, and at those times the sea was more like a friend. It would speak to him in hushed whispers, telling him that everything was going to be alright. The sea was immense, and yet it could be so wonderfully calm; somewhere to escape to and do his thinking, to share his troubles without fear of being found out. It had been like that yesterday. But now the waves were massive, their tops curling over with streaks of white appearing and disappearing, the sky dark and threatening.

Squeezing his eyes against a sudden squall, he saw a huge wave, bigger than all the others. It burst onto the shore some distance ahead, its breaking edge hurtling towards him like a big black wall tumbling down, spewing froth and spray as it advanced. He watched as the wave rushed past him, the surf hissing and roaring as it smashed into the beach, clouds of creamy white spume lifted by the wind and thrown high into the air. A torrent of sea water surged across the lane. It tore through his hair and sent an icy trickle racing down the back of his neck. For a moment he was blinded, trembling all over, unable to think or say anything. Tears began to flow down his nose and cheeks, the tang of salt harsh on his lips.

He glanced up at his mother. As she leaned into the wind,

the thin scarf around her head flapped like a torn sail in a hurricane. But her eyes… the brightness had gone from them. The gloomy look on her face reminded him of the horrible way Uncle Gorka had shouted at her last night, and again this morning. Uncle Gorka had got really mad during breakfast, swearing and hitting the table hard. It made Javier feel sick when Uncle Gorka got angry like that. He had that same feeling now. He gulped hard to make the acid in his tummy go away, but his mouth tasted of salt and he couldn't swallow properly. And that burning pain at the back of his legs!

"Mummy… my legs hurt!"

She came to a stop and knelt down beside him.

"Come along then," she said softly, flipping up the collar of his raincoat. "I'll carry you for a while."

She gathered him gently, her arms tightening around him.

"I don't want to go to school."

"Ssshhh…" She lifted him. "There'll be lots of other children at school. You'll make new friends."

But he didn't want new friends. All he wanted was for Uncle Gorka to go away. He just wanted Mummy to be safe and happy, so they could live quietly together in their little wooden cabin by the sea.

"I want to go home."

His heart burned with dread, caught between a ferocious Uncle Gorka at home and the idea of something perhaps even more horrible waiting for him at a place called school.

"Oh look, Javier! The sun's coming out! And I can see the village; we'll soon be there!"

He pressed his face against her neck and felt her warmth. Lulled by the rhythmic swaying of her body, he began to count in his head: One, *two, three, four;* One, *two, three, four;* One, *two, three, four…*

Slowly, it came to him; the music that was never far from his mind. He liked listening to music in his head. He could make the notes go high and low, soft and loud, just like the music he would sometimes hear on the radio. When he felt angry he would make short, sharp, stabbing sounds, but always keeping time with the beat so the music almost bounced along.

One, *two, three, four;* One, *two, three, four…*

The music had to stay in his head because Uncle Gorka would get mad if he made too much noise. Bedtime was best for making music. But would music ever be the same after last night? Would he ever forget the tears that had kept him awake until morning?

Uncle Gorka had grown very angry last night, yelling and breaking things in the kitchen. The noise had woken Javier, making him tremble with fear. He'd buried his head under the bedcovers to hide, and be safe. Then he'd heard Uncle Gorka thundering out of the house, and slamming the door behind him. The relief! Javier had crept out of bed. He'd stood quietly in the middle of his room, afraid to move. It was a long time before his mother had come to him.

"My darling," she'd smiled through her tears, cuddling him gently. "Yes, I know how Uncle Gorka frightens you. But we'll make it better, Javier, I promise. There's a surprise for you! Go and look under your bed!"

Reaching under his bed, he'd found something wrapped in a blanket. He'd uncovered it quickly, his heart leaping with joy at what he'd found there. Those beautiful deep warm colours; that dizzying scent of wood varnish and glue! It was like a living thing, trembling in his hands and humming softly as he'd lifted it from the blanket.

"It's a guitar, Javier." She'd sat him on the side of the bed and put the guitar on his lap. "Goodness, Javier, just look at you! If only you could see yourself!" She'd shown him how to stroke the strings using his thumb. "It's a very special guitar," she'd smiled. "It was made by a very special person. And one day, when you're older, it will be yours."

"Who, Mummy? Who made it?"

A faint shiver of apprehension had pinched his skin to see the brightness going out of her eyes. Javier always felt lonely and downcast when she looked like that.

"It was your father's guitar. Look…" She'd pointed to some tiny letters, beautifully engraved on the side of the guitar; MA. "They're your daddy's initials, Javier. Your daddy made it."

"My daddy!" How he'd fixed upon that blessed word! How he'd always longed for a daddy, a man he could be proud of, a kindly man who would love and take care of him! "Where is he? Where's my daddy?"

"He went away, Javier. It was long time ago, when you were just a little baby. He went to live in another country called Spain."

"I want to see him! I want to go to Spain and see my daddy!"

"We can't do that," she'd smiled. "Spain is very far away."

It had made no sense to Javier. He would gladly have walked to the ends of the Earth to find his father.

All night long he'd lain awake, an aching heaviness growing inside him. He'd thought of running away, of leaving his mother and Uncle Gorka behind and walking to Spain all by himself to find his daddy; a man who made beautiful guitars

142

that trembled and hummed with deep murmuring voices. But what if his daddy didn't want him? What if his daddy had a new family, other boys and girls?

Without a word to anyone, he'd tiptoed from his bedroom and out into the dark night. He'd stood at the water's edge, watching starlight shining on the glassy sea. He'd come so close to finding his daddy, but then had lost him again, forever. Weighed down by a horrible burden of grief, he'd crept back into bed. He'd wept as he'd never wept before, the scalding tears drenching his pillow until daybreak.

Now, as his mother carried him, he felt cold, wet and very tired. He drew a deep, sobbing breath.

"Why did daddy go away?"

"I don't know, darling," she said in a dead voice. "There are lots of reasons why fathers leave home. Sometimes they never come back. When your daddy was very young he had to leave Spain because of the civil war. He was just a boy; not much older than you, Javier. But then your daddy missed his own country so very much, and when the bombing eventually came to an end, he wanted to go back to Spain. He was born in Spain, you see; that's where he grew up and went to school. And soon you'll be at school. You'll be able to tell your new friends what a clever daddy you have, and that he lives in a wonderful country called Spain. I'm so proud of you, Javier."

Above the shrill of the wind, he heard the distant sound of a child screaming. Soon there were others, all shrieking together, the dreadful noise growing louder until he was almost deafened by it.

"We've arrived!" She lowered him to the ground. "Come on, Javier; let's go and meet your teacher."

He followed her through the school gate and into the playground. Some boys stepped aside, staring at him menacingly. One had a long face, dark sunken eyes and a very snotty nose.

"Mummy, I…"

"Keep close, Javier!"

She grasped his hand and swiftly led the way through into the school building. Suddenly, it was very quiet.

An acidic rise of disquiet rose up from his tummy as, once again, a familiar vortex of fear tugged at his fluttering heart. He stole a timid glance into a classroom. So many desks!

A tall, thin lady wearing spectacles approached.

"Aha!" she exclaimed. "Mrs Aguirre?"

"Yes. And this is Javier."

Another stab of panic went through Javier's chest as the teacher fixed him with a penetrating gaze. Her eyes moved slowly, right from the top of his head and all the way down to his welly boots.

"You'll have walked a long way, Javier?"

This was bad, *very* bad. Javier's breast took a shuddering heave. His lips felt stiff so he couldn't talk. And his nose was running.

"Come through, both of you." The teacher turned and strode purposefully into a classroom.

Suddenly there was a handkerchief under his nose; he gave a big blow. His mother smiled down at him, reassuringly… proudly. There were drawings and paintings on the walls, some with numbers and dots. This was a place of high hopes and heavy demands. The room had a funny smell, like old books. A crate of milk lay on the floor, close to an upright stove. He began to feel hot under his raincoat.

The teacher positioned herself behind a very tall desk. She opened a big book.

"Previous schools?"

"None. Javier has just turned five."

The teacher scribbled in the book.

"And your first name, Mrs Aguirre?"

"Maisie."

"Maisie," the teacher echoed. "And your husband's first name?"

"Michael. No, Mikel. My husband's name was Mikel. He was Spanish. Basque, actually."

The teacher glanced up, her eyes narrowing.

"Your husband is no longer with you, Mrs Aguirre?"

"No. I live with my brother-in-law now. His name is Gorka… Gorka Aguirre."

Javier shuddered at the mention of Uncle Gorka's name. He felt his eyes drawn towards the milk.

"Mr Gorka Aguirre," the teacher scribbled again. "Boy's uncle… and guardian."

"We don't *depend* on my brother-in-law," Javier's mother returned quickly. "Gorka is unemployed, you see. I receive a grant; a government grant on account of my husband's refugee status."

There was a long silence.

"Can you sing, Javier?" The teacher stared down at him. "Can you sing the Ayrshire song?"

"What's the Ayrshire song?" He felt lost… mystified.

"Oh, no! No, *no!*" The teacher frowned heavily. "We don't talk like *that*; not at *this* school. For one thing, pupils must always address the teacher as *Miss*."

She crossed over to the stove, pushed a straw into a bottle of milk, and offered it, smiling pleasantly. Javier sucked greedily; it was warm and tasted creamy.

"Aye, Javier," the teacher sighed, "we'll teach you the Ayrshire song. Now wait here while I call the class."

She lifted a big brass bell from the desk and walked off. Javier stood in a kind of dream, sucking up bubbles from the bottom of an empty milk bottle. Hearing the bell clanking in the playground, he looked around for his mother. She'd gone! His heart began thumping wildly, his mind thrown into a whirling frenzy.

"Boots off!" the teacher cried from the hallway. "Quietly now!"

Suddenly they were all around him; girls and boys, big ones and little ones, fat and thin. Javier stood completely still as they rushed past him and quickly sat down at their desks. Now they were looking at him. Faces everywhere; blank, expressionless faces, and all so very glum! He felt the weight of the teacher's hand on his shoulder.

"This is Javier," she announced. "Welcome to our class, Javier. Now, let's all say *good morning* to Javier."

"Good morning, Javier!" they chorused, but without the slightest flicker of happiness or welcome.

A girl seated on the front row began to giggle, staring accusingly at Javier's wellies. In a short moment, the whole class was laughing.

"Stop that!" the teacher cried. Then, in a gentler tone, "Do you have shoes, Javier?"

"No, Miss."

"Then take off your boots. We shall see what we can find."

She went to a cupboard and came back with a pair of

slippers. They felt warm and snug. She took his raincoat and led him to an empty desk at the rear of the class.

"Pay attention!" she cried, making her way back to the front. "How do we start lessons on a Monday morning? Marjorie?"

"With geography, Miss!"

The teacher unrolled a very large, coloured picture and clipped it to a blackboard.

"Here we have an atlas of the world. And remember, no-one is to call out. I will nominate!" There came a sharp crack as she brought the tip of a long wooden pointer down on the atlas. "Gregory?"

"France, Miss!"

"And what is France famous for? Ruaridh?"

"Wine, Miss!"

"And what else? Janet?"

Javier felt his body tightening.

"Cheese, Miss!"

"And the capital of France? Susan?"

"Paris, Miss!"

"Good, Susan! And what river runs through Paris?" Susan looked clever; she wore spectacles, like the teacher.

"The River Seine, Miss."

Questions, answers… more questions and answers; they flowed like a never-ending stream; questions about Germany, Italy, and the Second World War. There came a strange buzzing in Javier's brain. It felt as if the top of his head was coming off.

"Last question!" The pointer came down on yet another part of the atlas. "Who knows the name of *this* country?"

A forest of hands shot into the air. But this time the teacher was looking at Javier. He must get out of here! Run away! Now!

"It's Spain, Miss!" cried the boy next to him.

"Yes… Spain," the teacher said in a dull tone. "Thank you, Arran."

Lost in a muddle of fear and helplessness, Javier stared blankly down at the desktop. A black shadow had fallen across him, so heavy that he could hardly breathe. His heart burned with the pain of failure and shame.

"Fiona… James! The tambourines!"

Javier glanced up. The teacher was now seated at a piano. Someone struck a tambourine, and then another joined in. Soon the classroom was filled with a banging, jingling confusion of sound. Why wouldn't the teacher tell them to stop?

A girl with pigtails placed a tambourine on the desk in front of him. A smile flickered across her pretty face. And then she moved on, with several more tambourines tucked under her arm.

Javier inspected the instrument carefully. It was like a small drum with skin stretched across one side. There were slots around the edge and metal plates held loosely with wire. The plates were free to rattle against each other. He felt around the wooden edge, pressing with his thumb to feel the tension in the skin. Raising the tambourine close to his nose, he breathed deeply, his lungs filling with a scent that reminded him of his father's guitar. But this instrument was new to him. He began to think of the possibilities.

He tapped the middle finger of his right hand against the taut skin. Then he struck with his thumb and little finger in quick succession. There came a trembling sound. Within moments he'd learned to increase both the speed and strength of his right-hand movements.

He played on, trying hard to make the best possible sound, and soon he was able to improve the rhythm by adding extra beats. There was music in his head now. He made the beat of the tambourine keep time with the music. Loud and soft rang the tambourine, his fingers moving so fast that the music he made in his head began to flow smoothly, almost like the sound of a violin.

One, *two, three;* One, *two, three;* One, *two, three…*

A flame of excitement blazed up from deep inside him, his whole body warming to the rich, pulsating sound of the music. It was like a great door opening to reveal a whole new universe of sound. If only his daddy could hear him now… if only!

He would *stab* with the violin to show his anger! He would *make* his daddy listen.

Stab, *two, three;* Stab, *two, three;* Stab, *two, three…*

And now the music was *really* bouncing along! Even in Spain they would hear it! He would make the music come to an end with a final Stab, Stab, Stab*!*

It was so quiet that he could hear nothing but the sound of his own heart, the blood pulsing through his brain. Utterly absorbed in a world of his own making, he might just as well have been playing in a room on his own. But he wasn't alone. Lifting his head slowly, almost too frightened to look, he saw that every eye was upon him.

Chapter 8

SAN MIGUEL DE LOS REYES, MADRID

July 1953

Into the Darkness

Mikel searched for daylight through a tiny grille set into the wall high above his head, but all he saw was darkness. Forced to squat semi-naked on a cold stone floor, his wakefulness had been a silent torture. The muscles in his legs burned like hell. The blackness of early morning was heavy and sinister.

It was a miracle he'd survived for so long; five long years of ferocious beatings and suffocation to the point of unconsciousness. But survived he had, never deviating from his cover story; always insisting he was just an ordinary refugee kid from Bilbao, and seeking to return to the Basque Country under a repatriation scheme sponsored by the UK government. What had begun as a half-truth had become rooted conviction in his mind, establishing itself as fact. How else could he have lived through those agonising five years of misery?

But now he was done with it. Very soon, before the first sounds from the city streets came wafting through the grille above his head, he would call out to the prison guards and beg them to end his life.

Aware of his association with Ainhoa and Peli, the interrogators had questioned him remorselessly. Even the prison governor, Commandant Fortea, had taken a hand. Interrogation by Fortea was an appalling experience. It often involved the 'inversion in water' treatment; the prisoner's hands were lashed together behind his back, then he was suspended from a rope round the ankles and lowered slowly, headfirst, into a trough of water. Mikel would usually pass out on the second immersion. Yesterday he'd remained conscious well into the third. He shuddered now to recall being hauled out for the third time, coughing and choking, his lungs fit to burst.

"Come now, Señor Aguirre," Fortea had said. "Why put yourself through all this? Your colleagues have told us everything. A signed confession is all we need. And then you could be on your way home to England, and with our blessings!" He'd come closer. "The Generalissimo requires you to sign a piece of paper. It's as simple as that; a political thing. A way of facilitating an understanding between two countries, nothing more."

But they would never release him from prison. Not alive, at any rate. The Generalissimo would not wish the world to know what went on in places like this.

Leaning back a little, Mikel felt the cold stone ledge pressing into his shoulder blades. Sloping downwards at a crazy angle, the upper surface of the ledge was useless for lying on;

you couldn't even sit on it. In fact, it served no useful purpose whatsoever, other than to madden and frustrate. Setting his teeth against the pain, Mikel eased one leg forward, and then the other, slowly settling his backside on the cell floor.

Shards of broken glass embedded in the floor made walking highly dangerous, especially at night. Some years ago, he'd managed to clear a small area at the base of the ledge. It was somewhere to sit or squat; somewhere to exercise a little, and to brood a lot. The two-by-four-metre cell had been built to drive its occupant mad, to neutralise their will to live.

A sudden flurry of wings caused him to glance up. Pigeons! Their cooing and scratching on the prison roof was usually a sign of early morning. And sure enough, a smudge of deep crimson had begun to appear around the edges of the grille. He watched as the crimson glow spread slowly outwards across the ceiling. It opened like a fan, becoming richer in colour: first cherry, then deep pink, and finally orange. A wonderful contrast to the squalid, murky tone of the cell's interior.

Soon the daytime guards would arrive for duty. He would hear male voices, deep and guttural, echoing along the labyrinth of corridors deep inside the core of the prison. Their footsteps would come closer, accompanied by the clattering of keys turning in locks. Fellow prisoners would be dragged, sobbing, from their cells, shrieking as all manner of abuse was heaped on them in those ghastly interrogation rooms.

Eventually they would come for Mikel. But this time he would beg them to finish him off. He was ready for it. The thought of death brought a queer peace of mind. He must stay calm, settle himself, lean back against the cold stone ledge, let the body go limp. Say goodbye to Maisie and Javier in his mind, and in his heart. And then, perhaps… sleep.

Mikel's head began to droop.

Rude Awakenings

A loud crash sent a jolt hurtling through his body. He jerked upright and saw a guard standing in the open doorway, legs astride, his burly figure silhouetted by the blinding light of the outer corridor.

"Morning, dead man!" The guard turned and spat on the cell wall. "An early start for you! Something special!"

Another guard appeared, and in the next instant Mikel felt himself being hauled to his feet.

"No!" he gasped. "Please! Listen!"

"Save it for the Commandant!"

Manhandled in the semi-darkness, Mikel felt his legs giving way. He stabbed blindly at the ground with his bare feet, desperate to regain his balance; to support his own weight. He gasped in pain, his right foot viciously spiked by a shard of glass.

"Stop…!" he begged, his eyes smarting and filling with tears. "Please stop!"

It was no use. Seized by his upper arms, he was dragged out into the corridor, his legs trailing behind, the rough stone paving tearing at his knees and feet. God in heaven… the pain! The indescribable, bloody pain! Summoning his strength, he twisted himself from side to side, desperate to lessen the friction of stone against flesh. A ghastly sickness overcame him, the light growing dim around the edges of his vision; a tunnel of darkness closing in until he was consumed by it. Then he could see nothing, hear nothing. Death. Sweet Jesus, please let this be death.

With an almighty jolt he was wrenched up again, his body limp and powerless to resist. Now they were forcing him into a sitting position. He felt a tightening around his chest, then his fingers being stretched and squeezed.

"Keep still, you little bastard!" somebody yelled.

Through a shimmering haze he saw two crimson globes. His knees, the flesh exposed and glistening with blood. He tried to reach out to them, but his hands wouldn't budge. Blinking away the tears, he stared in disbelief as the guards, one on each side, levered his hands into massive metal clamps engineered into the arms of the chair.

"Stop! Please… Stop!" He shivered uncontrollably.

"Shut your mouth!"

The pressure increased around his hands and fingers as the clamps were tightened. They were like iron gloves, with each finger squeezed into its own narrow tube. He felt so desperately vulnerable, his arms, hands and fingers immobilised.

"There!" The guards stood back. "Get out of that!"

They moved out of sight behind him. A door slammed shut. There was silence… long and terrifying.

This was no ordinary interrogation room. No water trough, no racking apparatus, no electric cables or heating irons. Just a table bathed in the light of an electric lamp suspended from the ceiling. Squinting into the glare, Mikel saw a hammer on the table. And something else: a metal rod about a finger's width in diameter. He shivered as a wave of revulsion engulfed him.

Chest pains made it difficult to breathe; ropes had been lashed around his body, securing him firmly to the back of the chair. He glanced down, beyond his macerated knees, and saw his feet, the skin torn, flesh gouged and streaked with crimson. A dark pool of blood had started to spread outwards from under his right foot.

But those metal clamps!

Another sickening pulse of fear swept through him. He must think carefully, plan what he was going to say. Ask them… no… *beg* them to end his life. They must understand… he'd had enough of all this.

He tried to visualise Maisie's face… and young Javier. Mikel had estimated Javier to be around five years old.

Then he heard the door opening behind him. The silence was interminable, suffused by the anguish of uncertainty, of a faint unidentifiable stirring and an indefinable presence. His heart leapt into frenzy as he saw movement. And then a voice.

"Señor Aguirre… we meet again."

Commandant Fortea! The thought of Fortea's presence filled him with dread. Interrogators were always at their best with the Commandant watching.

He loomed out of the shadows like a monstrous evil, a smoking butt suspended between his fingers. He tossed a file of papers onto the table and sat down with a heavy sigh, his tunic buttons sparkling in the glare of the lamp above his head.

"Congratulations, Señor Aguirre," he said. "It is your anniversary, I think."

He opened the file and scrutinised.

"Ah, yes. It is five years to the very day since you were captured. Did you know that, Señor Aguirre?" His lips opened in what might have been taken for a smile. "Five years; isn't that a cause for celebration?"

"Please," Mikel whispered through his dry lips, "I've had enough. Just let me go."

"Let you go? But alas, Señor, that is something I cannot do. It is not in my gift to let you go. You see, you have made it extremely difficult for me. You have failed to pledge your support for the Generalissimo's mission... a united Spain, free and great. And that other little thing; signed a confession to acknowledge the purpose of your *own* mission." Fortea snuffed out his cigarette. "How many times must I tell you, Señor Aguirre? You will be detained here until we see an end to your obstinacy. Only then might the Generalissimo decide to let you go."

"No... no!" Mikel cried, a hot flame of terror burning in his chest. "You don't understand! I don't care anymore about going home. I mean... I'm ready to..."

"But I *do* understand," Fortea interrupted. "I hear them all the time, those heartfelt pleadings for death."

He rose to his feet, moved slowly round to the front of the table, and leaned back against it.

"What a pity. Clearly, you are in no mood to celebrate. Then I shall have to celebrate on my own. I am to be promoted, Señor Aguirre! The Generalissimo has appointed me to run another prison. And what is more, most of my guards have asked to come with me. Now that is what I call loyalty!"

The Commandant... going away? Was it possible this wretched existence might actually be coming to an end?

"To be honest with you," Fortea went on, "I have never been truly happy in this prison. The new establishment will be better equipped, interrogation swifter and more effective. But I have been asking myself... should I take Señor Aguirre with me? Or will he save me the trouble, I wonder? Will he tell me, here and now, everything he knows? Will he confess the truth, and sign a piece of paper to that effect?"

A breath of chaotic indecision trembled on Mikel's lips. But then, after a moment, he said, "I came here to look for a job, to find somewhere to live. I've told you everything... the truth."

"Repatriation to Bilbao with your wife and child? You expect me to believe that? And why have you said nothing about your affair with the Spanish guitar?"

"The guitar?"

"I told you... I know everything. I understand you were set to become an accomplished musician, Señor Aguirre."

"That was a long time ago."

"Yes... yes, of course, a very long time ago. Such a pity that you will never play the guitar again; and all because of your silly refusal to sign a confession." Fortea eased himself off the table. "Corporal!" he yelled.

The door burst open. A guard appeared. He made directly for the table, snatching up the hammer and metal rod.

"No...!" Mikel roared. "Oh God!" His head jerked back in a kind of involuntary spasm. He stared up at the ceiling, his eyes wide and searching. There had to be a way out of this! "Kill me! For God's sake, do it now! Kill me!"

Mikel felt something hard being pressed against the tip of his right-hand middle finger. He glanced down, stupefied. The metal rod had been pushed deep into the right-hand clamp. The guard was gripping the rod, holding it steady in his left hand; the hammer raised in his right hand, poised and ready to strike.

"Well, Señor Aguirre?" Fortea's mouth hung open, livid as a wound. "What's it to be? Your guitar and freedom, or a lifetime of incapacitation and endless pain?"

Mikel tore his eyes from the Commandant's gaze. Once again, he stared up at the ceiling, his mouth quivering and body convulsed with terror. No-one had the right to expect this of him. No-one... not Whitaker... not MI6... nobody! He would suffer it, if he must, for the sake of Maisie and Javier. They were so precious, so utterly dear to him that he could never be parted from them; not in life, not in death. He breathed heavily, squeezed his eyes closed and clenched his teeth. Then, blindly, he gave a frenzied shake of his head.

Suddenly, there came a loud metallic *CLACK!* A strobe of blinding light flashed through Mikel's brain as an indescribable burst of agony shot from his right hand. The searing pain travelled up his arm, thrashed across his chest, and impaled itself deep inside his quivering heart. A strange and harrowing cry seemed to come from somewhere deep inside him. Wrung from his soul, the sound of it hung in the air, unearthly, wailing unremittingly as if destined to last forever. The scream subsided slowly, ebbing away, exhausted and spent. Then, with his mouth agape, he drew a vast intake of breath, a grating, rasping ingestion of air.

He heard the unimaginable; another deadly *CLACK!* as the rod smashed into his index finger. Another explosive howl erupted from the very core of him. It stuck in his throat, his eyes bulging as if ready to burst into pieces. He saw another flash of brilliant light, the pain more terrible than he could endure. Mikel was losing control of his senses, descending into a sickening vortex of dismal oblivion. Almost overcome by an all-pervading state of stupefaction, there came the distant sound of unbridled retching. And then there was nothing; total paralysis; absolutely nothing. Mikel was gone... he was finished.

Chapter 9

IN THE COUNTY OF KENT, ENGLAND

8 Years Later, January 1961

A Palace of Music

Javier placed a recording of the Recuerdos de la Alhambra on the gramophone turntable. He set it spinning then leaned forward, his nose almost touching the disk, and counted the tracks; one... two... three... *there*! He positioned the pick-up arm with the needle hovering between the third and fourth tracks, and lowered it... gently. Gran would never forgive him if he were to scratch one of Grandpa's precious records. With a soft hissing sound, the needle settled onto the playing surface. Then, steadying the guitar on his lap, he quickly prepared himself; left foot up onto the rail at the end of the bed; straighten the back... get the posture right!

Curling his left hand around the neck of the guitar, he set his fingers ready for the opening chord, pressing down firmly on the strings. He'd been practising the Recuerdos all evening; his fingertips were burning like fire. But never mind; it was worth putting up with a bit of pain to get a really good sound. Javier lowered his head and waited. The composer, Francisco Tarrega, had set a lively pace for the beautiful Recuerdos. Keeping up with the recording was going to be tough.

Here it comes! Get straight into the tremolo and bring out the melody. Listen carefully; match the sound of the recording. Feel the music. Let it breathe!

He must get through this. He'd risen before dawn every morning these past few days, memorising several lines of the score before rushing off to catch the school bus. There was no excuse for failure. He'd learned all the finger positions. *So, concentrate!*

Yes, it was going well. And the repeat section had sounded good. *Now for the finale: ease the pace a little, slower… softer, slower still, and even lighter. Here comes that lovely broken chord to finish the piece. Make the notes rise cleanly upwards. Pause a moment; prepare for the last chord. Then play it quietly, like a whisper. There!*

He reached for the pick-up arm and swung it back onto its rest. Gathering the guitar close to his breast, Javier felt a rush of happiness, the warmth melting away the tension within him. He'd done it! There was no doubt that listening and playing along with Gran's records was helping to improve his sense of tempo and timing. If only his daddy could be here. What would his daddy have thought, hearing Tarrega's Recuerdos de la Alhambra being played on the very same instrument he'd built for himself all those years ago, and now being played by his own thirteen-year-old son!

Javier gave a sudden start as his mother opened the bedroom door.

"It's late, Javier… time for bed!" She looked a bit ruffled. "If only you'd spend as much time with your maths and English as you do on that guitar. Your form teacher said—"

"I know what he said! You don't have to keep reminding me! Choir practise! It's all they ever do! They never do any *proper* music lessons. I hate it!"

He'd only been at the school for a year, and they'd already rated him close to the bottom of the class. Why wouldn't they leave him alone to get on with his guitar playing?

Seething with frustration, Javier turned away from his mother and gazed down at the guitar, its shape barely discernible through a film of tears.

"You don't know what it's like!" he sobbed. "It's a waste of time going to that school!"

He felt the guitar trembling against him, almost as if it were trying to speak. If only he could be close to the man who'd built it, the father he'd never known. *"Keep calm, Javier,"* he would say in a kindly voice. *"You know the guitar won't sound good unless you control your temper."*

"You're very lucky to be going to that school," his mother said. "It's the best in the area. Most people aren't able to afford to send their children to a school like that."

"I don't care! What's the point of going to school if they won't let me study the guitar?"

He breathed a long, quivering sigh, as once again that mysterious trembling against his breast spoke softly to him. *"Easy, Javier… easy."*

"Anyway," Javier went on, "I don't care how late it is. I've *got* to practise. I promised Mr Vanderhorst I'll play the Recuerdos for him tomorrow morning."

162

"The Recuerdos!" she exclaimed. "Tomorrow morning? You can't, Javier! A week's practice isn't enough; not for music like that! What does Mr Vanderhorst expect? Guitar lessons are supposed to be fun, something different for you to do on a Saturday morning."

"It was my idea."

"Then you've only yourself to blame."

He felt her fingers lightly stroking the back of his neck.

Javier sat motionless, gazing down at the guitar. If only she would stop pestering him about school! How he hated that place! He'd tried joining in with the other boys on the playing field, but he was useless at sport. Even the games master had laughed at his skinny legs. From now on he would skip games. He would find somewhere to hide; a storeroom or a broom cupboard. And when the other boys went out to play football in the cold wet mud he would lie low and read about the great Spanish guitarists; Francisco Tarrega and Vicente Gomez.

"You mustn't let music get in the way of your schoolwork," she said tenderly. "Please, Javier, don't let it take over your life."

Javier quickly wiped the wetness from his eyes and cheeks. Maybe she was right. Hadn't Mr Vanderhorst warned against attempting the Recuerdos, saying it was for *professional* guitarists and well beyond the capability of a mere thirteen-year-old? Maybe he *had* been crazy to take it on. But he'd worked so hard over the past week. He'd memorised all the fingering. What would Mr Vanderhorst have to say about that? Wouldn't he be surprised, and pleased?

His face felt drier now. Swallowing down the torment, he glanced up. The sternness had gone from his mother's face, but there were dark shadows beneath her eyes.

"It's past bedtime," she smiled. "You need to sleep."

Sleep? Yes, he was certainly ready for sleep. But tomorrow he would perform his first major piece. Mr Vanderhorst would listen carefully to every note.

"Can't go to bed yet. I've got to practise the Recuerdos again, and without the gramophone this time. I can't mess it up, not in front of—"

"Yes, I know," she broke in. "You're a perfectionist, just as your father was."

Momentarily, her eyes appeared trance-like, her face swept with that doleful look that would often come over her when she spoke about daddy. But suddenly, her eyes brightened.

"Why don't you come and play for Gran? She would like that. Gran hardly gets to see you these days."

"Gran? What now?" In the back of Javier's mind there lurked the horrible certainty that he would puke with revulsion on entering Gran's bedroom.

"Why not?" she said. "Something simple. You could manage that, couldn't you? Just a few minutes?"

But Gran was so very ill! He would often hear her cry out with pain in the middle of the night. He would listen to his mother in the darkest hours of early morning, crossing the landing to try to help the old lady. And that bad smell of vomit hanging around the place like an invisible cloud... If only Gran would go into hospital, like the doctor had said.

"Is she in a good mood?" he murmured gloomily.

"Javier! You know Gran hasn't been well."

No, Gran wasn't well. And she didn't like him very much either; especially when she felt *really* bad. Gran could be horrible sometimes, pouring curses on his father for going off to Spain, deserting his wife and child, and not coming back.

If only Gran could listen to Mr Vanderhorst playing the Asturias from the Suite Española. It would take away all her pain. She would sleep all night.

Mr Vanderhorst was amazing. However hard the lesson, he would always make Javier feel like a true performer. "Never mind the nerves," he would say. "Just think of your guitar as a link between the music and the audience. Imagine turning that vast auditorium into a wonderful palace of sound and emotion. Go out there and win them over, Javier! Persuade the audience to forget themselves and put their cares behind."

Could he do that? Could he make Gran forget her pain and discomfort? It would be a huge challenge. But all that preparation… all those hours of practise…

"Okay, I'll do it."

"Good boy! Give me a minute to make her comfortable."

But what should he play for Gran? The Recuerdos? No. She would think him stupid if he broke down in the middle of a piece he hadn't learned properly. The Spanish Romance, then. Yes, the Romance would be better. Short and sweet; guaranteed to wow the ladies, according to Mr Vanderhorst.

Rising to his feet, Javier was about to make his way onto the landing, but shuddered to a halt as he heard a sudden cry from Gran's bedroom. What kind of fearsome agony was the old lady going through now?

He felt a burning in his stomach. Why should he have to live in this place? It was only because his mother had thought it best to be closer to Gran. He should have stayed behind up in Scotland, in that little wooden cabin by the sea. But how could he? For all he knew, Uncle Gorka might still be there, hiding away from all the people in London to whom he owed money. Javier would rather die than go back to live with Uncle Gorka. He would never forget those times when Uncle Gorka had lost his temper; that look of desperation on his mother's face, her tears of humiliation. It was hard on his mother, caring for Gran day and night, but at least she was safe from Uncle Gorka, living here in Gran's house.

The moaning began to subside. Now that awful gurgling sound; the coughing and spluttering as Gran tried to clear her throat. Javier lingered for several more seconds. Mr Vanderhorst had talked about what soloists had to go through before making a stage entrance; the loneliness they would feel whilst waiting in the wings. Javier felt like that now. He really *was* alone, *utterly* alone, and so very helpless. There was only one thing for it. He must disengage himself from the fear; confront and overcome the crazy situation he found himself in. Raising his head smartly, he took a deep breath and strode purposefully forward into Gran's bedroom.

"Ah, the music boy!" Gran croaked. She looked so ill, her face yellow and haggard, her lips almost purple. "Come to see your old Gran, have you? Come to play her a tune?"

"Sit here, Javier." His mother set a chair close to the bedside.

"No, Mam!" The sight of Gran's mean expression… it would put him off, for sure. "I always sit at the bottom of the bed when I'm practising." And that shocking smell of vomit!

"But Javier…" His mother sounded resentful.: "Gran won't be able to see you. Not if you sit all the way down there."

It was true. Gran's swollen stomach would be in the way.

"But I need to use the bedrail as a footrest. It's what I always do when I'm—"

"The pot!" Gran cried hoarsely. "The pot!"

"Mam?"

"Down there!" Gran gestured towards the floor. "There!"

"Oh right, Mam." His mother reached under the bed. "Javier, I think Gran needs to be alone for a little while."

"No!" Gran's eyes bulged. "It's for him! Give it to him! It's to put his stupid foot on!"

"Oh, I see, Mam!" His mother placed the pot upside down beside the bed. "Yes, that's perfect! Come on, Javier. Sit here, make yourself comfortable."

Slowly, reluctantly, Javier took his seat beside the bed and lifted his left foot up onto the upturned pot.

With the guitar cradled on his lap, he glanced round; first at his mother, and then at Gran. A sweat of anguish broke out over his whole body as he sat there in a frenzy of unrest. The two women gazed at him, waiting expectantly.

"I…" He paused to clear his throat. "I'm going to play the Spanish Romance."

"The Spanish *what*?" Gran wheezed.

"The Spanish Romance."

"Romance?" she echoed spitefully. "Who wrote it?"

"I… I don't know who wrote it. I mean, no-one knows. It's anon…" And then, with a strange lifting of his voice, "It's anonymous."

"Anonymous?" Gran gave a harsh, retching cough. "I expect it was a Spaniard that wrote it!"

"Mam!" his mother exclaimed. "Give Javier a chance!"

"I learnt it by myself," he said faintly, his tongue dry in his parched mouth. "Some people think it sounds happy."

"And what do *you* think?" Gran's eyes narrowed.

"I think it sounds sad. It makes me think of all the Spanish people living in caves. They do live in caves, Gran; I know they do. I read about them."

"What!" she flung out. "Spaniards, living in caves? Go on, then; try and make us feel sorry for the little blighters!"

"Mam!" his mother flushed with exasperation. "You're making Javier nervous!" She turned to him, her face strained. "Go on, Javier. Begin whenever you're ready."

Javier bit his lip and set his fingers for the opening, the silence around him dead and filled with foreboding. He began slowly. It sounded quite good, but he must be careful with the vibrato. Mr Vanderhorst had warned that too much vibrato would spoil the overall effect of the Spanish Romance.

As so often before when he'd played this piece, the image of a tiny farmstead took shape in his mind; the soil baked hard under a blistering sun, a pony hitched to a two-wheeled cart, a small boy dressed in rags, his face resting against the pony's neck. Reaching up, the boy would wave some flies away from the animal's eyes. If only this music could reach into Gran. If only she could see what it really meant.

And now... make the last note waver, just a little, as the sound ebbs away. And then be still.

Javier gazed down in silence, not daring to look up. He heard a sound, like waves brushing against a distant shore. Lifting his head slowly, he saw the bedclothes rising and falling as Gran breathed.

"Good boy, Javier," his mother whispered. "Gran's sleeping. Very well done…"

Trials and Tribulations

Glancing out from the top deck of a bus, Javier saw pavements teeming with people shuffling to and fro in the swirling sleet. The January sales must have drawn them in. The bus gave a sudden lurch as it turned sharply into St Dunstan's Street on the western edge of Canterbury. He tightened his arms around the guitar resting on his lap. It was well protected inside the tough canvas bag his mother had made. But what if it fell down into the aisle?

His mother sat beside him. Silent and sombre, she gazed through the slush-splattered window, the sky lead-grey, the rooftops spread with melting snow. He'd heard her flitting across the landing in the early hours. Oh, why wouldn't Gran go into hospital?

"You won't forget to pay Mr Vanderhorst, will you, Mam?" Javier spoke softly, reluctant to intrude too much on her thoughts.

"No, Javier," she replied, her attention still focused on the world outside. "I won't forget. When did I ever forget?"

"Last week. You didn't pay him last week."

She turned, fixing him with her melancholy eyes.

"I'd forgotten to cash a postal order last week. I won't forget this week."

"Don't then… please."

He'd felt embarrassed to see her rummaging through her purse at the end of last week's lesson. It would have been obvious to anyone that she didn't have the money. Mr Vanderhorst had dismissed the incident lightly. "Don't worry, Mrs Aguirre," he'd said. "It's quite all right. Pay me next time." But it wasn't all right. Mr Vanderhorst was a brilliant tutor, perhaps the best in the world. He deserved to be paid promptly. But those *postal orders*, they were a mystery to Javier.

"Where do they come from?"

"Where do *what* come from?"

"Postal orders; what are they for?"

"They're for sending money to people, so as not to put cash in the post."

"But who would want to send us money?"

"Ssshhh!" She glanced nervously over her shoulder.

"But who, Mam?"

"It goes back a long time," she said in a quiet voice. "Your father was paid to go and find somewhere to live in Spain. When he didn't come back, the money started coming to me. It's called a dependant's allowance."

"Does it pay for guitar lessons?"

"It pays for everything, Javier, including your education."

"So where do they come from… the postal orders? I mean, who actually sends them?"

"I don't know. It used to be the Spanish Refugee Council. They looked after your father when he was young. It's all changed now. They come from some government department or another. And please don't ask me which one, Javier. I get a postal order every month, and that's all that matters."

Javier hugged the guitar closer. What if postal orders were to stop coming? Would the guitar lessons have to stop? He'd worked so hard. Mr Vanderhorst had even suggested entering him for a music exam.

Glancing ahead, he saw the medieval arch of the city's West Gate looming into view. He must be ready to leave at the next stop.

"Good luck with the recital," she smiled. "I'll see you later."

"You won't be late, will you?"

"No, Javier, I won't be late."

Steadying the guitar, he rose to his feet and glanced down at her.

"And you won't forget to bring some money for Mr Vanderhorst, and for last week?"

"I'll have it with me. Mind how you go."

The compacted snow crunched under Javier's shoes as he stepped from the bus. It was bitterly cold, the wind raw on his face. He waved goodbye to his mother, lingering for a moment as the bus moved away. One day he would get a job so he could pay for his own guitar lessons. And he would buy a leather guitar case, with an inner lining of fur to keep the instrument warm on cold wintry mornings such as this.

Charged with enthusiasm and excitement, he set off at a brisk pace. By arriving a few minutes early he would have the waiting room all to himself; time for some last-minute practice while Mr Vanderhorst was still busy with another pupil... a chance to get the guitar warmed up.

He would be asked to play scales and arpeggios first. That's how every lesson started. Scales and arpeggios were important for developing a good fingering technique, and for passing exams. Then Mr Vanderhorst would request a short piece; something by Bach, Carcassi or Villa-Lobos maybe. But this week, he was in for a surprise. He would hear the Recuerdos de la Alhambra!

Turning into Pound Lane, Javier almost broke into a run.

Suddenly, a shock like electricity passed right through him. In a moment of sheer panic, he felt his feet sliding out from under him! Instinctively he clutched the guitar in both arms, fighting desperately to regain his balance. He stumbled forwards, and then sideways, his legs flailing as they went away from him.

Deprived of any grip whatsoever, he felt himself tipping backwards. Out went his left hand to break the fall; down came the guitar upon his chest as his body thwacked onto the pavement. Winded and shocked, his mind throbbed with a thought so terrible it was enough to split his skull. The guitar!

His breast heaved painfully as he made the effort to rise. Hauling himself upright, the sound of his heartbeat pounding in his temples, he struggled to his feet. The left hand felt numb. He probed quickly over the canvas bag, feeling along the whole length of the guitar's fingerboard, then around the sides and belly. The instrument seemed intact. But without actually opening the bag he couldn't be sure.

He felt blank and dazed, unable to fully comprehend what had just happened. Slowly, like an automaton, he moved on towards the big Georgian house where Mr Vanderhorst had his studio on the top floor. He climbed the steps to the double doors and pulled down on the heavy brass handle, flinching as the numbness in his wrist gave way to a sudden stab of pain. He stepped inside, closed the door behind him, and slowly made his way up the staircase. He felt sick and desperately weak, his mind in turmoil.

At the first floor landing he paused, just as always, listening to the busy clatter of typewriters and breathing the scent of the young women who came here to study at the school for shorthand and typing. But it was different this time. He felt like a mountain climber after a fall, unable to advance or retreat. And yet he must go on. He must present himself calmly, just like any other musician about to give a live performance. Javier took a deep breath and started up the stairs to the next level.

"Is that you, Javier?"

In the few seconds it took to realise that Mr Vanderhorst had been standing at the studio door, waiting for him, the shock of the mishap had all but vanished from Javier's mind.

"Yes, it's me!" he cried.

"Good. I've had a cancellation; we can begin right away." Mr Vanderhorst motioned towards the waiting room. "Leave your coat and come into the studio when you're ready."

Javier entered the waiting room, flung his raincoat on a chair, and turned his attention to the guitar.

"Please God; please don't let it be broken." He fumbled with the straps. "Please!"

Lifting the instrument carefully from its canvas bag, he inspected the join between the neck and belly. This was the greatest point of strain, where the tension of the strings could easily cause any guitar to break. But the joint appeared sound; there was no sign of damage anywhere. Thank God!

He moved quickly across the landing and into the studio. Mr Vanderhorst was sat at his desk, poring over a jumble of papers.

"Take a seat, Javier. Do your warm-up. And then we'll hear a scale; F sharp minor, I think. Three octaves…"

Javier sat for a moment. Lost in admiration, he watched Mr Vanderhorst at work. Mr Vanderhorst knew everything. Without even looking at a guitar he would know precisely where the left-hand fingers should be placed, and where alternative fingering could help to achieve easier chord changes.

"Harmonic or melodic scale?" Javier said, reaching for the foot stand.

"Both, I think. Start with the melodic."

That was fortunate. Javier had rehearsed those scales thoroughly; he could hear them in his head. But first he must tune the guitar. As he curled the fingers of his left hand over the strings, a flash of pain made him catch his breath. His wrist! Was it broken? He would brace himself to work through it. Straightening his posture, he tuned the guitar quickly, and then lowered the throbbing wrist to his side.

Now for the warm-up; some right-hand finger movements… let the left-hand rest for a while. Mr Vanderhorst had insisted on using letters to identify the thumb and first three fingers of the right hand: "*p, i, m, a.*" Caressing the strings in rapid succession, Javier played all combinations, whispering the sequences to fix the patterns in his memory: "p, i, m, a… p, i, a, m… p, m, i, a… p, m, a, i… p, a, i, m… p, a, m, i…"

He repeated the sequences over and over again, across all six strings, until from the corner of his eye he saw Mr Vanderhorst coming towards him and carrying his own guitar. Javier brought the warm-up session to a close as Mr Vanderhorst took a seat directly facing him.

"Try borrowing your mother's nail buffer," Mr Vanderhorst said, laying his guitar on the floor beside him. "The smoother the nails, the softer the tone." He leaned back and clasped his hands behind his head. "Now, let's hear those scales. Be sure to maintain a steady pulse, Javier. It's dangerously easy to begin too quickly, and then have to slow down for an awkward corner."

Javier positioned his left hand. With a slight adjustment of the forearm, the pain was a bit easier to bear. But would the fingers work properly? Would his wrist take the strain?

"Melodic scale of F sharp minor," he said firmly, just as he would have to do in an exam: "Three octaves."

He began at an easy pace, the fingers moving smoothly over the fingerboard. He must remember to play semitones between notes two-three and seven-eight ascending, and between notes six-five and three-two descending. He played the scale again. It had gone well both times.

"Harmonic scale of F sharp minor; three octaves!" he called out.

The wretched pain in his wrist suddenly returned with a vengeance. He leaned forward over the guitar, the fingers of his left hand tightening in a kind of spasm as they made fleeting contact with the frets. *Posture! And remember; semitones between notes two-three, five-six and seven-eight!* But the final sequence of descending notes was almost thrown together, his rendering of the scale sounding crude and slapdash. It rang harshly in Javier's ears for several moments after he'd finished. Held fast in the grip of self-condemnation, he sat with his head bowed.

"A little more practice should do the trick," Mr Vanderhorst said. "Aim for accuracy and quality of sound rather than speed. I've been wondering, Javier… that guitar of yours, you said your father made it."

"Yes."

"Your father is a very fine craftsman."

"He went away… when I was a baby."

"You never knew him?"

"No."

"And the guitar has stayed with you all that time?" Mr Vanderhorst breathed a deep sigh. "That's very impressive, Javier. But as much as I admire your father's skill, I think you should consider replacing the instrument. Even the best guitars will lose their tone eventually."

Javier ran his fingertips gently along an edge of the guitar's body. He felt numerous chips and dents, the result of many minor knocks and scrapes. And that tiny inscription: MA… the letters that had come to signify the creative power of the genius who'd built the guitar; his own father. How could he even think of abandoning such a treasured possession? He glanced up.

"I don't mind if it looks old."

"What it looks like is immaterial. Unless you're aiming to give recitals. Tone is what matters, Javier. Here… hand it to me for a moment." Mr Vanderhorst took the guitar and began to play; no chords, just single notes. "Recognise it?" he said.

Javier felt reluctant to say anything that might cause Mr Vanderhorst to stop. It sounded so absolutely perfect.

"Vivaldi's Concerto for Lute and orchestra. But without the orchestra!"

Handing the guitar back to Javier, he lifted his own from the floor and began to play the same piece again. The difference in quality was startling, the deep rich sound of every note booming gently in Javier's ears and touching him deeply.

"Notice any difference? Give it some thought, Javier."

Javier knew what was coming next. It was the moment he'd been waiting for. But that pain in his wrist! He drummed the fingers of his left hand nervously against the side of his chair.

"Remind me," Mr Vanderhorst said. "You were going to perform something for me… a short piece… a study by Carcassi, I think."

But Javier had already positioned his left hand ready for the opening of the Recuerdos, rehearsing in his mind the rapid right-hand finger movements that would carry the tremolo right through to the end: p, a, m, i... p, a, m, i... p, a, m, i...

Without further delay he was into it. Slowly and softly, he made the sound rise and fall to create that special effect that he knew would gain Mr Vanderhorst's approval. Pain? Yes, but hadn't the composer himself suffered pain? Francisco Tarrega's whole life had been plagued by an excruciating and incurable *dry-eye* disease. But despite that, he'd managed to produce some of the loveliest guitar music the world had ever known; including this, his beautiful Recuerdos.

Seated upright, and breathing in sympathy with the music, Javier moved into the final section. He kept it flowing at a gentle pace, playing from the heart, as if his father were listening in faraway Spain. He controlled the tempo nicely, maintaining the rhythm, the posture, everything. Almost choking with anxiety, he paused before the final chord, holding the silence for what seemed a very long time. And then he played the chord... softly.

His brain reeled with emotion as he slumped back in his chair, his left hand flopping down to his side, the wrist locked in a paroxysm of burning pain.

Mr Vanderhorst gazed back at him, his mouth open, the silence long and filled with foreboding.

"I warned you about that piece. Didn't I warn you, Javier?"

Yes, he had been warned. And he'd paid no heed. He'd gone blindly on; over-reaching himself, over-estimating his own pathetic ability. And the result had been a hideous, humiliating disaster.

"I thought I could play it. I tried... I really did try."

He gazed down at the floor, the pattern in the almost threadbare carpet blurred and shimmering.

After a few moments he heard the sound of the Recuerdos again: deep, sonorous, majestic and utterly immaculate. Mr Vanderhorst had taken up his own guitar. Swaying gently from side to side, his eyes appeared to sparkle as the music flowed from him.

This was the sound Javier had been trying so hard to create. The music seemed to embrace everything he'd learned about his father's country; a land where snow-capped mountains pierced the sky, where palaces and convents clung to craggy slopes. He could imagine it now: those deep ravines and sweltering desert wastes; busy city streets, where men and boys would be seen driving flocks of sheep and herds of cattle to market. There were villages too, nestling in the foothills; courtyards full of flowers, where people would quietly take their siestas; simple home-loving people, too poor to be going anywhere, and too sensible to try. The images began to fade as the sound of the Recuerdos slowly ebbed away.

"I know, Javier," Mr Vanderhorst said. "It's like searching for something that can't be described in words. You know, we guitarists owe a debt of gratitude to Tarrega, for the way we place the guitar on the left thigh, the use of a footstool, the positioning of the hands, and the way our fingers engage the strings. All of those ideas came from Tarrega."

There was a gentle knock on the door.

"Mrs Aguirre?" Mr Vanderhorst called out. "Please come along in!"

"I'm a few minutes early," she said.

"No, you're in good time." Mr Vanderhorst rose to his feet. "Actually, I'm glad you're here now. I'd like a word."

"And I with you." Javier felt a tightening in his throat. "To be perfectly blunt, Mr Vanderhorst, I'm rather worried about what all this music is doing to Javier's schoolwork."

"Ah yes, the schoolwork," Mr Vanderhorst moved over to his desk. "You know, Mrs Aguirre, one of the joys of my profession is that it brings me into contact with some very talented people."

"Yes, that's all very well, Mr Vanderhorst, but we can't spend all our lives indulging in music. There are other priorities, careers to work for."

"I quite agree, Mrs Aguirre. And yet, I sometimes wonder. You see, on very rare occasions I might find myself in the presence of a wonderfully *special* kind of talent. In all honesty Mrs Aguirre, I have to tell you that Javier is demonstrating an aptitude for music that is far more exciting than anything I have seen or heard in many years."

"Really!" The harshness of her tone made Javier blush. "But the school work, Mr Vanderhorst, the schoolwork must come first. I simply cannot allow Javier to—"

"Mrs Aguirre. I've taken the liberty of getting in touch with Cator Court. It's a college for gifted youngsters; a place where music studies are underpinned by a very wide range of other academic subjects.

"Cator Court?" she frowned.

"It's in the West Country. There are bursaries for successful candidates. Auditions are being held at the Royal School of Music in just a few weeks from now. Why not at least read about it?" Mr Vanderhorst offered a brochure. "Take it home with you. And one other thing: Javier must have a new guitar. I assure you, his success at audition would depend on it."

"A new guitar?" Her eyebrows lifted slightly. "I'm not sure we could run to that!"

A slight shiver, almost a convulsion, passed over Javier as a wave of doubt crept under his skin.

"Yes of course, I do understand. But Cator College is a highly respected establishment. It would be a signal opportunity for Javier. And as for the guitar, I doubt whether a brand new instrument would be entirely necessary. In fact, I'd be delighted if he would take mine, perhaps on a long-term loan. It's still a fine instrument; a product of the famous Esteso workshop in Madrid."

Javier gasped and leapt to his feet.

"Please, Mam! Please say yes!"

"The Esteso workshop?" She stood in silence, transfixed, as if conjuring a distant memory. "The Esteso guitar workshop?" she repeated. Then, after a long pause, "Well, Mr Vanderhorst, if you really think he's ready for it... How could I possibly refuse?"

Chapter 10

MADRID

3 Years Later, June 1964

Hope Springs Eternal

He'd seen it before, and so many times: that faint glow around the small grille above his head, the first sign of early morning. But this was a different kind of dawn. His aching body was in a more comfortable position; not slumped against the cell wall, but with his whole weight supported in a pleasant kind of way. He was actually lying on a proper bed! How could that be? The transformation was too weird. Mikel gave a shudder.

Here it came again, that agonising pain sweeping across his chest, a chilling reminder of the beating he'd received some days ago. His upper arms and shoulders still smarted from the flogging that had nearly killed him. And now *everything* was pain. His whole body was racked with it, raw and agonising.

There was no sense to it! Life had been bad enough ten years ago, with Commandant Fortea at the helm. Now it was worse. There was no control of any kind, nobody in charge of the prison, just a filthy bunch of savages dressed up like guards. Mikel wasn't even being interrogated anymore. Their behaviour had degenerated to the level of utter callousness, wanton cruelty. For how much longer must it go on?

Another flash of pain. His fingers! In God's name, why did they always go for his fingers? His eyes misted over as an excruciating bolt of fiery agony shot upwards through his arms, worming its way into every fibre of his body. He lay there in the semi-darkness, shaking and covered in sweat, straining in all his nerves. He must try to relax, regulate his breathing, give the ribs a chance to heal, and his shattered fingers.

Something scurried across the cell wall above him. Lizards! The lizards were his friends. There was a time in the very distant past when he would scoop them off the cell walls. He would watch as they twisted and squirmed in the palms of his hands, sometimes shedding their tails in a frantic effort to escape. A few discarded tails would lend a crunchy texture to a cup of cold, tasteless rice. But that was a long time ago.

He heard the sound of a guard's boots echoing along the corridor. They came to a stop outside his cell. Another sound came, like a forced whisper.

"Pssst… Maestro Aguirre!"

Mikel held his breath. Then he heard it again.

"Maestro!"

Slowly, cautiously, Mikel rolled his eyes towards the cell door. If only they would end it for him. Surely they must know he was as good as dead?

"No," he murmured. "Please… not again."

He rolled to face the wall, tears of despair flowing in rivulets down the side of his face and dripping onto the mattress.

A key rattled in the lock. And then… silence.

Cautiously, he rolled his head back and saw a large round face, the eyes wide and sparkling as they peered at him from around the cell door.

"So, you *are* awake, Maestro!" The door opened further and a short, paunchy, moustachioed guard loomed into view.

"It's alright, Maestro. It's only me… Sanchez." The guard moved closer, his boots scrunching on the thick shards of glass cemented into the cell floor. "You are safe now." He knelt at the bedside. "Here, Maestro… drink!"

Mikel felt a hand lifting his head gently, a deliciously cold fluid trickling down his throat. It tasted sweet, like honey. What was going on? Where were the usual guards?

"Goat's milk," the guard beamed. "Prepared by my wife. I will leave you now; you must rest a while longer." He turned to go.

"Guard!" Mikel croaked. "Wait… Who are you?"

The guard turned back.

"I am Corporal Sanchez. And please, do not mistake me for one of your prison guards. They are animals!" He spat into a corner of the cell. "I am a *real* soldier! I served with the Spanish Foreign Legion, the finest military force ever assembled!"

Mikel drew a sharp breath, the throbbing pain in his fingers heightened by a new sensation; a curious feeling of tightness around his hands and wrists. He glanced down at them, unable at first to comprehend what he saw. His fingers, hands and lower arms were wrapped in bandages. Bloodstains between his fingers contrasted sharply with the pure whiteness of the dressings.

"My hands…"

"Yes, they are in a bad way, Maestro. But I have seen worse

on the battlefield. Tomorrow I will look at your fingers again, and try to set them right."

This must be some kind of trick, a new method of interrogation.

"I... I don't understand. Who are you? Why are you here?"

Sanchez gave a little chuckle.

"You are one of the lucky ones, Maestro. The prison is almost deserted now. They have decided to keep it open for a few old jailbirds like you; prisoners they cannot decide what to do with. The communists have been transferred to other jails. Thank God you were not one of them. And as for me, I am finished with soldiering. But as I cannot afford to retire, the Generalissimo has given me the job of looking after what is left around here. The Generalissimo is a generous man, Maestro. He has even allowed me to keep my uniform... look!" Sanchez tapped his sleeve. "See this badge? A crack marksman! Oh yes, I shot many a Berber tribesman!"

"You killed people?"

"Of course, Señor! The Riff were threatening our colonial possessions in the Sahara! But they were no match for the Legion; the elite fighting force of Spain. And when Civil War broke out on the Spanish mainland, guess which army His Excellency the Generalissimo called upon to help him destroy the communists!"

Mikel heaved a slow, painful sigh. He'd thought about the Civil War many times, those powerful, wounding images so very graphic and utterly convincing. The nightmare visions had haunted him: Mama and Papa cowering under a barrage of heavy artillery fire; Mama's white blouse spattered with blood. Time after time, Mikel had tried to reach out to them in his dreams. But he'd been unable to move, his body locked in a kind of paralysis. If only they would turn and look at him… meet his eyes… just once.

"I don't know anything about the Civil War."

"Then you should *learn* about it, Maestro! The battle was a crusade! But look, I have something for you."

Loosening the top button of his tunic, Sanchez produced a bundle of papers.

"I've been looking through your personal file," he went on. "You were a guitarist, I think. Just like my mother; she too played the guitar. My mother was Italian. She was born in Rome on the same day that troops loyal to the King of Italy broke through the city walls, driving out the pope and making Rome the capital."

He laid the papers on Mikel's chest.

"My mother was a student of Oscar Chilesotti! But that was before my father arrived. My father was a Spaniard, you see; a traveller. He rode all the way to Italy on a donkey. And when he met my mother, he whisked her away and brought her back here, to Madrid! My mother played the guitar well. Oh yes, she played very beautifully."

Sanchez moved back towards the door.

"I will collect the papers later. Things would go badly for me if they were found in your possession. In two hours from now I will bring some food. Then I will help you wash and shave; some fresh clothes, maybe. But now you must rest!"

"Sanchez!" Mikel pushed himself up onto his elbows, but fell back. "What is it like? Outside, I mean."

"Outside? You must be patient, Maestro. All in good time, and then I will tell you everything. You will hear about the wide

Madrilenian boulevards; the wonderful bridges spanning the shallow Manzanares River; the ten streets radiating from the massive square at the city centre. And those women, Maestro; I will do my best to describe those beautiful Madrilenian women!"

As the cell door clanged shut, Mikel lay staring up at the ceiling. Wide-eyed and motionless, he felt lost in the grip of confusion. Then he felt movement across his chest. The papers! They were sliding away, cascading down to the cell floor. With a monumental effort, he managed to trap a newspaper under his elbow. He blinked to clear his eyes. Then, lifting his head, he read slowly:

PACO DE LUCIA MOVES TO MADRID

It was business as usual at the Esteso guitar workshop as the great flamenco guitarist Paco de Lucia paid a call last weekend to sample a few instruments. Founded by Domingo Esteso in 1917, the guitar workshop in the Calle Gravina continues to foster an enviable reputation. Following Domingo's death in 1937, the workshop was taken over by his three nephews, the brothers Faustino, Mariano and Julio Conde. Master craftsmen in their own right, the instruments they build under the Esteso banner continue to be sought by performers and collectors the world over. Paco de Lucia, who recently moved to Madrid with his family, intends to make the city his base. And he didn't leave the workshop empty-handed! So, the Esteso torch continues to burn. Paco de Lucia was heard to remark… "Esteso guitars are as light as a feather, and with a sound so beautiful that it is almost impossible to describe."

Mikel let his head flop back. One day, he would get out of here. He would build himself up, regain the use of his hands and fingers. Then he would go back to England, collect Maisie and Javier, and bring them to Spain. He would present himself at the Esteso factory on the Calle Gravina, show the Conde brothers the guitar he'd made, and convince them of his ambition to become a craftsman of the very highest calibre. He would ask them for a job, and serve his time as an apprentice at the Esteso factory. At long last, a dream fulfilled!

Cator College

Dr Lillian Walker chalked some chords on the blackboard. Her white lab coat tightened with her every move, bringing the subtle curves of her body into sharper relief. Seated on the front row, Javier's heart beat a little faster. He felt a blush in his cheeks and hoped she wouldn't notice.

Javier wasn't the only pupil who'd taken a fancy to Dr Walker. Fergus was crazy about her. But at least Fergus could joke about it. Fergus had called her *'the mistress of harmony'*; his *'princess of the supertonic seventh'*. Not to her face, of course. In return, nourished by the vigour of his Irish charm, Fergus had managed to capture Dr Walker's special devotion. It showed in the way she spoke to him, in the way she always made a point of sitting next to him in the dining room.

Fergus had become the college champion, and not just in Dr Walker's estimation. Throughout the entire three-year course, Fergus had outshone every other pupil, both in theory and in performance. He'd won the prestigious Jacques Thibaud memorial prize for his unaccompanied Bach Cello Suite at the Christmas recital. It was hardly surprising that Dr Walker had become so fond of Fergus. Why wouldn't she?

Dr Walker struck the blackboard with her chalk, dotting the final minim. Then, holding the chalk as if it were a conductor's baton, she turned and swept her eyes over the class.

"There!" she exclaimed, a smile flickering across her lovely lips. "Cadences like these were used by all the composers of the Baroque period: Bach, Corelli, Vivaldi, Handel; and just about every other successful musician since those times. You must be able to write chord sequences like these if you want to pass your finals next week."

Javier felt a twitching of his facial nerve, the mention of exams filling him with dread. Theory of harmony on Tuesday, orchestral writing on Wednesday, aural and stylistic analysis on Thursday. He would need to revise solidly over the weekend. His time at Cator was rapidly coming to an end, the last classroom session drawing to a close. Except for next month's début concert in the main hall…

Please God, let him be one of the six students selected to perform at the début concert. It was an important event, and not just for parents. Lots of people from the world of music would be there. Patrons, agents… talent spotters!

Fergus, of course, was destined for higher things. For the first time in the history of the college, one student would be chosen to perform at the Wigmore Hall in London. Everyone knew that Fergus would be nominated. Dr Walker had described his Bach recitals as inspirational, like breathing air. And how right she was. It was something about the richness of the sound he made; a kind of physicality that found its way into the heart of anyone lucky enough to hear him perform. Yes, Fergus was by far the best choice for the Wigmore.

But the début concert was no less important. A potential opening to a soloist's career, it was just the opportunity Javier had been waiting for.

Dr Walker was writing on the blackboard again. Javier glanced round at the rest of the class. They were heads down, frantically copying into their exercise books. Most of them were going on to study at higher levels, some seeking scholarships at the Royal Schools and Colleges of Music. But for an interpretive musician like himself, there seemed little point in spending more time on studying theory. He yearned to *reach out* with his music; to develop a rapport with his listeners, and persuade them to bathe in the harmonies of the finest pieces ever written for the classical guitar.

"I'd like you to study this passage over the weekend," Dr Walker said. "Fill in the bass and alto parts. Remember to use first and second inversions here and there. They always add interest, and will help to gain extra marks."

She was so utterly gorgeous; and so hopelessly unattainable, except to…

"Would you want us to modulate the piece?" Fergus called out from the back of the class. "And a cadence, Dr Walker? Would you want us to harmonise a cadence?"

Fergus had every reason to sound bright and cheerful. He'd recently won an unconditional scholarship to study cello at the Irish Academy of Music in Dublin.

"Modulate a phrase of this length?" she laughed. "No, I don't think so, Fergus. But you should certainly add a cadence. It could be a perfect or an interrupted cadence; you decide which sounds best. Come and see me on Monday morning if you want to discuss your ideas."

The bell suddenly sounded. Chairs scraped noisily across the floor, the room emptying fast.

Javier quickly copied from the blackboard into his homework book. He studied the line of music carefully, pondering over the chord sequences. The key signature was F sharp.

"Looks like a piece in G major," he murmured. "Or maybe E minor?" He searched in vain for an accidental in the leading note of the related minor key. "No, there's no D sharp; it can't be E minor. It *must* be G major, then." He tried to imagine the melody line. Yes, a perfect cadence would fit nicely; a simple five-one sequence to round it off.

"Got the idea, Javier?"

He gave a start, looked up, and saw Dr Walker gazing down at him.

"Oh... yes, I think so." It almost hurt to be this close to her.

"You've managed to get your head around all the theory?"

"Yes. Well... I mean, no. Not really." God, she must think him an idiot. "I mean, I'm not sure why I should have to..." He stopped short. What if she got the idea that her theory lessons had been wasted on him?

"You're not sure why you've had to put up with so much harmonic and stylistic analysis over the past year?"

"No... I mean... it's just that I'm not interested in composition. I want to perform. I've always wanted to perform. I think I'd be good at it."

"Another young hopeful," she said curtly, "so eager to catch the public gaze."

A rising sense of indignation choked Javier's heart. He didn't deserve that. Her lessons on supertonic chromatic sevenths had been a real slog, enough to destroy all thoughts of a childhood universe. But he'd put his mind to them and studied hard, maturing in leaps and bounds as the full emotional weight and colour of those more complex chords were made clear to him through the music of Mozart. And now she was making fun of him!

"We're all hugely impressed by your determination to play well, Javier," she went on. "But at Cator, we aim to establish a solid theoretical background of knowledge. We have to prepare our students for more advanced courses."

"I don't want to go on studying. There are lots of guitarists who've done well without having to learn loads of theory. Vincente Gomez, for example; Gomez started performing before the age of ten. I'm already sixteen and I haven't given a single recital."

"I hardly think Gomez would have been rated very highly at the age of ten," she frowned. "Gomez was playing in the taverns of Madrid at that age, struggling to make a living. He was self-taught, Javier, just like Andrés Segovia. It took many years for them to reach the status of front-rank musicians in the true classical style."

"But that's exactly where I want to be... in the front rank! I want to go on tour and make my way in the world." A maddening tightness in his throat made his voice sound childishly squeaky. "Anyway, I'm no good at theory. I just want to get out there and perform!"

"Do you, indeed?" she said rather stiffly. "Well, unfortunately, that's where things can go horribly wrong for a young musician. We're rather different from other artists, Javier. A painter might expect to produce hundreds of works, some good but mostly bad, before eventually going on to achieve recognition, perhaps even fame. But for musicians like us, it's different. A young soloist must either make a favourable impression at the very outset, or decline rapidly into obscurity. It's very tough out there. And besides, there's still much for you to learn. You'll need to know how to work with a conductor, how to interpret the mood of the orchestra when deciding on your approach to a cadenza."

"But I wouldn't dream of inventing my own cadenzas, especially not improvising during a performance. I'm no good at composing music. I would learn the cadenzas already written for the guitar. I'm good at learning new pieces."

"Yes, yes…" She turned aside and tossed the chalk into a cardboard box. "You've learned some great pieces, I'll grant you that. But ask yourself, Javier: what is it that makes you play the way you do? Is it *real* music you play, or is it just a collection of notes? What's the impulse? What's the driving force that carries your performance right through to the very end?"

What was Dr Walker getting at? Fault-finding was normal at Cator; even Fergus got a certain amount of criticism. But this was different. It sounded more like condemnation. Was she casting doubt on Javier's basic competence as a musician? With his repertoire now extending to well over forty major pieces, all playable from memory, he must surely be ready to face the public.

"Well, Javier?"

Then it struck him. He knew exactly what Dr Walker was getting at. Not a single pupil had ever failed the final exams. Cator had always prided itself on achieving a 100% pass rate. But that's because the *real* selection always came *before* the finals. It was generally believed that pupils falling behind during the run-up to exams would be sent packing. They wouldn't get a chance to sit their finals.

"I don't know what makes me play the way I do," he muttered. "I... I suppose its instinct."

What gave Dr Walker the right to see into his mind? Why should *anyone* know what it was that drove his fingers, filling his soul with the capacity to perform the way he did? He sat there in silence, unable to find words that might save him. A strange noise in his brain hissed and seethed with the dreadful notion of failure.

"Instinct? And is it instinct that motivates Fergus, do you suppose?"

That was it... the final nail in the coffin! It was all over for him now. To be compared with Fergus meant certain defeat.

"No," Javier answered bluntly. "Fergus does the analysis! Fergus studies the score! Fergus learns to recognise the exposition, the development and the recapitulation. He understands all the modulations from major to minor keys, and all that stuff!"

"And you don't?"

"It's not my way of looking at music! It would be like... like trying to describe someone by the shape of their face, or the colour of their hair. It's stupid! There's more to music than structure and form, just like there's more to people than the colour of their eyes!"

He gulped with apprehension.

"If you say so, Javier..."

She reached into the pocket of her lab coat. With an air of blank professionalism, she withdrew an envelope and placed it down on the desk in front of him.

"I've been asked to show you this," she said. "The college principal thought you should know about it... before everyone else does."

Javier swallowed hard. His moment of expulsion had

come. The shame! With a trembling hand he reached for the envelope, its flap already open, and withdrew the contents. It was a card. He read slowly:

CATOR COURT COLLEGE OF MUSIC

Debut Recital

The Principal, Academic Staff, and Governors of the College cordially invite you to attend a recital at

The Wigmore Hall in London

on Saturday 25th July 1964, starting at 7pm

where the young and exceptionally gifted guitarist
Javier Aguirre

will perform works by JS Bach and D Scarlatti.

Also, currently on tour from Budapest

The Salieri Ensemble

will perform the String Quintet D956 by Schubert.

RSVP

"Congratulations, Javier." The sound of her voice was barely audible through the deafening roar that filled his stupefied brain. "Some very important people are going to be there, including several members of the royal family."

Oh, the relief! The blessed relief! The absolutely boundless sense of overwhelming joy!

Fighting hard to control his tears, Javier glanced up into her lovely eyes.

"You were quite right," she smiled down at him. "Intellect and balance are so very important. But most of all... instinct."

Chapter 11

LONDON, ENGLAND

July 1964

A Close Shave

The carriage burst out from the tunnel and into the neon brightness of another underground station. People standing on the platform sped past the window in an indistinct blur. And now the brakes were on; the carriage lurching, swaying, and thrusting Javier sideways against the armrest. Steadying the small overnight bag on his lap, he caught a glimpse of the station name: *Piccadilly Circus*.

As the train squealed to a shuddering halt, he squeezed his knees around the guitar between his legs. With a loud blast of compressed air, the doors rumbled open. He felt a warm breeze wafting in from the platform; and with it a musty smell from the motors. He could almost taste the electricity.

More passengers piled on. He'd never seen anything like it. So many people... where were they all going?

In less than three hours from now, the Wigmore Hall would be full to capacity. Was this really happening, he wondered. A mishmash of apprehension and exhilaration swamped his brain so he could hardly think straight. Gazing down at his lean, sinewy fingers, a sickening wave of doubt rose up from his stomach.

It was within his power to stay on this train, ride out the journey until the very end of the line. He could get off at the last stop and find somewhere to hide. But what a crazy, stupid idea! How could he even think of giving up now? Of course, he must go through with it. He had to, if only for the sake of his father. That model of musical perfection that had rested within him for as long as he could remember, nurturing him, inspiring him to work tirelessly to wring the most beautiful sounds ever to be heard from a guitar. His father would surely have approved of what he was about to do. Wasn't that enough to spur him on? Javier breathed slowly, deeply, willing himself to relax, lessening the tightness around his neck and shoulders. He must be ready to get off at the next station.

An elderly couple entered the carriage. They hesitated momentarily, and then sat down in the last two unoccupied seats, facing him on the opposite side of the aisle. They were obviously well-to-do. The man was rather thickset, and with a white silk scarf tucked into the collar of an immaculate dark overcoat. The woman was well-dressed too. A reddish-brown fur thrown loosely around her shoulders seemed to emphasise her lofty demeanour. It was fox skin, judging by the tiny triangular-shaped head hanging down across her ample bosom. For a moment, the man's eyes appeared to settle on Javier's guitar case. The man suddenly glanced up, fixing Javier with a curious penetrating gaze. But conversation of any kind was the last thing Javier wanted now. He turned and stared blankly at some people standing near the open doors. Another hiss of compressed air, and the doors began to close.

There was a shout, and a loud thumping on the side of the carriage. The doors rolled open again, the standing passengers giving way as a pale, gangling youth leaped onto the train. The doors banged shut. The train gave a jolt, accelerated rapidly and plunged once again into the darkness of the tunnel. In a minute or two the train would slow down for the last time. The doors would open, just one more time… and then Javier would be there!

He lifted the guitar case, just a little, and set it gently down on the toe of his shoe to cushion the vibration. Three years had passed since Mr Vanderhorst had presented him with this wooden marvel. It would be interesting to know how the sound would carry through the vast emptiness of the Wigmore Hall. A guitar always sounded different in a hall filled with people. But Javier had chosen special strings for this occasion; a reputable brand from New York, especially strong and dependable. They could be relied upon to produce a gorgeous, robust tone in any sized theatre. And yes, he'd remembered to bring some spares, just in case.

Javier began to feel energised, the thought of gathering up the guitar and holding it in his arms sending a reassuring thrill through him. How he longed, with all his heart, to be on that stage!

He'd been right to come to London by train. Imagine travelling all the way from Dorset on the school bus! It would have meant sitting with all the academic staff and a lot of Cator College trustees whom he'd never even met. Dr Walker had tried to persuade him not to travel alone. She'd argued he was too young, especially with so much at stake. But he'd insisted. How else could he have found the inner peace he so desperately needed? Besides, travelling alone was an essential part of being a solo performer. So why not get used to it now, sooner rather than later? In any case, he'd wanted to arrive early. He would need to make himself known to the Wigmore's music director; find somewhere to practise, and change into his concert clothes. And he didn't need a bunch of college academics to tell him how to do any of that!

But if only his mother could have shared in the excitement and novelty of the occasion. Javier recalled that sorrowful moment when he'd been summoned to Dr Walker's office, just a few days ago.

"I'm terribly sorry, Javier," she'd said. "We were so looking forward to meeting with your mother at the Wigmore. But unfortunately, she's unwell and won't be attending. Your uncle has written to say that he is looking after her..." And then, as if his mother's absence didn't matter very much, "Now remember, Javier, don't over-romanticise the Bach Prelude. Try and fill every phrase with life and vitality..."

From thereon, her words had faded away, trivial and meaningless.

Javier had last seen his mother during the Christmas vacation. Since Gran had died a couple of years ago, his mother had become lonely, depressed and plagued by illness. There were money problems too. Maybe that's why she'd taken up with Uncle Gorka again. The thought of her being compelled to live with that monster filled Javier with hatred and rage. Uncle Gorka wasn't worthy of her. He was evil! And as for preventing her from travelling up to London to see her own son perform at the Wigmore Hall... it wasn't fair! It wasn't right!

Javier watched the cables at the side of the tunnel darting up and down, rising and falling rapidly, as if engaged in some crazy jumping dance. A chaos of emotions whirled and writhed inside him. He leaned forward, resting his chin on his hands, clasped together across the top of the guitar case. Sheltered by his drooping eyelids, he focused his mind on the opening bars of the Bach Suite in G major; the music with which he would begin the concert.

But now the brakes were on, the lights of Oxford Circus station streaking past. He waited for the train to stop, for the doors to open. Then, gathering up the guitar and overnight bag, he made his way out onto the platform and followed the crowd. According to the travel itinerary, Wigmore Street was very close, just a ten-minute stroll.

He must have a plan. A strategy for getting through those first few moments of brain-numbing fear before making his way out onto the stage. He would conceal himself in the wings, watch as the royal party took their seats, try and judge the mood of the audience. Then, lifted by his father's love, he would walk out and present himself boldly, but courteously. He would raise his left foot onto the pedestal, pause until there was absolute silence, and then... and then give the performance of his life. *Please, Daddy! Just be there; help me through those first few critical moments!*

Even now he could feel his father's presence, the faintest touch of a hand against his own, lifting the guitar gently and easing the load at his side.

But wait! This was *too* real! Javier came to an abrupt halt. He turned and saw a face, thin and pale with sunken eyes...

the youth from the train! Javier felt the guitar wrenched from his hand. He let out a stifled cry, but it was too late. In less than an instant, the youth had gone. The guitar... gone!

Something inside Javier snapped. In the grip of an uncontrollable rage, he let go of the overnight bag and lunged headlong into the crowd. Clawing his way forward, he spotted the youth stumbling awkwardly up some steps, just yards ahead.

"You bastard!" Javier yelled at the top of his voice.

Heads began to turn as a clear path of pursuit opened up before him. He hurled himself up the steps. The youth paused and glanced back, hindered by some passengers gathering at the top.

"You filthy rotten bastard!" Javier roared again.

The youth turned away and staggered on. Javier bounded up the steps, clearing two at a time. Then, within striking distance, and with a sudden outpouring of explosive energy, he lashed out with his fist. The blow struck the youth hard in the middle of his back. With a terrible moaning gasp, the youth sagged to his knees. The guitar case fell and struck the ground heavily, clattering away down the steps, and at such a rate that Javier had no hope of catching it. He just stood there, sobbing with emotion and fighting for every breath.

"Hey! Young fella!" It was a woman's voice... an American. "If you ever need a job in security, I'm gonna take you on... big time!" She stepped up and took Javier by the arm. Then, turning to the crowd, "Well? Don't just stand there gawping! Somebody call the metro cops!"

Then another voice. "Yep, great performance!"

Javier saw a man gazing up from the bottom of the steps. He was holding up the guitar case.

"And I'll bet you're glad to see *this* again!" the man called out.

"Please!" Javier cried. "Please open it for me. I need to know if... if..." He sank down and buried his face in his hands. "Please... just look inside."

There was an agonising pause, a dismal, interminable silence, as the man climbed the steps. And then Javier heard those familiar clicking sounds; first one catch, and then the other.

"Hmm... looks okay," the man said at last. "No *obvious* damage, I reckon. But hey! What's *this*?"

"Aw, go easy, honey. This boy's had one hell of a shock."

Catching the scent of an expensive perfume, Javier glanced up and saw a flattened fox's head dangling just inches from his face, its glassy black eyes sparkling under the neon lights.

"Just a boy, huh?" the man said in a tone that bit like acid. "Well I'm telling you, pal, this ain't no ordinary guitar. It's the very best, right? This is one great piece of Esteso craftsmanship! You don't lug this old lady around on the London underground. No sirree! This lady travels in style! She gets her own place in a cab, her own seat on a plane, her own darned cabin on an ocean liner if it comes to that!"

"Please. I just need to know... Is it alright? Is it damaged?"

"Nah!" The man laid his hand on Javier's shoulder. "She ain't damaged. She's in good shape... not a scratch. Great guitar case, too; can't beat good American leather!"

Javier drew a deep, joyful breath.

"Thank you," he murmured. "Thank you so much." A wave of gratitude, poignant with affection, flowed right through him. "I saw you! I saw you both on the train!"

"You sure did!" the woman laughed. "We got to wondering where you were headed, young fella!"

"I'm going to the Wigmore Hall. I've got to…" Javier heard footsteps; someone running along the platform down below. An instant later, two policemen were racing up the steps towards him.

"I guessed as much," the man said. "Now listen to me, young fella. You're about to be bombarded with agency offers. Don't be taken-in by 'em! My wife and I… we're different. We look after guys like you. Our musicians get to appear over the whole darn world." The man glanced down at the advancing policemen. "Keep your cool tonight. And be sure to look me up; either here in London, or at my place in New York." He slipped a small card into Javier's top pocket.

Javier leaned on his side and inadvertently sunk his elbow deep into the middle of the youth's back. There came a howl of pain so thoroughly chilling that Javier's body locked solid with the shock of hearing it.

"I'm so sorry!" he exclaimed. "I really am very sorry."

Thinking Positive

Pacing in the wings of the Wigmore Hall, Javier felt the weight of the guitar in his clammy hand. Dr Walker's introductory speech had been going on for ages.

"Please," he muttered. "Please God… make her stop talking soon."

Would he remember how to begin the Prelude? Would his mind trigger the correct finger responses, the patterns of notes and chord sequences, flawlessly, instantly, and without conscious thought? Would the new strings generate a good tone, with sufficient strength to carry the sound into every corner of the theatre? His whole future would be determined within the next hour. Would he survive by the elegance and quality of his playing or be branded a failure, another hopeful who'd been found wanting, his career in ruins even before it had properly begun?

Just one more peep through the tiny inspection window? One last look at the audience? No. Someone might spot him and see how nervous he was. Anyway, he'd seen enough already. In a flurry of panic, he turned away from the window, shuddering at the thought of what lay out there.

All this waiting, it was like torture. He might as well be in the dressing room, running through those trills in the Scarlatti Sonata, or practising the Gavotte to make it sound bright and bouncy. Why couldn't his mother have been here? His mother would have known how to comfort him. She would have taken his head between her hands. She would have held him close and told him how proud she was.

"Some water, Mr Aguirre?"

Javier spun round, nearly losing his balance. It was the stage manager. An hour ago, he'd been strutting around in an open-necked shirt, supervising the setting up of the sound and lighting equipment. He was formally dressed now, with a smart bow tie.

"Before you go on, Mr Aguirre; a glass of water?"

"Oh, no thank you." The words almost whistled between Javier's dry lips.

"Vocalists swear by it."

"Pardon?" Javier plucked at the stiff collar around his throat.

"Stage fright; it plays havoc with the voice. A drop of water usually does the trick. Are you sure I can't tempt you?" The manager nodded towards the stage. "You could be here for quite some time. Your college principal seems determined to attract a bumper slice of royal patronage."

"How many are there?

"Royals? Rather more than we'd planned, actually. The Palace is hosting a cultural delegation. There are guests from all over the world. They wanted a night out, so we've had to provide extra seats. And by the way, their Royal Highnesses are seated at the centre of the auditorium; second and third rows from the front. I'd extend a courteous bow in their general direction if I were you. Don't worry too much about trying to single them out. They like to spread themselves around a bit on occasions like this... mingling with the other VIPs."

"Ah... right. Yes please; a glass of water."

"I took the liberty, Mr Aguirre... lemon flavoured." The manager offered a tray covered by a white napkin. A half-filled glass stood in the middle. "And just one other thing. The Salieri players have arrived. They'll probably invite you to join them for an encore, just to round off the evening. I'm sure they'd be happy to accompany anything you feel like playing."

"Anything I feel like?"

"Absolutely; their repertoire is extremely broad. I've heard them play Giuliani, de Falla, Albeniz, Villa-Lobos... Rodrigo as well, I believe."

"Rodrigo? Oh no, I don't think so... not tonight." Javier gulped a mouthful of lemon squash.

"Really? Well, it's entirely up to you, of course. But this is your big opportunity, after all." The manager cast a speculative glance towards the stage. Then, in an almost pious tone, "I think you're on, Mr Aguirre. May I take your glass?"

The auditorium swelled with the sound of applause. Javier suddenly found himself alone, powerless to move, his muscles struck rigid. It must have lasted but a second or two, but felt like ages.

"Javier!" someone cried out.

He saw Dr Walker approaching, her face flushed and radiant.

"Just whenever you're ready!" she beamed. "Come along, young man. We're all waiting for you!"

His chest tightened. Then he was moving, almost gliding, towards the stage, his hand held aloft by Dr Walker. With a mighty surge, the applause grew louder, the noise unbelievable, deafening. And now he was out there! Hellfire! It was vast! It was bloody endless! How could he possibly cope with all this; the blinding lights, so many people? He felt the blood draining from his face, his heart fluttering like a dying bird. His father; where was his father? Please daddy, be here! Help me! Please! Oh daddy, please be here!

He sensed a gentle breeze, warm and instantly recognisable. He breathed it down; a slow, shuddering intake of air. He breathed again and felt his heart responding, pounding against his ribs, its rhythm strong and steady as the blood coursed through his brain like a raging torrent. He was smiling now, almost laughing in fact. He was coming alive, sustained by the intensity of his father's presence, which grew stronger and more tangible with every passing moment. He bowed low, raised himself up, and bowed again. He must gather himself now. He must retreat into himself and do what he must do.

The applause began to fade as he took his seat. It felt

strange to him that he was still smiling as he brought the guitar up onto his lap, positioning his fingers lightly over the frets.

Someone coughed. He held back. Another sound; a rustling from somewhere off to his side. He must have silence, absolute stillness. Was the time right? Yes… now.

He opened the Bach Prelude with a firm touch, listening carefully to judge the acoustic response of his surroundings. It sounded good. The Prelude could be performed in less than two and a half minutes, but he would maintain a smooth and leisurely pace and aim for a little longer.

He closed the Prelude with a flourish, and then adjusted his posture slightly in preparation for the Allemande. Not daring to look up, he listened for any sound from the audience. There was none. And that was good. The applause should come after the Gigue, at the end of the Suite. But this silence… it was weird, almost unnatural.

He began the Allemande at a lively pace, his fingertips skipping rapidly over the frets, his fingers propelled by a creative energy whose true nature and origins had always eluded him. Things were going well. He felt ready now to discover his audience, to reach out and engage with them. He stole a quick glance and saw a glitter of sumptuous jewellery; the royal party seated in the centre, their faces upturned towards him. His eyes flashed back to the fingerboard.

It was puzzling, but for some unaccountable reason he felt compelled to look again. Something, or someone, had caught his eye; but what, or whom? He waited for the right moment, and then glanced back towards the VIP area. He saw a woman, unadorned and more plainly dressed than the others. She was surrounded on all sides by a blaze of sparkling precious stones.

It was her very simplicity that had captivated his interest, her face a little thinner and paler than the rest. But those eyes; so wide… so bright! And there was something else about her. That familiar, gentle smile. The smile that had brought him comfort and warmth for as long as he could remember. And beside her, he saw another face… a man gazing up at him and beaming from ear to ear. It was Mr Vanderhorst.

Chapter 12

MADRID

11 Years Later, November 1975

The Parting Hour

"Wake up, Maestro! You must wake up… quickly!"

Mikel grabbed at his knees, pulling them tight against his chest. It was like a lightning bolt from the past. He might be dragged from his bed at any moment!

His eyes were open now, the cell wall just inches from his face. The security light had been switched on. But why? Then he felt himself being shaken hard. It had been years since he'd been woken like this!

"Hurry, Maestro! You must get up, right away!"

Rolling onto his back, Mikel looked up and saw Sanchez, his big round eyes filled with alarm as they stared down at him.

"Sanchez? What… what's happening?"

"Up, Maestro! Now!"

"But what time is it? It can't be morning already?"

"Never mind the time!" Moving frantically, almost beside himself with panic, Sanchez began collecting up some old discarded newspapers from the cell floor. "We are under investigation, Maestro! Someone is coming!"

"Who? Who's coming?"

"I don't know, but if they find these they will shoot me!" Sanchez waved a newspaper at Mikel. "There are officers in the investigation party!"

Mikel's heart gave a sudden heavy bound. Gathering the thin blanket around his shoulders, he eased his legs over the side of the bed. The air felt cold and dank as he gazed down at the bony feet protruding from the tattered hems of his prison trousers.

Sanchez looked distraught as he staggered around the cell collecting up the papers, stuffing them into a tight bundle under his arm. How could anyone even think of shooting Sanchez? For more than ten years he'd looked after Mikel. He'd brought treats from the local shops; fresh fruit, lovely artisan chocolates and tasty chorizo sausages on Sundays. He'd even installed a proper bed and cleared the cell floor of all those vicious glass shards to make space for Mikel to exercise. Life had become more tolerable in the company of this short, rotund little guard. Was it all about to change?

"What's happening, Sanchez?" Mikel was struck by a sudden thought so terrible he could hardly bear to utter it. "Is… is Fortea back?"

"Commandant Fortea?" Sanchez drew himself up, his fat cheeks glistening with sweat. "No Maestro. At least, I do not think so."

"Who then? Tell me!"

"I am sorry, Maestro, but I think…" Sanchez heaved a faltering sigh. "I think I may never see you again."

A bolt of terror shot down Mikel's spine. Dear God, he could almost taste the fear. He'd managed to keep going, the terrible past deeply rooted in his memory, the stuff of constant nightmares. He'd survived it all. So many years in this rotten cell, recoiling day and night listening to those harrowing screams; the torture meted out to so many other poor wretches. Prisoners he'd never even seen. For the past eleven years, even with Sanchez around, he'd lain awake, sometimes until dawn, plagued with anxiety about what the prison authorities might eventually have in store for him. And now, after all that, like a mighty unstoppable engine, his death was fast approaching. Soon, he would be crushed out of all existence. And who would know it? Who would remember him? Who, but Sanchez?

Mikel glanced up for the last time at the grille above his head. Squinting through the glare of the security lamp, he saw the familiar orange glow of morning. Oh, to be out there now, strolling along the streets of Madrid. The shops would be opening, people sitting down to breakfast in smart Madrilenian cafés.

If only he were a bird. He would hop between the iron bars of the grille, launch himself into the air, fly right across Spain and over the Bay of Biscay to England. He would search for Maisie. He would find her, wherever she was. He would settle close to her, watch her rising from her warm, cosy bed.

And he would look for Javier. Judging by the many annual calendars supplied by Sanchez, Javier would now be twenty-seven years old. Young Javier might be gazing into a shaving mirror at this very moment, studying his youthful features whilst contemplating another day of honest work. Maisie… Javier! Never in their wildest dreams could they imagine a place like this; bleak and squalid cells, interrogation rooms with walls stained black by the detritus of a thousand executions.

"It's all over. It's finished, isn't it, Sanchez?"

"Yes, Maestro…" Sanchez gave another profound sigh. "The end has come. Spain has lost its leader… His Excellency, the Caudillo, is dead."

Mikel struggled to understand what he'd just heard. The Generalissimo… dead? The dictator who'd murdered tens of thousands of Basque people? The tyrant who'd driven so many Spaniards into concentration camps, innocent people who'd lost homes and families in the civil war? People who were now quarantined, living in exile without work and without a country to call their own.

He heard footsteps in the corridor. They sounded brisk, purposeful. For Mikel, each echoing stride trod a measure of inexorable pain, like an agent of death come to claim him.

In a lightning move, Sanchez snatched up the last newspaper. Then, snapping stiffly to attention, he stared trancelike towards the open door. There, framed against the brightness of the outer corridor, stood a young officer, smartly dressed, his epaulettes sparkling. With a jerk of his head, the officer motioned for Sanchez to leave, and then turned his gaze on Mikel.

"Señor Aguirre?"

Mikel rose unsteadily to his feet and let the blanket fall to the ground. Fortea's guards had made him stand like this. After several long hours of waiting, sick with fear and cold, they would drag him away for another round of interrogation. He must endure it again one more time, await the first blow from a guard's baton. But this time, please God, they would drag him out to die, quickly.

The officer opened a file of papers and began to read aloud.

"Señor Mikel Aguirre! Captured on 7th July 1948 whilst engaging in a plot to sabotage the holy Nationalist cause in Bilbao. Tried by court of justice; found guilty of conspiring to store explosives and war materials in the centre of Bilbao, of encouraging the Red campaign, inciting revolt and strike action with intent to paralyse the life and unity of the city. Condemned to life imprisonment. Sentence confirmed and countersigned by..." He glanced up: "Countersigned by His Excellency, the Head of State." Then, after a moment's pause, "So what do you think of *that*, Señor Aguirre? You are lucky to have been kept alive for so long, are you not?"

"It's not true," Javier croaked. "There was no trial. I saw no judge."

"But the case against you is overwhelming! Utterly convincing. I have the report right here in front of me. And I should say that your interviewer was highly accomplished, his investigative skills exceptional."

"Fortea? Fortea couldn't find anything against me. How could he? I only wanted to bring my family to Spain. I was looking for somewhere to live, that's all."

"Ah yes... your family. Many Basque people were seeking repatriation at that time. Most of them were genuine refugees, of course, but not you, Señor Aguirre. Alas, the investigation found against you. It concluded that your real purpose was to, and I quote..." The officer glanced again at the file. "... '*to gather information for the British intelligence services with the undoubted aim of obstructing the Caudillo's intention to guide his nation to greatness and prosperity.'"*

"I told you… it's not true."

The officer snapped the file shut and stood gazing at Mikel.

"Well, Señor," he said at last. "I do not doubt that your treatment here has at times been a little harsh. Such is the way the Spanish authorities are entitled to deal with those who conspire against our country's best interests. However, considering the gravity of your transgression, you will be thankful at least that your life was spared. You must get dressed now. Some people are coming to see you. Visitors, Señor Aguirre! Visitors!"

"Visitors?" A painful lump rose up in Mikel's throat.

"A delegation from the British Attaché…" The officer glanced down at Mikel's trousers. "I have ordered some new clothes for you. We cannot have you looking like a common tramp in front of important embassy staff." He stepped back into the corridor. "Corporal Sanchez! See that Señor Aguirre receives a good breakfast! And make sure his new suit is a good fit!" He glanced back at Mikel. "In one hour from now, you will be released from this prison and placed into the care of the British consulate. I wish you every success for the future, Señor!"

With a click of his heels, the officer turned away and was gone.

Mikel felt faint, his body cold and trembling. A circle of darkness began to gather around the periphery of his vision. It closed in, squeezing out the glare of the security light. He felt his legs giving way. He was falling, descending into insensibility, and there was absolutely nothing in the world he could do to stop himself.

An Old Acquaintance

Drifting back into consciousness, slumped forward over a tabletop with his head resting on his arms, Mikel heard voices. He would keep very still, pretend to be asleep and listen carefully to what they were saying. They were male voices, the first words of English he'd heard spoken in nearly thirty years. There seemed to be two of them.

"Can he be moved?" said one.

"Moved?" the other threw out contemptuously. "Of course he should be moved! I simply cannot understand why the British embassy has taken so long to act! He's one of *us*, for God's sake!"

"We have been trying, I assure you," said the first. "Foreign Office officials always do their best to—"

"Do their best to sit on their fat arses and do nothing all day!" interrupted the other. "Bloody diplomats! Thank God I'm a medic. I'd go crazy working with you lot!"

"So, going back to my first question," said the first calmly. "Is it safe to move him?"

"Why not? There's nothing I can do for him here. And there's no point in calling for an ambulance; they won't come anywhere near this place. I suggest you use an official car. Get him over to the embassy as soon as you can. I'll treat him at the clinic there. But take it easy. His heart is very weak. You've seen for yourself the state of his hands. Bloody sadists!"

"You'll come with us, of course?"

"Unfortunately not. I've got more work to do. There are others like him at the other side of the city. I'm going to raise merry hell about all this. It's a bloody outrage. I'll see you back at the embassy. Give me a couple of hours."

A door slammed shut, and after a long silence, the first man spoke again.

"Mikel? Can you hear me?"

Mikel sat motionless, hardly daring to breathe.

"Look, I'm awfully sorry about the way all this turned out. I've come to take you away, old chap. It's all over now."

The very Englishness of that voice conjured up an image in Mikel's mind; of vast orchards, fruit trees set in rows with grassy avenues between, parallel lines of blossom, marvellously pink and white, drenching him in springtime fragrance. The vision ended abruptly.

"Now look, Mikel. I know it hasn't been easy for you."

What was it about that voice? So utterly refined... compelling... coercive...

Raising his head slowly, cautiously, Mikel saw a figure seated at the other side of the table.

"Remember me? I'm with the British Embassy now."

Whitaker? Was it possible? He looked older... balding at the front, his face fuller. But yes, it was Whitaker all right. Mikel searched Whitaker's face for a sign; anything that might convey an understanding for what Mikel had been made to endure over the past twenty-seven years. But there was nothing; just a lofty, superior smile.

"Please..." Mikel mumbled hoarsely. "Please could I have some water?"

"Water...? Yes, of course, old chap. It's right here."

Whitaker pushed a tray forward. There were slices of ham, chunks of soft fruit, and a glass, smooth and heavy as Mikel lifted it to his lips. He choked at the first gulp. Orange juice; acid against the inner lining of his dry throat.

"Easy, now! Easy!" Whitaker leaned forward and prised the glass from Mikel's fingers. "You know, Mikel, there hasn't been a single day when I haven't done something to try to secure your release."

"My wife... my little boy!" The words tumbled out in a raucous whisper.

"I gave you my word, Mikel. I kept my promise. Your wife received a regular income; your son a good education. He's a fine young man."

"Maisie... I want to see Maisie. Where is she?"

Whitaker's expression turned sombre.

"I'm terribly sorry, old chap. But you must try and keep in mind the length of time you've been away."

Gorka! A bolt of pain flashed through Mikel's clenched fists. Gorka had achieved his goal; he'd won Maisie over!

"I'm afraid there's no easy way to tell you this..." Whitaker paused for a long moment before going on. "Sadly, Mikel, your wife passed away ten years ago. It was cancer."

Mikel slumped back in the chair, his senses annihilated. Maisie... gone...

"She lacked for nothing," Whitaker droned. "She received a generous income right to the very end. And as for your son, I expect you'll want to hear all about him."

"No!" Mikel cried in a strangled voice. "Please... no more!"

Gripped in the surge of a heavy downward sinking, lost in a whirlpool of devastating grief, Mikel flopped forward onto the table and buried his face in his arms. He began to sob uncontrollably. Oh, the utter loneliness of his miserable life.

Through a strange high-pitched hum surging through his

confounded brain, he sensed the persistent sound of Whitaker's voice.

"Yes, I know how you must be feeling, old chap. We lost some good people. But not you; you're a survivor, Mikel. And we've found work for you at a guitar workshop on the Calle Gravina; the Esteso factory. They're offering you an apprenticeship. Isn't that what you always wanted, Mikel? To be a craftsman?"

Chapter 13

AIRBORNE OVER MADRID

23 Years Later, September 1998

Flying High

The muted tone of a woman's voice reached out to Javier as if from another world. He heard it again, coaxing him back from the brink of sleep.

"Señor Aguirre. We are approaching to land, Señor."

He opened his eyes and gazed out through the cabin window. He felt so tired… exhausted, in fact. He saw the wing of the aeroplane swathed for most of its length in a grey watery mist, the wingtip totally obscured. A flashing red light pulsed from somewhere deep inside the nebulous gloom. The strobes must have been switched on; it would be dark down below. Suddenly, the cloud was gone, whisked away in the blink of an eye, the sky now clear. He glanced higher and saw the tiny glint of another aeroplane, its thin vapour trail brilliantly illuminated by the setting sun.

"We'll be on the ground in a few minutes, Señor Aguirre. You slept well?"

He turned to her, sensing her delicate perfume as she leaned closer.

"No, not really. But you've looked after me very well, thank you." Since when had he ever managed to sleep on an aeroplane?

Squeezing the button on his armrest, he felt the sumptuously wide seatback moving upwards, restoring him to the vertical. He could see her better now. She was gorgeous; cherry-picked, of course… selected for her good looks to wait upon the VIP classes choosing to fly with Iberia, the Spanish national airline.

"And your friend? Does she *always* travel first class?"

"My friend?" Javier reached out and placed his hand on the brown leather guitar case resting by his side. "But my friend *is* the first-class passenger. I'm just along for the ride."

"Really, Señor," she chuckled. "My boyfriend is a fan. And my father too. In fact, my father has collected every one of your recordings." Reaching down, she tightened the seat belt around the middle of the guitar case. "My family tried to buy tickets for your concert tomorrow night, but they were sold out weeks ago." She gave a final tug on the buckle, and then stood back. "I will have so much trouble convincing my boyfriend that I have been this close to Señor Aguirre's guitar!"

"I'm sorry. I mean, I'm sorry about the tickets. They really shouldn't be so hard to come by."

"Oh, no matter," she smiled. "The concert is being broadcast live on radio, and on national television."

Javier's heart almost skipped a beat. He disliked TV cameras. Especially the mobile ones. Careless movement around the stage could be as distracting to an audience as it was to the soloist.

"Unfortunately, I am on duty tomorrow evening," she went on. "But my family and friends will be watching. I have asked them to record the whole performance."

"Well, I'm sure the Madrid Symphony Orchestra will put on a fine show. Let's hope I can manage to keep pace with them."

She gave another little chuckle, her bright eyes shining with delight.

"You'll be no stranger to Madrid, Señor Aguirre. I think you will have played in all the great cities of Spain."

"You'd be quite wrong to think so. I have never set foot in Spain, not in my entire life."

"But you *are* Spanish, aren't you? We'd always believed you were born in Spain."

"Wrong again; I was born in England. Solidly British, I'm afraid. I hope it's not too much of a disappointment."

"No, Señor!" She blushed slightly. "It's just I remember reading somewhere… and your name…"

"Ah yes, my name…" It irritated Javier slightly; the never-ending association of his name with a country he'd never seen, and had never even wished to see. "Actually, my father was from the Basque Country."

"Basque!" she smiled. "Just wait until I tell my family. They were so sure about you being Spanish! Well, I hope you enjoy your time in Madrid, Señor Aguirre. And please… you must fasten your seatbelt now."

Moving on, she paused beside a young man with rolled-up shirt sleeves and flashy braces. He'd been banging away on a laptop computer for ages. After a brief exchange in Spanish, the man handed over the laptop. Arching her back in a graceful curve, she reached up and pushed the laptop into an overhead locker.

Javier turned away and gazed down at the darkening landscape. He fixed his eyes on a solitary pinpoint of light, a remote farmhouse perhaps, and followed its steady progress until it disappeared under the leading edge of the wing.

He should never have accepted this engagement. He'd been invited to perform in Spain so many times, but had always managed to find excuses for not doing so. It was cowardice, of course. A reluctance to face up to that maddening dilemma; the twin fires of hatred and love that had seethed and simmered inside him since childhood. He should never have agreed to come here, torn as he still was between a brutally callous objection to the father who'd deserted him as a baby, destroying his mother's life, and a strangely obsessive intimacy with that same man, whose shadowy spirit had inspired Javier to wring such wondrous sounds from the guitar.

Could he have avoided coming to Spain on this occasion? No, of course not. Turning down an invitation to perform at the official re-opening of Madrid's prestigious Royal Theatre might have had disastrous consequences for his career. Could he have faced being disowned by his agent, and cold-shouldered by the world of music? And all those Spanish devotees; wouldn't they be eager to see him, and to hear him play for the very first time in their own country? Huge numbers of dignitaries would be present, the auditorium filled to capacity.

The worry of it had contributed to his lacklustre performance in Berlin last night. The applause had been rapturous enough. Members of the Berlin Philharmonic had commented very favourably on his playing, their feedback verging on the rhapsodic. But on being chauffeured away from the Berlin Philharmonic Hall, he'd begun to feel dissatisfied, convinced in his own mind that he'd failed to convey the notion of Spain that Joaquín Rodrigo had wanted to engender in the listener's imagination; an impression of those ancient gardens of Aranjuez.

Joaquín Rodrigo was Spain's most highly regarded composer, a national hero in his native country. Rodrigo had done much to keep the spirit of Spanish music alive during the Franco period. He had a home in Madrid, and there was a good chance he would attend tomorrow's concert, despite his great age. He would listen critically to Javier's rendering of the Fantasia for Guitar and Orchestra, a work Rodrigo had written many years ago for the legendary Andres Segovia. A bolt of anxiety, crisp as pain, shot through Javier's body. The obligation on him to play supremely well at tomorrow's concert was frighteningly awesome.

He reached out again and felt the reassuring touch of the leather case at his side. Snugly cocooned inside was one of the finest guitars ever to emerge from the workshop of Domingo Esteso Lopez, the late master craftsman of Madrid. With a rosewood backing, mahogany arm and ebony fingerboard, it was both a performer's delight and a collector's dream. Its very closeness would induce in Javier a kind of personal affiliation with the highest-ranking maestros of Esteso's time; performers like Andres Segovia, Manuel Ramirez, and still earlier to Francisco Tarrega, the composer and performer who'd done more than any other to confirm the guitar as a miniature orchestra within itself. Javier needed that spiritual contact with the past, especially at times like this.

He glanced through the window again. There were city lights now, millions of them. He was about to set foot in a country he'd only ever read about. A land of smoke-filled bars, sherries of every description and taste, fresh octopus and tapas. A culture that left plenty of time to eat and drink, or so he'd heard. How different it would be from the sweeping pace of life he'd become accustomed to. A career of constant travel. Performances at every type of establishment; concert hall, cathedral, church and school.

Music schools were a joy. He always felt at his best amongst music students. He would laugh at their searching questions, their eagerness to find within him the key to winning genuine applause from discerning audiences. He would joke with them; reminding them that praise makes a good musician better, and a bad musician even worse. He would tell them that preparation was everything; that a failure to prepare was a preparation for failure. Yes… preparation was everything.

And so he would choose to disregard the trembling moan of the aircraft engines, the steady hiss of chill cabin air. He would conjure the presence of that great audience filling the dark void beyond the footlights. It was good to rehearse like this, in his mind, even without the guitar on his lap. It always left him marvelling at the capacity of the human mind to call forth all the notes, conceptualising every finger position and sensing every dynamic.

He visualised himself moving out onto the stage, giving his customary brisk acknowledgment of the thunderous applause, taking his seat at the centre, and willing himself to overcome that harrowing sense of fear that always raged in the pit of his stomach moments before starting to play. Even now he could feel the mighty power of the Madrid Symphony Orchestra as it burst into life behind him, his body trembling to the opening bars of Vivaldi's R93 concerto in D major.

He glanced down at the fingernails of his right hand, inspecting each of them in turn, feeling their round smoothness with his thumb. One final polish and they would produce a superlative tone when brought into contact with the strings of his Esteso guitar.

A reassuring thump from below signalled the undercarriage locking firmly into place. With the soloist's moment of entry almost upon him, Javier closed his eyes and drew a deep breath. Then, gathering his mental faculties, he began the D major with an exultant flourish... all in his mind. He resolved not to open his eyes again until the aircraft had come to rest outside the terminal building at Madrid airport.

Just Another Day

Eliana stood gazing at the flight arrivals board. The information on IB452 hadn't changed in half an hour. She turned to the elderly chauffeur at her side.

"IB452 has landed!" she flamed. "Isn't that what it says, Julio?"

"Yes, Señora Eliana."

"So, where are they?"

Julio shrugged his shoulders. He looked profoundly bored.

"Maybe they haven't landed at all, Señora. It was simpler

in my day. No computers and fewer problems. But you are too young to remember."

She glanced at her watch… 8.45pm. This whole day had been a complete waste of time. Turning abruptly, she gazed into the crowd. Had someone called her name? Standing in the hustle and bustle of a busy airport terminal, it was difficult to be sure. She heard it again.

"Eliana! Eliana!"

Benita, a friend from school days, waved from behind the airport information desk. Eliana smiled and waved back.

"Shall I wait in the limo, Señora?" Julio wiped the shiny peak of his cap on the sleeve of his uniform.

"You may as well, Julio. Please be back in ten minutes. I need to know where to find you."

"See you at the car, Señora Eliana." He sauntered off.

"Oh, and Julio…" she called after him, "please don't smoke in the car; it leaves an unpleasant smell."

She gave the arrivals board a final scan before steering a meandering path across the busy concourse towards Benita's desk.

"Still mixing with the high society?" Benita grinned.

"At this time of day? Where are the passengers from Berlin?"

"Berlin. That'll be Flight 452… one moment." Benita's fingers rattled on a keyboard. "Delayed on an inbound taxiway. They're starting through immigration now.

"Thank heavens for that."

"How many this time?"

"Just one. And before you ask, Benita… Yes, he *is* quite dishy. That's if his photograph is anything to go by."

"Well done, you! What's his line of business?"

Eliana hesitated. It was a question of striking a balance between discretion and good manners when chatting with friends.

"That's classified information, Benita. You know we're not supposed to reveal client identities."

"Eliana! You're the only VIP escort from the Foreign Office who never tells me anything!"

"Really? Well then, I'll tell you this much: I've spent a lot of time over the past few days arranging a business tour for a party of Japanese industrialists. They're due to arrive early tomorrow morning. You wouldn't believe the amount of preparation… so much coordination! But then, just as I was packing up to go home this evening, it all changed. Suddenly, I'm supposed to be looking after an unaccompanied UK national! No explanation; no time to prepare. You can take it from me, Benita; it isn't easy working as a VIP escort for the Spanish Foreign Office!"

"Threaten to resign!" Benita laughed.

"It's not funny! Actually, I'm beginning to get quite fed up with it."

"Put up a fight, then. Complain to your boss; that's what I would do."

"No, you wouldn't… not when the Minister himself has insisted that you take the lead."

"The Foreign Minister?" Benita's face lit up. "Gosh, Eliana! You *are* a bright spark!"

"Oh no, I don't think so." Eliana darted a quick glance towards the arrivals area. A few people were coming through; business types, mainly, one striding purposefully forward, a jacket casually slung over his shoulder. Nobody looking lost.

"They're starting to appear. Must dash, Benita… can't afford to be late. I'll see you another time, okay?"

Eliana moved quickly to the arrivals gate.

Time for one final look at the briefing notes. She peered again at the black and white photo clipped to the inside cover of the visitor's file. Javier Aguirre had posed seated, his left foot up on a footstool, a guitar resting on his lap. His hands were clasped across the body of the guitar, his elbows hanging down loosely at the sides. He was looking slightly away from the camera. There seemed no pretence about him, none of the fake posturing she'd seen in so many other VIP photos. Eliana felt drawn to his large dark eyes and the neatly trimmed hair, receding slightly at the front. His mouth bore the suggestion of a smile. He looked like a quiet, self-effacing man; probably highly intelligent.

She turned to the itinerary page but was distracted by the sound of her mobile phone.

"Hola?" she answered brightly.

"Eliana! It's Maria, from the office. Have you met with Señor Aguirre yet?"

"No, but very soon; his aircraft was delayed."

"We've received a call from his agent in London. It's urgent. Aguirre must contact his agent as soon as he arrives."

"Yes, of course, I'll tell him. But Maria, it's nearly nine! You're surely not still at the office?"

"Afraid so! I'm looking after those Japanese visitors. Reading the briefing notes you left behind!"

"Enjoy the tour…" Eliana felt a twinge of resentment. "Take care, Maria."

"Wait! Eliana! Señor Aguirre… do you know who he is?"

"Yes, of course. He's a guitarist."

"No Eliana, not just *any* guitarist! You've scooped the big one! People went home from the office feeling very jealous!"

"Is that so? Well I'm sorry, Maria, but I'm not a guitar aficionado. See you in a few days' time."

Eliana pitched the phone into her briefcase and scanned the arrivals area. Still no sign of Aguirre.

Turning back to the file, she ran her eyes quickly over the itinerary:

Transport:	Chauffeured.
Accomm:	Hotel Adler VIP suite (pre-booked).
Day 1:	Collection from MIA 20.00hrs (IB452).
	Convey to hotel.
Day 2:	Convey to National Palace for 12.00hrs.
	Royal reception (formal).
	Return to hotel.
	Convey to Royal Theatre for 19.00hrs.
	Return to Hotel Adler around 23.00 hrs.
Day 3:	Convey to MIA for 09.00hrs.
	Flight to London Heathrow 10.30hrs (BA230).

Turning quickly to the biography section, she scanned the leading particulars. Aguirre was half Spanish, born 1948, aged fifty… unmarried. She read on:

Javier Aguirre came to international prominence in 1964 after his debut at the Wigmore Hall in London, England, was lauded by the press. He went on in that same year to win first prize in three of the world's most important guitar competitions, an unprecedented achievement for such a young performer…

Eliana estimated he would have been around sixteen years of age at that time. Almost a child. There was more:

> *In 1965 he was awarded a coveted Young Musicians'*
> *Prize in London, which led to his first major concert*
> *performances outside his native country. His formidable*
> *repertoire includes more than twenty concertos and most*
> *of the important works for guitar, including adaptations*
> *of all the Vivaldi lute, violin and cello concertos. Javier*
> *Aguirre is also a leading authority on Bach and…*

There was a sudden flash of light. A crowd had gathered; cameras were popping everywhere. She'd allowed herself to become distracted from what had been going on right in front of her.

"Mr Aguirre!" someone yelled in English. "How long are you planning to stay, sir?"

"Can you confirm this is your first visit to Spain?" cried another.

She spotted him. Microphones were being pushed close to his face.

"What other activities are you planning, Mr Aguirre? Apart from your appearance tomorrow night?"

Another voice rang out, "Can you name your sponsor, sir? Is it true that you are here at the personal request of the Spanish royal family?"

Smiling and nodding politely to the reporters on either side, Javier moved steadily forward, guitar case in hand. He approached Eliana, coming to a stop right in front of her.

"Excuse me," he said. "Are you waiting for me by any chance?" The very Englishness of his voice seemed in marked contrast to his sloe-dark eyes and the saffron flush of his skin, which so obviously identified him as a Spaniard.

"Yes…" Momentarily stunned, Eliana felt lost for words.

Then a porter appeared, pushing a trolley neatly stacked with luggage. Eliana sprang into action.

"I'll take that, thank you!" she cried. "If you follow me, Mr Aguirre, we have a car waiting."

Seizing the bar of the trolley, she pressed hard, but the trolley refused to budge. She pressed again, and with all her weight. Damnation! It wasn't moving! And where the hell was Julio? The limo… what if it wasn't where it was supposed to be?

Reporters were closing in fast, more cameras flashing and buzzing all around her. This was turning into a nightmare!

"The brake, Señora!" The porter reached across in front of her. "You must release the brake! There, you see?"

She pushed again, and the trolley moved forward smoothly.

"All this fuss, Mr Aguirre!" She headed for the exit. "I'm so sorry!" Another ripple of blinding lights.

"No, it's not a problem. Just so long as I don't have to talk to them. I can never read what they say about me in the newspapers. Unfortunately, they seem incapable of telling the truth."

She stole a sideways glance. He was immaculately dressed, his light grey suit matching nicely with a white collar and broad-striped tie. Rather odd that he should be wearing gloves, she thought.

"Mr Aguirre!" A man stepped out in front. Eliana released the bar and the trolley came to an abrupt stop. "We'd like to run a feature in our celebrity magazine, Mr Aguirre. If you could spare a little time to talk to us whilst you're in Madrid…"

"Move away!" Eliana thrust forward again, and the man leapt aside.

Thank God… the exit doors! They parted, and the limo was there!

"Señor Aguirre!" Julio stepped forward, touched the peak of his cap and reached for the guitar case. "Please, allow me, Señor."

"No, but thank you!" Javier ducked down and promptly disappeared into the back of the limo, still carrying his guitar.

Photographers surged forward.

"Madrid Radio, Mr Aguirre! Please… just a word or two!"

"Julio!" Eliana yelled: "Quickly! Put the luggage in the back!"

Pushing aside a microphone, she lunged towards the limo, leaned forward, and almost fell onto the back seat. The door closed behind her, and suddenly there was complete silence.

"I'm late," Javier said. "I hope I haven't kept you waiting too long."

"Oh no… not at all."

She heard a muffled thump as the boot slammed shut behind her.

"So… where are you taking me?"

"To your hotel, sir. The Foreign Office has prepared an itinerary." She handed Javier the visitor's brochure. "I'll see you are collected and delivered at the appropriate times. I'm afraid your schedule allows little opportunity to explore the city."

Julio climbed into the driving seat beyond the glass partition and started the engine.

Aguirre flipped open the brochure.

"Two nights…" he said. "But what's this… the National Palace?"

"Their Majesties have requested the pleasure of your

company tomorrow afternoon, sir. I gather they are very fond of your music. You'll be one of several guests at the reception. The others are mostly embassy staff, or so I believe."

"Hmmm… Then we mustn't disappoint them, must we?"

The limo began to accelerate smoothly, as if floating on air.

"I'll try to make sure you leave the palace early, sir. I expect you'll need time to prepare for the concert later in the evening."

"Your English is very good." He smiled warmly. "Javier Aguirre. Please… call me Javier." He extended his gloved hand.

"Eliana," she replied.

"And what other languages do you speak, Eliana?"

"Most of the European ones. Japanese, a little."

She glanced down at his gloved hands.

"I'm always being asked about these," he laughed. "You'll probably think it odd in a hot climate, but I'd rather wear gloves than risk a calamity."

"Calamity?"

"Absolutely! It's so easy to lose the tip of a fingernail. Happened to me once in South America, opening a cab door… Bit of a disaster really."

"Losing the tip of a fingernail?"

"The tone, Eliana. It gets ruined if the nails aren't right. You should take up the guitar. It will get you out of all sorts of menial tasks: no more opening doors, no washing dishes, or ironing clothes."

"Oh, but that would be a shame," she chirped. "I love to iron. Actually, I find ironing quite relaxing."

"You do?" Aguirre showed his beautiful teeth in a wide grin. "Remind me to try it some time. But first you'd need to show me how."

Eliana was herself again. Her great passion in life was making foreign VIPs feel at home in her country. She was already doing well with Javier.

"So, what happens if you *do* happen to lose the tip of a fingernail?"

"A spot of glue will often save the day. Provided, of course, that you can manage to find the missing piece."

"And did you find the missing piece... in South America?"

"In the middle of Buenos Aires? And with less than an hour to go before walking on stage?" Javier's smile faded. "I was just a teenager in those days, completely alone in a foreign country, and with no support whatsoever. You'd have thought my agent would have been on-hand to offer support. It left me wondering why we bother to employ them."

"Agents?" Eliana murmured. "They sound like a necessary evil." A shock of discomposure suddenly shot down her spine. "Oh! Your agent, sir! You must contact your agent in London... without delay."

"Was there a message?"

"I don't think so." She lifted the courtesy phone from the recess between the seats and offered it.

Javier produced a card from his top pocket.

"If you wouldn't mind, Eliana. Would you dial this number for me?"

She entered the digits carefully, waited for the dialing tone, and then handed Javier the phone.

"Diane? Yes, I'm in Madrid." A slight pause. "Hello Jonathon! What's happening?" Another pause. "Singapore? Direct from here? Standing in for whom?"

Eliana felt a rage inside her. She'd botched it twice this

evening. It was so completely unlike her! Reaching up, she adjusted the air conditioning louver; the blast of cool air passed over her face, cool and refreshing. They were approaching the Plaza Independencia now, the hotel just minutes away. She glanced round at Javier. He appeared confident, unshakable, as he spoke into the phone.

"And what are they asking for? The Malagueña by Albeniz? Yes, I could manage that. I'll probably offer the Asturias as well; the Chinese are very fond of Albeniz. Presumably Diane will make the arrangements?" A pause. "Very good. Speak soon. Goodbye for now."

"Well, Eliana," Javier handed back the phone, "it seems I'm destined to spend even less time in your beautiful country. Off to Singapore straight after the concert tomorrow night. Confirmation of the revised flight bookings to arrive at your office tomorrow morning. You'll need to strike *Day 3* from your timetable."

"I'll make sure everyone's aware," she said, "including the hotel manager. Speaking of which; here we are, sir."

"Eliana," Javier touched her hand lightly, "the name is Javier… okay?"

As the limo swept up the hotel's floodlit driveway, a concierge and a porter appeared at the main door. Eliana stepped out and led the way up the steps into a marbled reception area.

Rogelio, the manager, was standing behind the desk. He perked up and removed his glasses.

"Señora Eliana!" he beamed. "And Mr Aguirre… what an honour, sir! Would you care to sign our visitor's book? A meal? I could have something sent to your suite."

235

"Kind, but no thank you." Javier transferred the guitar to his left hand and scribbled in the book. "Breakfast in the room would be nice. Say, at nine?"

"At nine, sir."

"Rogelio," Eliana said. "A slight change of plan. Mr Aguirre will only stay for one night. He will leave Madrid on a late flight tomorrow evening, but would you please retain his room until midday on Wednesday?"

"Of course, Señora Eliana, the suite will be held for as long as Mr Aguirre requires it." Rogelio turned to Javier. "I wonder, sir; would you be so kind as to provide an autograph?"

"An autograph? Certainly."

"Ah… but it is not for me, sir. It is for Paco, our porter. Or rather, I should say it is for Paco's daughter.

"Señor!" Paco stepped forward and bowed courteously.

Eliana had seen Paco many times in the past. He had always cut a lively dash amongst the other hotel porters, but now he seemed overwrought, his face thin and strained.

"And your daughter's name, Paco?"

"If I may, sir," Rogelio cut in, "Paco speaks only very little English. His daughter's name is Rosa."

"Rosa Ortega Vásquez," Paco said, a little nervously.

"And how old is Rosa?"

"I believe that she is nearly ten," Rogelio answered again. "And she is very poorly."

"Oh, I see. I'm really sorry to hear that." Javier's expression bore the look of genuine compassion.

"It is immensely worrying for Paco and his family," Rogelio went on. "The treatment doctors say that Rosa has very little hope of recovery. We are all extremely upset about it."

For several moments, Eliana heard nothing but the gentle sound of water trickling from a fountain in the foyer off to her side. She kept her eyes fixed on Javier, and wondered how he would respond.

"How unbelievably sad," he said at last. "Is she confined to bed?"

"Apparently not, sir," Rogelio replied. "Paco says that Rosa is trying to lead a normal life, at least while she can."

"Then she must come to the concert," Javier said decisively. "Eliana, would you please see that Paco and his family receive complimentary tickets?"

"Yes, of course, sir."

How on Earth was she going to achieve that? The theatre was already solidly booked with a capacity audience!

Javier turned to face the porter.

"And Paco, you must remind Rosa to bring her autograph book. I will sign it after the concert, but only if she manages to stay awake during the whole performance."

"Señor!" Paco beamed with happiness. "My wife, Señor! My daughter! My friends!"

"Yes… yes, of course. You must bring them all. And be sure to sit near the front."

"The elevator is waiting, sir," Rogelio said. "Your luggage is already in the room. I hope you have a very good night."

Eliana slid her hand across the desk and took hold of the room key. She dithered for the briefest moment. Germany, Spain, Singapore, and all in the space of three days! What a wonderful way to spend one's life… how absolutely fascinating! And there he stood, so amazingly attractive in his striped tie and light grey suit; so totally in command.

But perhaps a career like that wouldn't always be quite so wonderful. A lifetime on the world's stage might easily become a trial, monotonous and bereft of gladness. Eliana had experienced it herself; the business of constantly having to engage with the upper classes, educated men and women, unsatisfied, smug, and perhaps not nearly as tame as their outward appearance would at first suggest. She'd felt it keenly; a yearning to break away from it all, the amorphous sterility of a job spent exclusively in the company of the high and mighty. Wouldn't Javier sometimes feel the same?

"Shall I see you to your room, Javier?" she said.

"There's really no need," he smiled. "I've detained you for long enough already."

Paco reached out. She felt the key slip from her grasp.

"Please, Señor Aguirre," Paco said, "I take to your room."

Eliana felt rather blank. It would have been nice to have stayed with Javier Aguirre for just a little longer, perhaps to know him better.

"Yes," she murmured: "It's been a long day. I'll see you tomorrow."

Chapter 14

MADRID

The Morning of the Concert

Journey's End

The workshop was officially closed for the weekend, but Mikel would often come in on a Saturday. He preferred working alone, undisturbed. Although, right now, he longed for the closeness of another human being. He didn't feel at all well.

He lifted the guitar that lay before him. It would soon be allocated a serial number and entered into the production catalogue under his own name; the fiftieth guitar to be designed and built by Mikel Aguirre, master craftsman, employed by the Esteso-Conde guitar factory.

A fine guitar. He'd decided to manufacture the back of the instrument using two pieces of African walnut, inserting three alternate strips of ebony and sycamore to secure the join between the panels. The sides of the guitar were of solid rosewood, the front of Cyprus pine. He'd used a veneer of multi-coloured woods to produce a Spanish-style mosaic around the sound hole. His efforts had certainly paid off. The bridge looked good too, with its mother of pearl inlay.

Yes, the overall effect was quite stunning. It was a beautiful guitar… perhaps his best. And Mikel knew in his heart that it would also be his last.

He felt happy for what he'd achieved during his twenty years at the Esteso-Conde guitar workshop. The medics hadn't expected him to survive much beyond the age of fifty. And here he was… aged seventy-one! He'd even managed to outlive the three Conde brothers.

The brothers had been dubious about taking him on at first. And who would have blamed them, given his general state of health, and the dreadfully poor condition of his fingers? But through hard work and commitment to the trade, he'd quickly won their confidence. Mikel's output was slow by normal standards. He'd managed to turn out perhaps only two or three new guitars each year. But the brothers had demanded quality, and quality is what he'd given them. They were gone now. Faustino Conde had died first, then Mariano, and finally Julio just three years ago. Mikel felt ready to meet them again in another world; to suffer the loss of his earthly self.

He must gather himself and complete the last two remaining tasks.

First… the strings. One by one he secured each of the six strings to the bridge, and then tightened them gently onto the pegs. The tuning would come later, perhaps after an hour or two. The guitar must have time to adjust to the tremendous forces that were about to be imposed upon it.

Finally, and always the most pleasurable task, he reached for the engraving knife. Pressing down hard to steady his hand, he moved the blade carefully and inscribed his initials into the neck of the guitar... MA. Using a narrow pencil-brush, he ran some glue into the channel. To finish the job, he drew a short strand of fine gold thread from a spool, and set it firmly into the groove to highlight his initials. It was done.

He pushed the guitar away, flopped forward onto the bench, and lowered his head onto his arms. Mikel was exhausted, totally unresponsive, rapt in silence and weary of the world. He was done with it.

A telephone rang in the front office. Let it ring. It would go away, eventually. But it didn't go away. It just kept ringing. On and on it rang, remorseless and unrelenting, until he could bear it no longer.

He moved slowly, as if in a trance, the joints of his fingers locked in a flame of torment. He pushed open the door of the office, the sound of the telephone beating in his brains, and lifted the receiver, balancing it between the palms of his hands to save his fingers.

"Esteso-Conde guitars..."

"Thank goodness!" It was a woman's voice, and she sounded mightily relieved. "Are you the manager? I need to speak with the manager. And right away, please. It's very urgent."

"I'm sorry, but there's nobody here." He felt cold, as if in transit between life and death.

"No-one? So, who am I talking to?"

"I'm just a worker. Not the manager."

"Then perhaps you can help me. I'm with the Foreign Office. I'm looking after tonight's soloist at the Royal Theatre. Look, we're absolutely stuck. The poor man opened his guitar case this morning and found the instrument completely ruined.

It imploded, apparently. He doesn't know why. Might have been too much time spent travelling in high-flying aeroplanes. The guitarist is beside himself. He's passionate about Esteso guitars; says nothing else will do."

"A guitar? For tonight?" Mikel felt like a dead man, the reality of life outside of himself.

"Yes, tonight," she echoed. "And the very best you can offer. I know its short notice."

Was this a hoax? A hand-crafted Esteso was worth a king's ransom.

"Please," she pleaded. "It's absolutely vital. Isn't there something you can offer?"

The new guitar. Its playing qualities had yet to be determined. And it had yet to be priced.

"Call round in one hour," he croaked.

"Joy!" she exclaimed. "That's marvellous! I simply cannot tell you how grateful we are. I'll reserve a seat for you at tonight's concert. That's if you don't already have one. You'd have pride of place, right next to the royal box!"

"No. That's quite unnecessary. Not tonight. It's impossible."

"But you must! We'll send a car around to your home, pick you up! It's formal, of course. Everyone's going to be there. It's the Madrid Symphony Orchestra. The soloist is absolutely world-class. What's more, it's your Esteso guitar he's going to be playing!"

"One hour. I'll let you have a new instrument. But I must have an hour to bring it up to full pitch." Mikel lowered the phone.

Could he do it? Tension the strings, but in discreet steps. Check the alignment of the frets beneath the strings. Adjust the positioning of the bridge. So much; so little time. He felt the blood draining from his face.

A Royal Reception

That dreadful moment! Opening the guitar case and seeing his beloved Esteso in ruins! It burdened Javier's mind and tore at his heart. There was nothing in the world he could have done about it. But that initial feeling of shock and utter despair still haunted him, the anguish heartrending and timeless.

He glanced around the sumptuous anteroom of the Royal Palace. Forty or so other guests were assembling in small groups and making polite conversation. Javier stood apart from them.

The replacement guitar should have been delivered to the hotel by now. How he longed to be away from here! He could hardly wait to hold the new instrument in his hands; to investigate its acoustic behaviour; to examine its tonal response across a range of finger positions, from the soft liquid notes produced by lightly plucking the strings far from the bridge, to the harsh rasgueado sound so emblematic of the Spanish flamenco guitar. It was immensely irritating to Javier that official protocol should prevent him from getting acquainted with the new instrument. It was eating into his practice time!

Two massive doors swung open to reveal the splendours of the throne room beyond. Javier gazed down the whole length of the chamber, a place where the Spanish monarchy had held court since the reign of King Philip V in the eighteenth century. The room was magnificent, staggering in its grandeur.

"Ladies and gentlemen… if you will kindly come forward!"

A senior officer of the Spanish armed forces beckoned with ceremonious formality. "Two lines, if you please." He outstretched his arms. "One line to my left, and one to my right!"

The guests drifted slowly into the throne room. For no particular reason, Javier joined the column processing to the right. Stepping noiselessly across the luxurious carpet, he marvelled at the embroidered crimson velvet that covered the walls, at the huge mirrors framed with gold and elaborately carved. He glanced up at the frescoed ceiling. The depth of perspective achieved by the artist was absolutely mind-blowing. The whole impression was that of being inside a great hall or temple, whose ceiling was at least three times the real height of the chamber. The procession came to a halt with Javier about halfway down its length.

His eyes were drawn to four lions standing at the foot of the throne. They were about two feet high and exquisitely sculpted, each with a front paw resting on a globe.

"They're made of bronze," a man next to him said. "Rather splendid, don't you think?" He was elderly, very distinguished in his white bow tie, long-tailed jacket, and blue sash draped across his chest.

"Stunning."

"Bonicelli," the man went on. "Seventeenth century. There are twelve lions altogether. They were intended as supports for a decorative table at the old Alcazar Palace. Four of them were brought here. The others are on display in the Prado. You should visit the Prado whilst you're in Madrid."

"Unfortunately I won't have time. Nor to see the Alcazar, for that matter."

"Ah… that's a shame. What do you make of the ceiling?"

"Now *that's* something else. I think it's fantastic."

"Giovanni Tiepolo; he was a Venetian. Most of the rooms have frescoed ceilings by Tiepolo. This one shows the old kingdoms of Spain, parts of the world that were once under Spanish colonial rule. You should take a look at the fresco he did in the Queen's antechamber. The job lot took four years, apparently. Poor old Tiepolo. He died shortly afterwards; probably wore himself out. They had to transport his body all the way back to Venice for burial."

Javier studied the man for a moment. He was quite good-looking for his age; partially bald, his face handsomely hewn and resting easy. Their eyes met.

"The name's Whitaker," the man smiled, extending his hand.

"Aguirre… Javier Aguirre."

"Yes, I know." They shook hands. "And I'm much looking forward to your concert this evening."

"You're English," Javier said. "British Embassy?"

"Good God, no. Retired from the embassy years ago. Diplomatic service now, advisory capacity only. I'm much too old for anything else."

A small group of musicians began taking their seats in a corner of the chamber near the throne. A respectful silence descended on the company, the atmosphere vibrant with expectation. Javier felt like a leopard in a cage, the passion of resentment growing stronger inside him with every passing second. He needed to be back at the hotel, practising and getting to know the new guitar!

"The king will make his way along one side of the chamber," Whitaker said in a hushed tone. "The queen will come down the other. They'll reverse sides before making their way back. You can never tell who you'll shake hands with first. Of course, if they're pushed for time you'll only get to meet with one of them."

Javier dared to hope.

The musicians, a string quartet, opened with a light and very attractive dance by Schubert. Drinks were being handed around on silver trays. Javier chose a glass of sparkling lemon. A more relaxed atmosphere began to fill the chamber, the noise level rising as a buzz of conversation began to flow. The royal couple entered.

"Ah… looks as if we're going to meet with the queen first," Whitaker said. "She's very fond of music, you know. A personal friend of Rostropovich. Ever cross paths with him?"

"Rostropovich?" Javier said, gazing up at the beautiful image of a cherub winging its way across the open space high above his head. "No, I've never met Rostropovich."

"Ahem!" somebody coughed.

Javier glanced down. And there, in front of him, stood the king and queen of Spain. They were gazing at him intently, the queen flanked by two ladies-in-waiting, the king by his aide-de-camp. A waiter reached over and, with the dexterity of a master magician, slipped the glass cleanly from Javier's fingers.

"Mr Aguirre," the queen smiled warmly. "We were advised to come to you first. We are so delighted that you have travelled to Spain at last, and that you will be playing for us."

Bowing from the neck, Javier took the queen's hand lightly. When he looked up, her expression had changed to one of grave concern.

"We've been hearing about your poor guitar. How terribly upsetting for you; what an awful shock."

"A tremendous loss, Your Majesty. I shall miss the instrument for a very long time. It's rather like losing an old friend."

"And so close to this evening's performance," the king said. "Have you managed to find a replacement?"

"Yes, Your Royal Highness, thanks to the efforts of your Foreign Office."

"Well, that's some comfort anyway." The queen smiled again. "I do hope they have found you a suitable replacement. Something with a long and distinguished history, perhaps."

"Actually, no, Ma'am. I understand it will be a new guitar; straight out of the Esteso factory."

"New?" The queen raised her eyebrows.: "But a wooden instrument will take years to mature, will it not?"

"Very true, Ma'am; a guitar will often improve with age. But I've performed live with many a new instrument. The results can be excellent. For me, the problems usually arise in the recording studios. Microphones can be very unforgiving."

"Ah! All that modern electronic equipment," the king said. "I have a very fine recording that features the Madrid Symphonic. In fact, it is so good that one can even hear the conductor's shoes squeaking! Listen out for those squeaky shoes tonight, Mr Aguirre!"

"I will, Sir," Javier smiled broadly. "Unwanted sounds can certainly be a problem. And as you say, today's microphones are extraordinarily sensitive. I've known studio engineers to become completely baffled when they hear the sound of a nervous heart beating away in their earphones."

"Oh!" The queen's lips parted in a wide smile. "And now you are joking with us, Mr Aguirre! But we must detain you no longer; you will be anxious to prepare. We are very much looking forward to your concert later this evening. We do so enjoy your music; a little slice of heaven."

Javier bowed again as the royal couple moved away. The king's aide-de-camp lingered for a moment longer.

"Señor Aguirre, if you wish to leave now, you may exit by the door to your right. A member of the chamberlain's staff will show you to your car."

"Yes… thank you." With a sense of grateful relief, Javier turned to leave.

"Well done, Javier," Whitaker whispered, with a kind of familiarity that Javier could not quite comprehend. "And good luck for tonight."

Chapter 15

THE ROYAL THEATRE

Winning Them Over

Javier stood close to the footlights and absorbed the full force of a standing ovation. They'd demanded an encore, and he'd executed it flawlessly: Rodrigo's In The Wheat Fields. The choice had been something of a gamble, steeped as it was in the rich musical folklore of Spain. Javier had been uncertain as to whether the new guitar would cope with the rapidly repeating notes of the outer sections and the deep singing base of the inner parts. But he needn't have worried. The sound had come through beautifully, without blemish.

He glanced over at the royal box, framed by a huge velvet curtain, its gorgeously rich colours blazing in red and gold. Even Their Majesties were standing now, signalling their appreciation. Javier bowed low and held the position for several moments, the air around him vibrating to the sound of thunderous applause.

Then he straightened himself, smiling openly, and cast his eyes around the animated crowds in the stalls. They were all on their feet, clapping and waving to him in their hundreds. He gazed higher, acknowledging the cheers from the line of sumptuous boxes at the first level. His eyes wandered up to the second line of boxes, and then higher still to the third and fourth levels. Madrid's Royal Theatre was Spain's most important classical music venue, and surely one of the finest he'd ever seen.

He turned to the musicians behind him: the Madrid Symphonic, the oldest orchestra in Spain. They too were standing, the violinists registering their appreciation by tapping their bows gently on their music stands.

And now the audience were chanting, "Rod-ri-go! Rod-ri-go! Rod-ri-go!" Once again, Javier turned to face them. The elderly composer had joined the royal party; the king was lifting Rodrigo's hand high in the air for all to see. Javier nodded politely, smiled again, and offered Joaquín Rodrigo a respectful, unpretentious wave.

It was time to leave the stage now, his duty done. Javier turned away and moved into the wings, the conductor following closely behind.

"Listen to them, Señor Aguirre! Please, Señor, one more encore, and with the full orchestra this time!"

"I'm so sorry, but I really must be on my way. Believe me when I say that I have an aeroplane to catch."

The conductor shook his head emphatically.

"They will not let you go, Señor. Truly, they will not let you leave this theatre; not without another encore!"

The roar of acclamation from the auditorium filled Javier with an almost overpowering fear of himself.

Eliana would be waiting with the car to take him to the hotel. A quick change of clothes and he would be speeding off to the airport. And yet how could he, with an audience still going wild?

"What do you have in mind?"

"The Concierto, Señor! The Concierto de Aranjuez. Joaquín Rodrigo is here. I know he would wish to hear you play it."

"The second movement only?"

"Perfect, Señor! The Adagio is the best known of the three movements. It lasts for little more than ten minutes; a good way to end the evening!"

"Yes… ten minutes. I'll forgo changing into my travelling clothes if necessary."

A familiar voice rang out.

"Javier!"

It was Eliana. She looked lovely in her blue evening gown, a splendid orchid pinned close to her breast.

"There's no need for you to rush, Javier. Everything is in the car. We can leave for the airport just whenever you're ready. And there's someone else to see you. She was worried that she might have missed you." Eliana ushered a little girl forward.

The child was small, her face thin and pale, but there was a glint in her dark eyes that seemed to express her undoubted right to be here. She was holding a small posy of flowers. Javier smiled reassuringly and knelt down in front of her.

"The flowers are from Rosa's garden," Eliana said. "She picked them herself. Aren't they beautiful?"

The posy was simply presented, unadorned and without frills. Javier buried his nose in the flowers, pretending to catch their scent, and handed them to Eliana.

Rosa drew a quick breath and thrust out an autograph book.

"Here, Rosa…" Javier pressed the guitar into her hand. "Keep this safe while I sign your book."

"Rosa doesn't speak English." Eliana offered a pen.

He quickly sketched the outline of a guitar and scribbled a quick message: *To Rosa… my heroine… from Javier Aguirre*. The little girl stared at him silently, her dark eyes sparkling with a kind of pride in what she had achieved.

Javier gazed up into Eliana's smiling eyes. If only there could be more time. Just a little more time to know this woman better…

"Listen to them," she said. "My God, Javier; just listen to them. They're waiting for you."

"You've done so well, Eliana. I've performed with so many wonderful instruments over the years. But this… this is the greatest of them all. The very best."

"Off you go, then. And take your time. Enjoy the last few moments of your time in Spain."

It pricked him with a pleasant sensation to think she might actually be concerned for his wellbeing.

"Come, Maestro!" The conductor grasped him firmly by the hand. "We go on together!"

His senses almost overwhelmed by the ear-shattering roar of two thousand people, all cheering and crying out together, Javier took his seat quickly. He was ready for action.

The Adagio would open with four majestic spread-chords from the guitar. He must create the right mood for them; capture the feeling of quiet regret that should permeate the start of the movement. He waited for absolute silence; it came quickly. Then he glanced round at the conductor, and received a subtle nod. It was time to begin.

Javier played the four chords smoothly, and with such a controlled intensity that even he was surprised at the marvellous quality of sound. The guitar was continuing to perform magnificently. The music flowed easily, a dialogue gradually opening up between the guitar and each of the other instruments in turn; the cor anglais, bassoon, oboe and horn.

According to some, the Adagio had been inspired by the bombing of Guernica in 1937. Others had suggested it was an evocation of Rodrigo's sense of devastation at the loss of his first child. It hardly mattered, because whatever had galvanised Rodrigo into writing this concerto, it was a masterpiece; music fit for the gods; a banquet of pure harmony.

With the climactic build-up now underway, Javier applied an off-tonic trill on the bass string to create the first seeds of tension in the piece. He was playing alone now, without the orchestra. The solo passage would demand the utmost intensity of expression and depth of sound from the guitar, building up towards that mighty crescendo, the majestic climax of the Adagio movement. The instrument responded beautifully, the whole experience very emotional and awesomely powerful. Then the orchestra took the lead, driving the crescendo on to even greater heights, and allowing Javier a few moments of respite before the guitar would re-enter in preparation for the finale.

He glanced down at the audience, his gaze settling on an old man seated in the stalls very close to the stage. A small, frail figure, his face wrinkled, eyes red-rimmed and filled with sadness. The old man gazed up at him, captivated, enthralled, and abandoned to his melancholy. The finale drew ever closer, and with a twinge of regret that he could hardly fathom, Javier disengaged his attention from the old man and set his fingers back on the frets.

As the orchestra broke into the main melody for the last time, he entered the concluding section, molto appassionato, the music resolving into a calm arpeggio from the guitar and coming to a close with a slow and gentle run of ascending notes. The silence in the hall was deep, profound beyond words. Yes, it had been a good way to finish.

The Final Cadence

Clutching the guitar in his hand, Javier followed the stage manager along a dimly lit corridor of the Royal Theatre, the sound of the audience still audible through the thick walls.

"This way, Señor Aguirre," the manager said. "We must stay clear of the crowds."

Javier was led to a small, elegantly decorated room.

"In here, Señor. This is where our important guests are invited to gather before taking their seats in the main auditorium."

Javier glanced round at the gilded Regency-style chairs, richly carved and upholstered in purple velvet. A glass cabinet displaying some exquisite blue porcelain stood in one corner, an ornate long-case clock stood in another. Several classical paintings were hung around the walls.

"We like our high-ranking guests to feel comfortable," the manager smiled. "I will leave the key in the door, should you wish to change, Señor. I will go now. Your escort will be along shortly. I gather she is trying to arrange a meeting?"

"Yes. And with a very important man: the craftsman who

made this." Javier lifted the guitar. "I must hand it back to him. The meeting shouldn't take long."

"An inspired performance, Señor Aguirre; and may I wish you a very pleasant journey to Singapore." The manager gave a courteous bow and left the room.

Javier breathed an immense sigh of relief. It was so good to be alone again. Eliana had arranged for the luggage to be brought from the hotel. He would return the guitar, change quickly, and then go directly to the airport.

Spain wasn't such a bad place after all. In fact, the notion of having to leave Madrid actually saddened him now. Over the past few days he'd thought he would go mad from coming here, his mind turning in upon itself and casting a spell over him, beating him down in a spiral of contest between those two mysterious opposites: the callousness in his father on the one hand, contrasting so starkly with the creative genius of the man on the other.

But Javier had given the Spanish people a good and honest account of himself, and they in turn had made themselves alive to him. There were no brute monsters in Spain; none but those that had dwelt in the tangle of his mind. It wasn't that the immorality in his father had suddenly become virtuous, because the bad had *not* become good. But at least Javier now felt ready to move on with his life. Perhaps not quite able to forgive, or even to forget; but simply to move on, unhindered by the thought of his father's wrongdoing.

He raised the guitar up again, breathing the heady scent of fresh, sweet wood and varnish. It reminded him of that very first guitar, the one he'd inherited from his father as a child all those years ago, and which had launched him on a career of world travel and command performance. His heart went black at the thought of having to part from this beautiful instrument. He would offer to buy it. But what if the guitar had already been promised to another?

Javier heard movement at the doorway. He drew a deep breath and turned, eager to meet the craftsman from the Esteso factory.

Eliana appeared. She stood for a moment, her expression fixed and solemn. She moved slowly towards him.

"I… I'm so sorry," she said in a low intense voice.

"Why? What's wrong?" Javier felt a pang of regret. Were his hopes of meeting the craftsman about to be dashed? "Don't tell me; it's the man from Esteso, isn't it? He didn't turn up. He didn't make it to the concert."

"Oh, but he did, Javier! He was elderly and very frail. I had so much difficulty trying to win him over; believe me, I had to work hard to persuade him to come. But he did eventually make the effort. We offered him one of the best seats in the house. He chose instead to sit in the stalls, close to the stage."

"So where is he now?"

Eliana looked as if her heart had been wrung.

"I went to find him. People were leaving the theatre, but he was still in his seat. He looked so desperately ill, Javier. We called for an ambulance and they came quickly, but… he just seemed to slip away. I keep thinking I was to blame."

"Blame? That's silly. It's not your fault, Eliana. How could you possibly blame yourself?"

"When I saw him at the workshop… maybe I pushed him a little too hard. I told him how much you were looking forward to meeting him, and that you wanted to return the guitar, to thank him personally. He was such a lovely man, Javier. And he wanted to know everything about you. He seemed almost overcome when I told him."

"No, Eliana. You're not to blame. Nobody's to blame. He'll pull through, you'll see."

"Oh, no… I don't think so," she shook her head sadly. "I think he was already gone when they carried him away. And to think I may have been the last person to speak to him. Javier, I can hardly bear to think of it."

Javier struggled within himself. He longed to reassure Eliana, to comfort her. But a measure of moral conscience forbade him from stepping forward, from gathering her into his arms.

"Well," he sighed, "there's nothing more we can do now. I suppose I should hand the guitar back to you. Return it for me, Eliana. Tell him… tell him that Javier Aguirre fell in love with his magnificent guitar. And thank him for me."

For just one last time, he ran his eyes over the beautiful soundboard. Turning the guitar over, he felt the weight of the instrument, feeling with the tips of his fingers along the whole length of its neck.

At that moment, something caught his attention. There were initials, embossed in gold… MA.

His eyes narrowed as he peered closer. He caught his breath as a cold sweat of disbelief broke out over his whole body, his heart thrashing wildly against his ribcage.

"Oh my God…" he gasped, his mind a maelstrom of confusion. "Oh my dear God…"

"Javier? What's wrong?"

Eliana's voice sounded distant, her words almost drowned by the pounding of blood coursing through his stupefied brain.

And then another voice: "Where words fail, music speaks…"

It was like a remote echo from the farthest reaches of the universe, faint and nebulous.

He glanced up and saw someone standing at the doorway, gazing back at him. He'd seen that face before, at the Palace reception.

"Your father was a wonderful man, Javier," Whitaker said. "He spent almost thirty years shut away in a Madrid jail. And if it hadn't been for the memory of his wife, and that little boy he'd left behind in England, I doubt if he'd have survived and gone on to become such a fine craftsman."

The knot in Javier's throat grew ever tighter as he gathered the guitar close to his breast, and felt it vibrating softly against his heart.

 Matador